Praise for *Deviant Acts*

"In *Deviant Acts*, J.J. White has reinvented the amateur sleuth. His reluctant PI, Jackson Hurst, is crazy as a loon, funny as hell, and deadly serious. He's as outside normal life as a man can get and somehow still solidly on the side of the angels. This is a great read. Let's hope Jackson Hurst goes pro and we get a string of novels about this original and compelling character." —Sterling Watson, author of *Fighting in the Shade* and *Suitcase City*

I0636065

DEVIANT ACTS

DEVIANT ACTS

J.J. White

OPEN ROAD

INTEGRATED MEDIA

NEW YORK

Copyright © 2015 by J.J. White

ISBN: 978-1-5040-7793-4

This edition published in 2022 by Open Road Integrated Media, Inc.
180 Maiden Lane
New York, NY 10038
www.openroadmedia.com

To Pamela Ruth and my daughters,
Elizabeth and Kathleen.

DEVIANT ACTS

Chapter 1

JANE FONDA

Charlotte, North Carolina, 1973:

Jane Fonda shot ten feet up the screen and then ten feet down.

It pissed him off that she was selling out to the Man after risking her career sitting on an NVA antiaircraft gun. When the photo had come out, it was a big middle finger to the establishment, but now she was back making shitty movies for money, ignoring the cause.

Jackson Hurst hadn't always felt this way. In '68, he had supported the war so strongly he enlisted in the Corps. He believed all that stuff they beat into him in boot camp, until his tour changed his mind. Funny how a year of fighting jungle rot and fending off inconsiderate bastards trying to kill you changes your attitude.

Hoots, hollers, and whistles floated up from the smoky theater. Jackson kicked the projector until the steady click-click-click began again, Jane's mouth and voice back in sync.

He leaned forward in the chair, set the lighter between his legs, and cooked the last of the smack. He still called it "smack." The platoon sergeant who had introduced it to him in Da Nang called it that, so Jackson would call it "smack" to honor his dead sergeant.

Every bone in his body ached. Sixteen hours since his last hit and it felt like a goddamn truck sitting on his chest. He used to go three days between hits. Why couldn't he do that anymore?

More hoots from the seats. Jackson ignored them, wiped the hypodermic needle on his jeans, then dipped it into the hot spoon of liquid god. As he was sucking it up into the hypo, a pounding behind him drowned out the whistles and shouts from below.

"Open the door, Hurst."

"What?" Jackson flicked the vein in the crook of his arm. It filled with blood and then popped up as if anticipating the needle.

"The film's stuck. Open the goddamn door."

Jackson looked out through the smoky glass window at Donald Sutherland's thin face, cooked brown by the high-wattage lamp. It reminded him of the marshmallows he and his father used to roast at a campsite near Icy Knob Hill, back when he still had a father. He flicked the switch off and the lamp went out. Boos filled the grand movie theater. Surprising, considering there were maybe thirty people there, tops.

"I got it!" he yelled to Maxwell, the whiny son of a bitch.

"Open up."

"I got it! You know, Max, who gives a shit about *Steelyard Blues*? I got it. Go away."

Jackson pulled the burnt celluloid loose and fed the film back into the projector. Christ, he was dying, sweat covering his forehead, the pounding in his head worsening. He had to hurry before the smack cooled or he'd have to cook it all over again.

He flicked the switch and then, thank Christ, the movie started, slowly at first, and then up to full speed. Max finally went away.

Jackson sat in the chair and lined up the needle. He'd have to do a direct deposit, shoot it right into the vein instead of the usual skin-popping. The hippies and dicks downtown liked to skin-pop to save the vein, but it left you with abrasions that looked like the acne he had hated so much in high school. A direct deposit would hit his brain in seconds.

He pushed the plunger and felt an almost instant euphoria. When he did this, he was never sure if it was the heroin or his anticipation of the high that gave him the quick rush. He stood and leaned against the wall until his legs gave out, and then he slid to the floor. A cigarette would have been nice, but he didn't have the inclination or the motivation. His body was at peace, without pain, highly sensitive, though without much tactile pleasure, if that made any sense.

He could never explain how it felt to Karen as she asked for the millionth time why he wanted to kill himself. It just felt so damn good. After work, he'd stop by her place and try to explain it to her again, but even in his haze, he realized that wouldn't be possible, since they had broken up over six months ago. Still, he might ride by to see if he could get a glimpse of her through a window.

Jane once again filled the screen, emoting to Donald Sutherland. She was supposed to be a prostitute in the piece-of-crap movie, trying to reprise her role from *Klute*, he guessed. The flowery blouse, leopard pants, and frizzy perm made her look more like his mother than a whore.

He'd had enough. Jackson threw a metal trashcan at the projector. It bounced off and the film continued unabated. He flung the trashcan again and the film froze, this time as small pieces of the projector fell to the carpeted floor. Still sitting, he bowed to his imaginary audience and said, "It would be her last movie. A shadow of what she once was, my fellow Americans."

Max pounded on the projector-room door for half a minute, or maybe it was an hour. Who the fuck knew? The sound of fumbling keys, and then Max and Vincent Holmes, the Flynn's big, black facilities engineer or technician or whatever, came striding in like John Wayne and the cavalry.

Vincent picked up scattered pieces of the projector. "Broke. He broke it. Goddamn junkie did it this time." He booted Jackson in his outstretched leg to emphasize exactly which junkie he was talking about.

"Hey, man," Jackson said. "Ease off, brother."

"I'll ease off your hippie-loving ass, boy." Vincent tried the power switch. Nothing.

Max waddled over to confront the perpetrator. Jackson pulled his long blond hair back out of his eyes and met the kid's gaze.

"That's it, Hurst. You're fired. Do you know what the projector cost? I don't care if your mama knows George or if she's sleeping with him, but that's it. Get your ass out of here."

Jackson shook the bats from his brain. "You gotta pay me what you owe me, Maxwell."

"Fuck you. You owe *me* for the projector. I said, get out." He kicked Jackson's leg. It didn't hurt like Vincent's kick had.

"Dude. Little respect for your elder here. I'm an armed services veteran, man."

Max gestured to Vincent. "Throw him out."

"Don't touch me," Jackson warned Vincent. "I'll get up in a minute. Just let me rest for a second."

Vincent grabbed Jackson by his shirt and jacked him up against the wall. Jackson hadn't been man-handled like that since his birthday, five years ago in Vietnam. He could still smell the jungle . . .

The platoon had been in an earlier firefight and they were exhausted, including Jackson, who had watch. The men lay in a circle around the fire, somehow managing to sleep amidst the cacophony of nighttime jungle noises. Jackson was reading the second page of Karen's letter when the monkeys and birds and whatever else was out there went quiet. He stood and scanned three-sixty with his M16, the attached Starlight NVD scope painting the jungle green. His heart raced, despite his having smoked some smack earlier—good stuff that kept a middle-class boy's head level after seeing your buddy's brains on your shirtsleeve.

Nothing. Jackson turned in a circle one more time and, as he aimed the rifle over heavy scrub nearby, he saw green eyes staring back. He emptied the clip on auto and then ducked as the other twenty-six men woke and stood as one, also emptying their clips into the black void. Nothing should have lived through the fusillade, but two VC rushed into the circle of Marines, bent on suicide and taking as many of the enemy with them as they could.

One of the VC screamed as he fired twice into Jackson's sergeant. Jackson butted the man, but then the insurgent came up, thrusting with an antique rifle taller than he was. Jackson sidestepped the bayonet and wrestled him to the ground, only to be thrown over on his back. Before Jackson could stand, the VC thrust three fingers into his Adam's apple. The pain paralyzed Jackson. He watched helplessly as the soldier prepared to run him through, until someone's M16 nearly cut the bastard in half.

After seeing what the VC could do to him with just bare hands, Jackson swore he would someday learn the martial arts himself. Two months after they kicked him out of the Corps, he'd kept his oath . . .

Jackson's skills in the ancient arts kicked in as Vincent Holmes reared back to punch the shit out of him. Despite the heroin, despite the euphoria, despite the feeling of equanimity that enveloped Jackson, he knocked Vincent out cold with a kick to the ribs and an elbow to the temple. He turned to Max, who trembled behind the damaged projector.

Max pointed to the door. "Get out of here."

Jackson jerked his head back to get his hair out of his eyes and moved in close on little Max. Although Jackson weighed nearly nothing, a result of the drugs, his six-foot-two-inch frame towered over his portly young boss.

"Forty-two fifty, man."

"What?"

"That's what you owe me for the week. Forty-two fifty."

"It's going to cost more than that to fix the projector. I'm calling the cops."

"Call the pigs, man. I don't give a damn. You gonna pay me?" Max flinched when Jackson patted his cheek. "Whatever, man."

Jackson walked out of the projector room and down the stairs to the lobby. He shakily made his way behind the concession counter and pressed the "No Sale" button on the cash register.

"What you doing, Jackson? You can't touch that, you know." Millie was the nicest of the girls who ran the concession stand.

He counted out two twenties and a five. Close enough. "Max said it's okay, Millie. Besides, I quit anyway. Howard Hughes wants me to run his company, so I said, 'Okay, man, I can do that.'" He stuffed the bills in his jeans pocket and shot her the peace sign.

Outside the Flynn, Jackson fumbled with his key to unlock a chain that held his rusty Schwinn to the signpost. As he pedaled down the sidewalk, he wondered how many hits he could get out of the forty-five bucks. He knew of two streets on his way to his mother's house where he could stop and negotiate. They cut the stuff so much now, he was sure he could score a nice price.

The neighborhoods changed from somewhat black to almost all black as he neared his mother's house. She had lived in it since she married thirty-three years ago, and she said she would be damned if she was going to move out, even if everyone else in the quaint neighborhood was black. Her parents had lived in downtown Charlotte all their lives and Jackson's mother intended to do likewise. He didn't give a damn as long as he had a place to crash.

Chapter 2

CAMILLE CALLS

"Adele—Adele, dear. Are you there? I know you're there, Adele. I can hear you breathing."

Adele Hurst held the telephone receiver out and looked at it as if it might tell her what to say.

"Adele."

The last person, no, the *very* last person she expected to hear on the other end of the line was her older sister, Camille. It had been five years since she had talked to her. No call, no letter, not one word from Camille up there in her Vermont mansion. What could Adele possibly say to her?

"Hello."

"You already said that, Adele. Let me explain to you how phone etiquette works. You say, 'Hello.' I say 'hello' back. And then I say, 'This is Camille,' and now—it's your turn."

"I know how to talk on a phone. I just wasn't expecting your call and all."

"Well, how can you be expecting my call if you didn't know I was calling? I swear, I am so glad I left Charlotte. Is there anyone in that town who can talk and think at the same time?"

"There're a lot of good people here."

"Yes, I'm sure. I guess you're still living with all those Negroes in that horrible neighborhood."

"They don't like being called *Negroes*, Camille. Why do you say things like that?"

"Because even in this enlightened time, I don't care for the government telling me how I have to talk and how I have to act and how I have to think. If I wish to say *Negro*, I shall."

"Why are you calling me?"

"I didn't want to, but it was a necessity."

"You said you never wanted to see me again."

"And I don't, dear. I am angry at you and I will stay angry at you until the day I die for what you did."

"I couldn't leave work to go to Vermont, Camille. Not everyone marries a rich husband like you did—"

"That wasn't it at all and you know it. You didn't come to Cheryl's graduation because she isn't my real daughter and—"

"That's not true."

"I sent you plane tickets."

"I had to work."

"People can take time off from work."

"It was a high school graduation, not a wedding, for God's sake."

There was a long silence.

"It wasn't work, was it, Adele? You never liked me because we are seventeen years apart. That was it, wasn't it?"

"Is this why you called? Because if it is, I have things to do."

"No, it's not. That's not why I called and I'm sorry I brought it up. I—I need your help, or more specifically, I need your son's help."

"Jackson?"

"How many sons do you have, Adele?"

"I know. I'm sorry. I'm confused. It's this call and all. Why do you need Jackson?"

"I am having some trouble. Something I'd rather not go into over the phone, but let's just say it's some matter that I need handled by someone I can trust."

"It's not Cheryl, is it?"

"Yes, it is."

"Oh, dear God," Adele said.

"It is something I must do to ensure her safety, but with discretion. My nephew is the only one I believe can help me with the situation."

"What is it?"

"I will tell Jackson when he gets here."

"But he has a job."

"You're not using that excuse again, are you, dear?"

"He runs a projector at the Flynn, but he said the manager liked his work and he should be promoted soon."

"I will give him a job when he gets here. He was in the war, wasn't he?"

"Yes, you know he was, but—"

"Adele, I have money, you know."

"Yes," Adele said.

Camille had money but had never offered any to help out when Travis died or when Jackson was sick. Yes, she had lots of money.

"When Jackson arrives I will fund a business for him. The delicate matter I need resolved will be best handled by a private investigator. You do not need a license in Vermont to be a private investigator and I'm sure Jackson would like a steady income and an office. Let me talk to him."

"He's at work."

"When he gets back have him call me and we'll discuss the details. You *do* want him to have a better job, don't you?"

"Yes, but it's up to him."

"He's twenty-four, Adele. It's time for him to move out of your house."

"How did you know he's living here?"

There was a momentary silence. "Didn't you say he was at work? I assumed that meant he still lived with you. Now, he can pick up the ticket at the airport."

"When?"

"Wednesday. It's desperately crucial he's here by Wednesday."

"But that's only two days from now."

"Yes, Adele, I have a calendar. Now tell Jackson that after he has helped me I will pay for advertising for his new business and provide a salary until he gets enough clients to survive on his own. I believe an ex-soldier would make a good investigator, despite Jackson's shortcomings, and we both know what I'm talking about. Tell him to call me immediately."

"I will, but not for you. I'll do it for Jackson."

"Fine. I don't care. Just have him call."

Chapter 3

TIME TO SPLIT

Jackson pulled into his mother's driveway and threw the bike down on the front lawn. Who the hell would steal the thing, anyway? You could get a better one in the junkyard.

On the walk to the carport, he fingered the bag of heroin in the pocket of his jeans. The neighbors' black faces followed him all the way to the back door. They blamed the longhaired hippie for all the recent break-ins in the neighborhood. Not true. He had been involved in only two of them. Let's see them try to deal with a hundred-dollar-a-week habit making forty bucks a week at the Flynn, he thought.

Oh yeah, he didn't work there anymore.

"Hey, Ma," he said and walked by her to his bedroom.

"Jackson. I have some—"

"Not right now. Be out in a sec."

He hid the bag of heroin under the pillow. Safe enough. His mother would never enter his room without his permission. One lousy bag was all he could get with his forty-five dollars' absconded pay from little Max. Thirty-five dollars a hit and it was getting worse, the way the Feds were cracking down. If it was thirty-five in Charlotte, what was it in New York City or wherever he might go? He had to get out of Charlotte. There'd be no more jobs with his reputation and one of the neighbors might be armed the next time. He needed a car. He needed Ma to buy him a car.

His mother shut the television off when he walked into the living room. The furniture needed replacing and the room smelled as old as it looked. Jackson grabbed his mother's cigarettes and lighter from next to the lamp on the glass end table, sat across from her on Grandmother's old sofa, and lit up.

"I need a car. I can't keep riding that piece-of-shit bicycle in town. It's embarrassing." He sucked on the cigarette and flipped the pack back on the end table.

"I've bought you five cars since you've been out of the marines. You wrecked three and God knows what you did with the other two. I can't afford another. You should have made enough by now at the Flynn to get a used one. I saw one of those Bugs you like for a few hundred at Cline's."

"I quit the Flynn."

"Oh, Jackson. Why?"

"They kept giving me hell about my hair. Max is an idiot, anyway. I'm getting out of here. There's nothing in this hick town worth—"

"Your entire family has lived here since before the Civil War. There is nothing wrong with Charlotte."

"You know what's wrong with Charlotte, Ma?" Jackson emphasized his point with his cigarette. "Every white person here still thinks the South should have won. They live in the past while the rest of the world moves by them. I've had it. Gonna go to LA or San Francisco, where the kids my age think about the future, instead of living in the past. That's why I need a car and some feed money. Hell, they pay bag boys four dollars an hour out there. You give me a little cash to live on, Ma, and maybe I can get a band together. Just a thousand. That's it."

"I just can't afford any more cars, Jackson. I can't. Now your Aunt Camille called."

"I thought she was dead."

"No. She's not. She called a few hours ago and she said she wants to offer you a job."

"She wants to offer me a job?"

"That's what I said."

"What kind of job?"

"She said she would discuss it with you. There's some trouble with Cheryl and she needs your help."

Cheryl. Aunt Camille's adopted daughter, although they were never allowed to say that in front of his aunt. Cheryl was a good kid. The last time they'd come to visit he was twelve and Cheryl was eight. She was the first girl he had ever kissed. Actually, it was the other way around. They were out back, shooting dragonflies with a BB gun, when she pecked him on the lips and ran into the house.

"Is she all right?"

"Camille wouldn't go into any details. She said she needed you to do something for her discreetly. She said she would put the money up to help you start a business."

"What kind of business?"

"She said as a private investigator."

"Me? Man, that's something. She know I have a record?"

"She just said you won't need a license. Maybe you should call her. You said you want to go away. Well, here's a chance. Vermont's not Los Angeles—"

"Not even close."

"But it couldn't be bad for you. It would help me out with finances. We barely get by, Jackson. I can't keep giving you money I don't have."

Jackson lifted the receiver off the phone.

"What's her number? I need to split this town, anyway."

Aunt Camille had a throaty voice similar to his own, though she had very little of her Carolina drawl left after living most of her adult life in Shrewsbury, Vermont. Jackson's mother never seemed to get along with her older sister. Odd, since they were both widows. All he knew about his Aunt Camille's husband was that his last name was Hebert, pronounced "Eh-bear," and he made a fortune in Montreal before marrying Camille and settling in Vermont. Aunt Camille was the rich aunt who wanted nothing to do with her hick sister and her little brat, Jackson. Well, he'd forgive her for some cash.

"I don't have much to say, Jackson. I am offering you an opportunity to start a business here, or near here. I have a situation with your cousin that I believe only you can help me with and I am willing to pay you for your services."

"What situation?"

"I'd rather not say, but I will need you here Wednesday to start."

"Couldn't someone there help you?"

"I have already explained to you that I need *your* services. It is important that it be someone I can trust. May I assume I can trust you, Jackson?"

"How much money?"

"We'll discuss that when you arrive. Now, I have purchased an airline ticket for you. The plane leaves Charlotte Wednesday at six a.m. Will you be on it?"

"I'll need some money now."

"Why is that, Jackson?"

"For clothes, food. Stuff like that. Ma won't have any help from me with my paycheck."

"How much?" she asked.

"A thousand."

There was a pause.

"I'll wire six hundred and I'll subtract it from your final pay. Tell Adele to pick it up at the Western Union tomorrow. I will have someone meet you at the Burlington Airport. Now, are you coming or not?"

"Okay, but I'll—"

The phone clicked.

"Jesus. What's her problem?" Jackson lit another cigarette.

"She's never liked me," his mother said. "Your grandmother made her babysit me when she wanted to go out instead and she blames me. Are you going?"

"Yeah. She's wiring six hundred to the Western Union. You need to pick it up."

"All right. When do you leave?"

"Six, Wednesday morning. You have to drive me to the airport, but I'm ready to go now. I'm sick of this house and sick of this town."

There was a knock on the door. Adele looked out the peephole and unlatched the chain lock. She turned back to Jackson.

"It's the police."

Jackson put out his cigarette.

"I'm not here," he said, but his mother had already swung open the door.

"Yes?" she asked the policeman.

The big one in front ignored her and stared at Jackson. "You Jackson Hurst?"

"Yeah."

"Let's go, boy. Seems like you in a little trouble again. You know the drill." The cop held the cuffs out. Jackson turned around and placed his hands behind his back. The cop cuffed him and walked him toward the door.

"What's it for?"

"Something different this time, boy. Battery."

They led him down the steps. Three of the neighbors stood on the sidewalk and smiled as the cops led Jackson to the patrol car.

"Hey, man," Jackson said. "This couldn't have come at a worse time, you know?"

"When's there a good time to get your ass busted, hippie?"

He had a point.

Chapter 4

FLASHBACK

Sergeant Lawrence Becker made him point man and Jackson loved his sergeant for it. The squad was on a search-and-destroy mission, which was an official way of saying mind your own goddamn business and stay out of firefights unless Charlie makes a point of engagement. Jackson wanted to be the point man since the Viet Cong rarely attacked the column from the front and, since he and Becker shared smack and whores, Jackson always got point. Everything was cool until they reached a narrow path bordered on both sides by rice paddies. Jackson turned and yelled to his sergeant in the back of the column.

"What do you want to do, Sarge?"

There was a calm silence as the entire squad turned their heads to the sergeant to hear what he'd say.

"Keep going, damn it. Jesus, Hurst, you want me to carry you?"

That got a few chuckles. Jackson shrugged and pressed on. They'd make camp in an hour anyway. He felt his right foot sink slightly into the path and knew he had stepped on one of the VC's tennis ball–sized anti-personnel mines even before he heard the click. The explosion sounded like his daddy's shotgun with that loud, low boom that rattled your brain. Jackson flipped twice before landing on his ass in a rice paddy. His M16 was gone, along with his helmet and two grenades. He patted his head, body, and legs and grinned.

"Christ!" he yelled back to the squad. Most of the men, except for Johnson and Riggs, lay prostrate on the grassy path, their hands on top of their helmets. "I'm fine! Not a scratch!" Jackson stood and sloshed through the shallow water back to the path. He came up on Riggs, who sat with his legs pulled in close to his chest, like something a little kid might do.

"Ya okay, Teddy?" Jackson lifted Riggs's helmet over his eyes. A chunk of frag was lodged in the corporal's chin, the other end jutting out obscenely through his right eye . . .

* * *

Jackson jerked back as he woke, banging his head on the cell bars. It got some laughs from the other drunks and dopers who filled the retaining cell of the Charlotte-Mecklenburg Central Jail. He rubbed his arms to stay warm and to hide the shakes. It had been a while since they so unfairly incarcerated him and it was hard not to think about that baggie under the pillow at home.

He had the worst damn luck. A rich aunt calls out of nowhere to offer him money and a way out of Charlotte, and it just happens to be the same day he gets his ass arrested. His life was one long string of bad luck that began when his daddy died. Things would have been different if he had lived. Jackson wouldn't have joined the marines, he wouldn't have lost Karen, and he wouldn't be a junkie. He was sure of that. And now, he wouldn't be flying to Vermont. The worst damn luck. At least he'd be housed and fed in prison—if he lived through withdrawal. When the hell was his mother coming down to bail him out?

An overweight cop looked up from his clipboard. "Which one of you is Hurst?"

"I am."

"Well, get up, princess, and put your hands through here." The cop pointed to a waist-high rectangular opening in the bars. Jackson put his hands through.

"Back up to it, asshole."

Jackson placed his hands behind his back and through the opening. The cop roughly handcuffed him and then unlocked the cell door.

"C'mon. We're going on an elevator ride."

"Where to?"

"This ain't twenty questions. Just shut up and don't try nothing."

They went up three floors to a room full of small offices. The cop led him into one with a sign on a smoked glass door that read, "Detectives." He sat him in front of a desk where a large man with thinning black hair and broad shoulders ignored them as he read a file through reading glasses. The detective looked up at the cop.

"Thanks, Bo."

"Can I take my cuffs?"

"Yeah. We won't need them, will we, Jackson?"

Jackson shook his head and rubbed his wrists after Bo took his cuffs off.

"You got a cigarette?" Jackson asked. The detective pulled a pack from his shirt pocket and threw them on the desk.

"Lighter's over there." The detective pointed to another desk near him. Jackson lit up and put the lighter back on the vacant desk. He had smoked half the cigarette by the time the detective looked up from the file again.

"Quite a record, Jackson. Dishonorable discharge in '69, pot smuggling in early '70, and then downhill from there with four possessions and two break-ins."

Jackson blew out smoke. "Only one conviction."

"That's right. Momma always came to the rescue with pretty good lawyers, but sooner or later your luck was bound to run out, boy, and I guess this time it has. What would ol' Travis think about you if he could see you now?"

"You knew my dad?"

"I did. Travis and I hunted. Quite a bit. I cried when he died. I was at the funeral, and back then I felt pretty bad for you, boy. You remember David Kenton?"

"From Jefferson? Yeah."

"You boys went with us to Icy Knob a few times."

"Yeah, I remember that, man. I didn't know you were a cop. How's he doing?"

"Out of college, working at Deere. He's doing good. So what fucked you up, Jackson? Vietnam?"

"Nothing wrong with me. Got me a job waiting in Vermont if I ever get the hell out of here."

Detective Kenton put his hands behind him and scratched his head. "Well—it don't look good, Jackson. Seems you have a few problems here that might delay your plans for a few years. A Mr. Holmes said you attacked him at the Flynn. Knocked him out, he said, and he definitely wants to press charges. Now, what made you think you could knock some nigger around and get away with it? Your momma ain't gonna be able to help you with this one, Jackson."

"He pushed me against the wall."

"Says you were mainlining."

"I've been clean for a year."

Kenton leaned over and pulled back Jackson's sleeve. He shook his head. "A year, huh?"

Jackson said nothing and finished his cigarette. He remembered David's dad had been a good guy. He hadn't treated them like kids, showing them how to hunt and handle the deer rifles. Those were good times—until the accident at the factory. Could the detective use his influence to get Jackson out of this? Maybe he'd do it for his father.

"Is there any way I can get on that plane Wednesday?"

"Maybe," Kenton said. "Your victim said you pay the damages for the projector, he'd drop the charges."

"It's not his projector."

"That's what he said, boy. I'm just repeating it."

"How much?"

"A thousand."

"Is he out of his mind? There's maybe fifty dollars' damage. Hell, I could fix it."

"Listen, Jackson. If I hadn't been a friend to your father, you'd still be in holding. You want out, then get Momma to foot the thousand. Otherwise that boy's gonna fry you. My preference would be to see you board a plane to Vermont and never come back. You been enough trouble for your momma and she don't need any more of your shit. So what is it?"

"Can you ask him if he'll take six hundred? My aunt's wiring the money tomorrow."

Kenton shrugged. "Won't hurt to ask. Sit here until I get back."

Ten minutes later, Kenton still hadn't returned. Jackson grabbed his chest to try to stop the shivering. Everything hurt. The clock on the wall ticked louder as the minutes passed. Finally, Kenton returned.

"He'll take six hundred. Cash. Western Union, right?"

"Yeah."

"I'll pick you up in holding in the morning. I'm doing this for Travis. It's a onetime deal, Jackson. After this, you're on your own. You understand?"

"Yes, sir. Thanks."

Chapter 5

A BICYCLE RIDE

Tuesday morning, Detective Kenton drove him to the Western Union, but they wouldn't give Jackson the six hundred because his Aunt Camille had wired it to his mother. An hour later, they had the cash from his mother and paid Holmes and Max a visit at the Flynn. Max also demanded the forty-five Jackson took from the register, but Kenton told him not to press his luck. Like Jackson, Kenton must have noticed a movie was showing, which meant by some miracle the projector had healed itself.

Once home, Jackson shot up the baggie and went for a wobbly bicycle ride. He had something he had to do before leaving Charlotte for good—something he had thought about every day for the last six months, something he had hoped would come true since the day he and Karen had split.

It was two miles of slow pedaling to her apartment and, by the time he had reached the complex, he was exhausted. Jackson crouched over and sucked air for a couple of minutes or more until he felt steady enough to walk through the parking lot to her apartment.

Should he put his hair back in a ponytail? She had once said she liked him to wear it that way when they made love. His favorite memory of her was when she lay naked atop him, her long, auburn hair draping his head, cocoon-like, as she bent over to kiss him.

That was six months ago, after she had stopped her drug use and asked him to stop his, but he hadn't. Then one night after making love, they argued and he'd threatened her and that was it. Why was he like that? Why didn't he at least try to do what she asked, instead of saying she was the problem and not the drugs?

Since then, he thought about her every day. When he was high, he dreamed of bumping into her somewhere; their small talk and awkward conversation would lead them both to confess they missed each other and wanted to get back together.

But he hadn't bumped into her, though he saw her almost every day. Karen worked the three-to-eleven shift at the hospital and Jackson knew if he rode his bicycle to the Piggly Wiggly parking lot each day at two thirty he could see her drive by in her red '65 Mustang, her hair blowing through the window she kept cracked open to let cigarette smoke out.

Jackson walked the Schwinn over to the high brick steps of the apartment building. He hid the bike at the side entryway and walked up the steps. He hesitated then knocked on the screen door. An eyeball blocked the peephole. She was home.

A man his size, but with more weight and short black hair, answered. "Yeah?"

"Is Karen in?"

The guy shook his head. "She doesn't live here anymore."

"Let me talk to him, Sam." Karen's voice. She moved Sam aside and came out the door to the stoop. Her hair was short, just to her chin now, and she had her pink nurse's aide uniform on, the hem sewn three inches over her knee. Jackson had never seen her look so beautiful. She had gained a little weight, but it looked good on her. She smelled of raspberries.

"I thought you understood, Jackson."

"No, really. I'm not going to bother you. I came to say goodbye."

"Goodbye." Karen turned to go back in.

"No. Wait. I meant I'm leaving tomorrow for Vermont. I got a job up there as a private investigator and—"

"Jackson, you have a record. You've been to prison. No one's going to hire you as a private investigator—"

"No, really. Listen. I've changed. I'm clean. I've been clean since we broke up and I wanted to ask—"

"That guy is Sam. He's my fiancé, Jackson. What don't you understand? You're not clean. You'll never be clean. I am. I haven't even had a beer since we broke up and I want it to stay that way. You're bad for me. Maybe I was bad for you and I loved you once, but not anymore. I don't want you coming by here. I'm not going anywhere with you, and I don't want you sending me any more flowers or calling me and hanging up. I just want you to go."

She went back inside. Jackson stood there for a few moments until an eye filled the peephole again. He got back on the Schwinn and pedaled home.

Chapter 6

A FLIGHT TOO FAR

The flight from Charlotte to Burlington, Vermont, wasn't long, maybe four hours with the stopover in Newark, but that's an eternity for a drug addict. Jackson had no money and no smack, and it was killing him. Worse than that, he was in Vermont. Would he have any opportunity to score in such a backward state? Maybe. Every town supported its vices, wherever you went, and people everywhere had addictions like his. He'd have to hold out until the old lady gave him some cash.

He nearly froze to death on the long walk from the plane to the terminal. A heavy, wet snow fell and the light clothing that had been fine in Charlotte did nothing to ward off the bitter cold that blew in relentlessly from Canada. The terminal was warm, thank God, but had a musty smell of evaporating snow and slush. A cup of coffee would have been nice, though vodka would have been nicer. A cab driver came up to him just as Jackson sat down to warm himself.

"You Jackson Hurst?"

Jackson nodded.

"I'm to take you to your aunt's house in Shrewsbury, if you'll follow me. Luggage?"

Jackson had only one suitcase, a plaid monster that held everything he owned, although most of its contents his mother had bought for him, so he didn't really own anything, did he?

The cab weaved through small streets and then finally onto a two-lane freeway that headed away from Burlington. Large drifts of white snow lined the roadway, the frozen moguls blocking rows of Craftsman houses that delineated the towns from the endless birch forests behind them.

"So—what's your name?"

"Ralph," the taxi driver said.

"Yeah, okay, Ralph. How far to this place? What'd you call it?"

"Shrewsbury."

"Yeah, Shrewsbury. How far?"

"Eighty-five miles."

"Jesus. I thought she lived somewhere near civilization, for Christ's sake. So, Ralph. Y'all think you can find a liquor store or something."

"*Y'all.* You must be from the South, eh?"

"Yeah. Charlotte, eh?"

"North Carolina?"

"You know of another?"

"I guess I don't. About a mile back is Gracey Liquors."

"Well then, Ralph, turn this yellow cab around. Oh—and, Ralph?"

"Yeah."

"I'm gonna have to borrow a couple of bucks from ya, man. The old lady'll reimburse you. Cool?"

"She's going to have to, *man,* or I don't ever pick her up again. Only cab that'll go to Shrewsbury."

Jackson had drunk half a pint of the vodka by the time they reached Rutland, a town that surprisingly had restaurants and gas stations. Just outside the city, the driver turned left toward a mountain and drove what seemed straight up on a road that couldn't have fit more than one car at a time. Thankfully, the cab had it all to itself.

It was a half-mile drive up the mountain to his aunt's place. For the entire way, a stream paralleled the road. It was frozen ice, but he imagined that, during the thaw, the stream would flow like rapids because of the steep incline.

Not far from the top, they took a sharp left turn onto an even smaller road that had no name, apparently. When the snow covered the wheels of the cab, they stopped. The driver pointed to a huge Victorian a hundred yards or so away.

"There you are, son. This is as far as I can drive without getting stuck, even with the chains."

Jackson pulled his thin jacket around him. "You want me to walk in that? I don't have boots, man. She has to pay you anyway."

"Nah. She paid in advance. Paid me good too, eh? You tell her she owes me two-fifty for the pint. Tell her to mail it to me. Sorry, but all I can do is drop you or take you back."

Jackson took a quick swig and opened the passenger-side door. It stuck fast against a drift, so he pushed it hard with both feet until he could inch out.

"Thanks, pal," he said as he slammed the door shut.

Jackson started slow, sinking to his knees in the snow at each step, the weight of the suitcase slowing him as he dragged it behind him. There was a good possibility his benefactor would find his frozen carcass outside her mansion the next day unless a miracle happened or he suddenly grew snowshoes. The miracle turned out to be a large man with a Santa Claus, yellow-stained beard driving a fire-engine-red snowmobile. Santa lifted Jackson onto the snowmobile with one arm, not a difficult feat, since Jackson was down to a hundred and forty.

"Thanks, man," Jackson said, but Santa said nothing and brought him right to the doorstep of his aunt's looming mansion. It was three stories and a pale yellow, something he hadn't been able to make out through the falling snow. He tried the doorknob. It was open, so he walked in. His feet were frozen, or at least they felt like it. Blessed heat filled his lungs and warmed his body. The snow melted instantly, drenching his clothes and hair.

Aunt Camille strode into the foyer. She eyed him head to toe and expressed her disapproval with a frown that seemed fixed to her face. He knew she was in her seventies, but she looked much younger.

"They have no winters in Charlotte, I suppose, or have you not heard of our climate in New England?" She shook her head. "You can change in the first bedroom on the left." She pointed down a carpeted hallway. "Leave your wet clothes in the mudroom, two rooms farther down the hallway and then come back to the den." She gestured to a large door on her left.

After he changed, he slipped the half-empty vodka bottle into his jacket and hung it on a peg. You had to admire the opulent rooms along the way to the den. Uncle Edward must have made a shitload of money in the lumber and maple syrup industry to have Aunt Camille so well off twenty-five years after his death.

Jackson pulled his belt tight, but he was going to have to add another hole if he kept losing weight. It was the heroin, he knew, but there was nothing he could do about it. Ask Karen, she'd tell you.

The den walls were lined with shelves of books. Why call it a den? Why not a library? The wood paneling and shelves were a light color, probably constructed from poplar or maple. Aunt Camille sipped coffee and sat in an upholstered colonial high-backed chair. She looked over the rim of the cup and pointed to a chair opposite her.

"Jackson, my wonderful sister's only boy from lovely Charlotte. I escaped that dreadful place fifty-three years ago and never looked back. A pleasant trip, I hope."

"It was pleasant enough," he said.

She had always looked down on his family in her condescending way. Someone needed to tell her it wasn't her money, it was her husband's, until he kicked off early. Someone needed to tell her to shut her pie-hole until she earned the right to talk to him that way. Someone, but not him. He needed cash and he needed it sooner, not later. He'd probably have to drive to Boston to score, but if he didn't do it soon he was going to die. Be nice to her. Find out what his cousin did wrong and find out why Aunt Camille wants him to fix it, but for God's sake get her to pay in advance. "Santa Claus came to my rescue out there or I'd have frostbite. I can get winter clothes, but I'll need a little advance."

"What happened to the six hundred I wired?"

"I left it with Ma. She don't get paid until Friday and I didn't want to leave her without some cash. I could probably get by with three or four hundred."

"Is that what it costs for a fix nowadays? I thought heroin was much cheaper than that, but perhaps I'm wrong."

Jackson flinched. How did she find out? Had his mother told her? "What do you mean?"

"I mean, Jackson, exactly what I say. I always mean exactly what I say. You're wondering how I know. You're wondering if that's all I know. Well, it's not. I know about your dishonorable discharge. I know about your arrests, and I also know your neighbors suspect you broke into their houses, and they'd be right to suspect you, because you sold the stolen goods to a pawn shop. I even know your ex-girlfriend, Karen DuPree, wants nothing more to do with you despite dating you since high school. And I know you are in desperate need of that fix. Well, I hate to disappoint you, Jackson, but Vermont is not known for its heroin trade. Perhaps the alcohol will fend off your demons."

"How do you know all this?"

"I know all *this* because I hired a private investigator in Charlotte three days ago. He had no trouble tracking down your history. My boy, you are a damn mess and that's why you are presently invaluable to me."

Jackson fumbled for a cigarette, but he hadn't brought any with him.

"You said you'd start me in a business if I helped you with a problem with Cheryl. You said you'd pay me."

"And I will, if you do as I ask. Now excuse me. I'll be right back."

His aunt slowly lifted herself from the chair and walked across the den. While she was gone, Jackson looked in the lamp-table drawers for cigarettes. None. You'd think a rich widow would smoke with no husband around to nag her. As he sat, his aunt came in holding a glass jar filled with a greenish liquid. She placed it on the table in front of them. Jackson stared at a brown object lying on the bottom of the jar.

"What the hell's that?"

"That, Jackson, is Cheryl's ear."

Chapter 7

KIDNAPPED

It looked more like a pork rind than a human ear. How long had Aunt Camille stored it in the jar? And why?

She rubbed her head and cried, her pale complexion now a bright red. "They cut my child's ear off. Why would they do that? I would have given them anything they asked for without them having to hurt her."

Jackson had come for the money, not this. He'd thought, at worst, Cheryl had gotten pregnant and he'd have to threaten or pay off the father. Cheryl was a good kid and had treated him like a brother when she and her mother came to visit. Except for the kiss, but that didn't mean anything, did it?

"Kidnapped?"

"No, Jackson, they accidentally cut it off at the beauty salon. Of course, she was kidnapped, for Christ's sake! Is there a brain anywhere in your head?"

"Okay. Just asking, is all. Why do you have it in a jar?"

"That is my business."

"Okay, okay. You said 'them,' so you think there's more than one of 'em did this?"

"The note said 'we,' so yes."

She sat up, wiped her eyes, and composed herself. The concerned mother had metamorphosed back into the controlled business woman who had run her husband's factories for twenty years.

"Can I see the note?"

She shook her head. "Later. First I need to know if you are going to agree to do what I ask and also if you are physically able to do what I ask."

"I'm cool."

"Your hands are trembling, there's sweat on your brow, and you're pale. You obviously need drugs. It's evident you can't go on much longer without a hit, as you dopers call it. I do not care if you do, to tell you the truth. All I care about is getting Cheryl back."

"Why don't you call the police or the FBI?"

"As I explained earlier to your mother, it must be discreet."

"Well, then a private investigator, a local one. Even hick towns in Vermont must have private eyes."

"They can't help me. Only my poor excuse for a nephew can and that is why I have rented you a small office in Burlington and incorporated the business in your name. Hurst Private Investigation Agency. And I will fund your business at two thousand dollars a month for two years, if you live that long." She threw a bank envelope on the table. "There's a thousand dollars cash in that envelope. It's yours to do with as you please. After you leave here today, you can try to find a pusher who will sell you the heroin you need or you can give the money to a church. I don't care. But first, you must agree."

"Agree to what?"

"It will take some time to explain. Will you be able to last that long, Jackson?"

"I *could* use a drink."

She went over to a cabinet near the fireplace, removed a bottle, and poured two drinks. She walked as if balancing a book on her head. Was that how she landed the maple syrup magnate, perfect posture, Southern charm, flawless manners? Or did she throw herself on ol' Uncle Ed like Jackson's mother said she did?

"It's brandy," Aunt Camille said. She sipped. Jackson gulped. When he finished, he shoved his shaking hands into his pockets. His gut felt like someone had kicked him.

"I can't call the police or the FBI, because Cheryl isn't adopted, despite what I have told everyone, and I am afraid they might find out. She is nineteen now and it probably doesn't matter to the authorities anymore, but it would kill me if she found out. I can't hire a local investigator for another reason I will tell you about later."

Jackson went to the cabinet for a refill. As he poured, she said, "You might ask for another drink instead of helping yourself. You are just like your mother."

"Sorry." He sat back down.

She continued. "Edward died in '52. I was fifty-four at the time. I desperately wanted a child to quell the loneliness, but, of course, they won't let you adopt at that age and I could not see acting as a foster parent to a child I'd never be able to keep. I needed my own child, one that I raised from infancy. Have you read the Bible?"

"Forced to. King James."

"Then you know the story of Moses, how Jochebed placed him in a wicker basket when he was a baby and floated him among the reeds until the Pharaoh's daughter found him."

"I saw the movie."

"Well, that is exactly what happened to Cheryl. Sometimes, when the loneliness was too much, I walked near Meader's Pond to feed the ducks. One day, I saw a young couple place a galvanized washtub in the pond, and after checking to see no one was watching, they pushed it toward the stream that flows down the mountain to Rutland. They drove away right after that."

Jackson was headed back for the brandy when Aunt Camille said, "Sit down and listen. Do you want your money?"

Jackson sat. Her story, though interesting, was agonizingly slow, as she enunciated each word as if reading a picture book to a child. He needed a cigarette.

"Naturally, I looked in the wash bin to see what was inside and there was—"

"Cheryl."

"Yes, though I did not name her for a week. At first, I thought of going to the police, for she would have died if I hadn't saved her, but then I thought this must be God's way of giving me the child Edward and I had prayed for. I didn't bring her out in public for a year, but by that time it was easy enough to convince friends and family that I had adopted her. False papers were easily obtained over the years, and Cheryl, in my eyes, is my child, but that's why I can't involve the authorities. If Cheryl found out, she might think differently of me. Lately she has been expressing her independence while at college and I wouldn't want to alienate her any further."

"And me?"

"You," she said and sighed. "The kidnappers have given me a week to obtain a hundred thousand dollars. I have done so. You will be delivering the money to them tomorrow."

"You could have done that."

"I am not finished, Jackson. You were in Vietnam."

Jackson nodded.

"You've seen death—fired guns—killed the enemy."

Jackson nodded again.

"Then I will tell you why I asked *you* to come."

Aunt Camille opened the lamp drawer and took out a revolver. She placed it in front of him.

"They are *my* enemies. After we have Cheryl, I want you to kill them for what they've done."

Jackson picked up the gun and hefted its weight.

"You're shitting me, right?"

"I am most definitely not shitting you."

He spun the chamber. "Man. She might be dead already."

Chapter 8

THE NOTE

The note from the kidnappers had each letter of each word cut from a magazine or newspaper, glued to make sentences on a sheet of college-ruled paper. The FBI could have easily lifted prints from it if his aunt had gone to them instead of him, but then she might lose Cheryl and her precious chance for vengeance.

Jackson did not want to kill anyone. After this was all over, Cheryl would still have one ear and she could grow her hair long enough to cover it, so why make it worse? But if he wanted the money, and he did, what choice did he have? He'd need a plan and, so far, the only one he had was to take the thousand and bug out as far away from his crazy old aunt as he could. But then, there was Cheryl.

He read the note:

We have your daughter. You have her ear. If you call the police, we'll send you the other one. If you don't pay us one hundred thousand dollars by Thursday, we'll kill her. Place a briefcase with the money on the floating bridge at 11:45 p.m. Thursday, and then drive away. If we get the money we'll release Cheryl on Friday.

He gave the note back to his aunt. "And I'm supposed to kill 'em. How am I going to do that?"

Aunt Camille's expression was stoic.

Why didn't she kill them herself? She was mean enough.

"I have no idea how you'll kill them, Jackson. I just know that if you do not, there won't be any more money and I'll ask for the rent deposit back on your office. Then you can go back to my sister and live off her for the rest of your life, however short that is."

Aunt Camille filled her brandy glass and then his. He had to wrap this up, take the cash, and head south. But he'd need a car.

She continued. "You will take the money to them."

"A hundred thousand."

"Yes. You'll take the money to them tomorrow and, after they give us Cheryl on Friday, you will hunt them down and kill them and then you will bring me back my money."

Jackson sipped the sweet brandy. "I got no experience with that, you know, investigation stuff. Just firefights in 'Nam. How am I supposed to find them?"

"That's your problem, but I know someone of your suspect morals would have no problem killing for money and drugs. Especially drugs. Right now you are thinking of a way to steal my thousand dollars and blow it somewhere on heroin and whatever else cretins like you do for excitement. Of course, it will break your mother's heart when I tell her you stole my money and my car."

"Your car?"

"My Jeep. It's out in the garage building next to my Lincoln. It's the only way out of here, besides Ethan's snowmobile."

"Santa Claus–looking dude?"

"Yes. He helps out. He knows nothing of Cheryl's abduction. He thinks she is still in Burlington attending the university. I don't want him to know."

She picked up the envelope with the thousand and handed it to him. "Here. Be back here tomorrow, by dusk. Tomorrow night, you will drive to Brookfield and drop the briefcase off at the bridge. I know you will do it because you are fond of my daughter and she is fond of you. I saw that when we visited you. After the drop-off, drive away. Do not kill them in front of Cheryl, if she's there. When she is home, you can start your new investigation business by tracking down whoever maimed my daughter. If you kill them, and you prove to me you killed them, I will give you an extra twenty thousand dollars."

She handed him car keys. "Take the Jeep. It's full of gas and somewhat warm with the sides up. It has four-wheel drive. I want it back."

Jackson finished his drink and put the money in his jacket pocket. He reached for the gun.

"I'll keep that here, until tomorrow," she said. "Now leave and try not to overdose. Will you be here tomorrow night?"

Jackson nodded. "Yeah. For Cheryl."

Jackson went out the backdoor and slogged to the garage shed. He pulled the large wooden doors open and then drove the old Jeep out into the snow. As he was shutting the garage doors, he saw Ethan throwing firewood into a wheelbarrow, probably for the huge fireplace in the den. Jackson rubbed his hands together and slogged over to him. He hoped the heater in the Jeep was warming up.

"Ethan."

"Yes, sir, Mr. Hurst. What can I do for you?"

"Nothing, man. Just wanted to thank you for keeping me from freezing my ass off earlier. Dude, you rescued me."

"I did, indeed. Are you leaving?"

"Yeah, for Rutland—or maybe Burlington."

"Well, then, wait a second." Ethan walked in the backdoor of the mansion and came back with a coat. He handed it to Jackson. "That Jeep never really warms up. Now drive carefully."

"Thanks, man. I will. Peace."

"Peace to you, son. And go with God. And Mr. Hurst?"

"Jackson, Dude. Call me Jackson."

"Jackson. Miss Camille can be harsh sometimes, but she would give her life for her daughter. I assume you're here because of her."

"You know about that?"

"A little. Miss Cheryl has been gone a long time and Miss Camille has said nothing about it. Something has happened to Cheryl. I have known her since she was a child and she wouldn't stay away from here this long unless something's happened."

"Yeah, man—there's some trouble, but I'm taking care of it. Don't tell my aunt I told you, cool?"

"Cool. And please. Tell Cheryl that her Uncle Ethan misses her."

Chapter 9

ANGELS

The snow was getting worse and it was a hundred and fifty miles to Boston, the closest city large enough to have the smack he needed. There was no way in hell he could make it there and back in time for the money drop to save his disfigured cousin. What kind of hell was she going through? Had they done anything else to her other than cutting her ear off? Would she be able to conceal the injury by covering it with her hair? In 'Nam, he'd seen plastic surgeons work on grunts who had lost an ear.

The surgeon would remove skin from other parts of the body and try to shape something out of them, but it still looked like shit.

The Jeep's wipers struggled to rid the windshield of the heavy snow. He had to crane his neck out the side window to see the road. The withdrawal symptoms were worsening. Already weak from not eating and drinking too much vodka and brandy, he had to fight the nausea, runny nose, and, despite the freezing temperatures, the sweats.

This self-imposed detox wasn't working. He'd have to crash in a Burlington hotel room, his only hope, until he saw the angels on the side of the road in Brandon.

Two thin blondes in thick jackets and watch caps, thumbs out and gesturing wildly, jumped out from a side-road bakery as each car passed. Jackson stopped. What the hell? Company.

The first one in said, "Thanks, man. Christ, it's like a freezer out there. Is it like this all winter? They didn't say anything about this in Hartford."

"That where you ladies from?"

The girls looked maybe eighteen and were identical in every way: body, face, hair, clothes.

"Yeah," she said, "I'm Julie and she's Jane, but those are the Man's names. We changed them to Sky and Rain. With this weather, maybe I should be Snow instead of Rain. Hey, can you take us to the Red Maple. We've got a little weed, but no cash."

Jackson rubbed the windshield with the sleeve of his jacket.

"Let me do that," Sky said. He knew it was Sky because Rain had wedged herself into the small backseat. Sky leaned over the steering wheel and rubbed the windshield with her watch cap. Her hand touched his face. She was warm despite Rain's earlier protestations.

"What's the Red Maple? A restaurant?"

"No," Rain said. "A commune. You're not from here, are you? We had to sneak off for coffee and danish. A definite no-no at Red Maple, but we didn't know we'd get stuck in a snowstorm and we thought we'd get back before they noticed."

Maybe the girls would know where he could get a few baggies of smack. It wouldn't hurt to ask later. His head was throbbing. "If it's on the way to Burlington, I can drop you off."

"About twenty miles from here, near the state park," Sky said. She rubbed his arm. "We hitched all the way." She turned to Rain. "C'mon, girl. Light a joint. Dude needs something."

After Rain took a few tokes, she leaned over the seat and held the joint to Jackson's lips. He kept the smoke in his lungs for a few beats and then blew it out with a wheeze. It had a sweet smell and was easy on his throat.

"What's this commune like?" he asked. "Red—"

"Maple," Rain said. She grabbed the joint from Sky. "Ex-SDS, couple of Black Panthers, but mostly middle class, like us. We're gonna change the fucking world and we're gonna start here in Vermont. There're sixty communes within a hundred miles of here. Most started after Chicago in '68. There were a couple of hundred then but, you know, dudes gave up and went home to their racist world. Everyone's equal at Red. No sexism, no racism. We all work together. They'll take you in if you believe."

"In what?"

"A free society. The end of racism, imperialism, capitalism."

"What do you eat?"

"We grow our own on the farm. Everyone has a job. I grow carrots and preserve jams. The food's good."

"But no danish."

"No," Rain said, a little sadly. "Hey, you wanna fuck?"

They spent the next three hours at a cheap motel. Jackson wasn't much of a lover in the condition he was in, but he felt better after a few more joints and some candy bars from the vending machine. He had forgotten about the thousand he had in his jacket when he had pulled into the inexpensive motel. He had the money to stay somewhere better but had gone to a dive instead. Bad habits were hard to break.

Sky and Rain were able to amuse themselves when he had given up on their acrobatics.

He was afraid to ask if they were twins. Maybe he didn't want to know.

When the snowstorm ended, their *ménage a trois* headed for the Red Maple Commune, since he had agreed to take them, but also because they had assured him Freedom and Phoebe, the commune's leaders, had heroin. The girls had seen others shoot up, but they couldn't see why anyone would when they could safely drop acid. Maybe he'd stay at the commune. Why not? Pocket the thousand and live among fellow freethinkers. Then he wouldn't have to kill anyone for his psychotic aunt.

After a mile, he surrendered the wheel to one of his new lovers. He wasn't sure which one. He hadn't kissed a girl since Karen left him and as far as he could remember of the last three hours, he still hadn't kissed a girl. On the lips, anyway. The monotone hum of the snow tires lulled him to sleep, transporting him back where he didn't want to go . . .

Sergeant Becker finished with the Saigon hooker. Jackson had been with her first and she had refused to lie on the concrete of the bombed-out bunker, so he screwed her against the wall and then smoked some near-pure smack that whacked the shit out of his brain. He slumped against the wall and watched Beck work her over like a master until she begged him to stop. He was a mean son of a bitch with hookers. Mean as hell.

Then the whore started giving Becker hell over the price. Normally for a boom-boom, which was just a wham bam, the girl would charge five dollars tops, but this one was giving him shit because he plowed her for at least a half hour. She had a point.

"Give her what she wants, Beck," Jackson said. "Hell, I'll pay. Hang on." Jackson tried to unbutton a pocket in his Ks but then gave up.

"Fuck her," Becker said. "She wants twenty. Said she didn't do two of us for the price of one. Since when?" He smiled at the diminutive girl. She slapped his arm.

"Twenty dollar. He not free here." She pointed to Jackson, her voice rising in pitch to a screech. "You always pay too little. No more. You no good, anyway. Like little boy."

She reached for Becker's shirt pocket, where he kept his roll. He pushed her against the wall. She fell on her ass but got up and charged the six-foot, two-hundred-and-forty-pound Marine, swinging her arms like a runaway windmill, beating on his chest.

"You give me my money!"

Becker grabbed her neck with his left hand and lifted her against the wall until they were at eye level. Her eyes bulged as she tried to cough or scream or something, but only squeaks of air came out. Jackson wanted Becker to let her go but didn't have the strength to stop him. The smack was so pure Jackson would probably OD about the same time the whore suffocated.

"What's that, Giang?" Becker said, his face an inch from hers. He had that DI voice going. It hurt your ears the way the words resonated and vibrated in the burnt-out hallway. "How much did you say? One dollar? Is that what you said?" He squeezed so tight her tongue shot out, her arms and legs flailing like a marionette. "How much? A dollar?" She nodded, but then a few seconds later, it was too late. She had gone to join Buddha. Giang's little sister saw everything and ran like hell, screaming at the top of her lungs.

Chapter 10

RED MAPLE

Freedom was black.

He and Phoebe sat in high-back chairs in a meeting room that looked like it was once a large meat locker, the rusty eyebolts still hanging from the ceiling.

"Brother Hurst," Freedom said in a deep voice. "Sky Three and Rain Four said you are looking to score some heroin."

"I have money," Jackson said. There were folding chairs against the wall, but Sky, Rain, and about thirty others sat cross-legged on the floor, so he did the same.

"Well, my friend, you are not in Harlem, this is the Red Maple Commune and I am not a pusher. If you are in need of opiates to quell your addiction, then you are welcome to what we have, which is little, as we have successfully weaned off two in our family who craved the drug." Freedom held three baggies of heroin in his huge hands. He threw them to Jackson. "I assume you have nothing to administer the drug?"

Jackson shook his head. Freedom threw a kit to him. "Belonged to a dead man. He succumbed to his vice and fought rehabilitation. And you?"

"I just need it, man. I'll do my thing and bug out."

The big man pondered that. Jackson wondered whether he was one of the Black Panthers Sky had talked about in the car.

"Rain Four says you are an employed junkie. I find that difficult to comprehend."

"Why do you keep calling her Rain Four?"

"We have three other Rains and two more Skys. Popular names for our sisters, yes, Phoebe?"

Phoebe nodded and finished the thought. "At Red Maple you may choose the name that best fits you." Phoebe was a lighter shade of black than Freedom and spoke with a slight Caribbean accent. She had a freckled face that gave her a childlike look. "Why don't you stay with us, Hurst? The rehab is only three or four months and we work with city men from the hospital in Burlington who supply us with methadone so that the shock is not too dear for your system. If you want to contribute that thousand dollars then, that is okay."

Jackson gazed over at Sky or Sky Three or whatever her name was. She grinned. So, the girls had checked him out while he slept. He was lucky they hadn't robbed him.

"I'm a private investigator," he said.

Freedom laughed. "You? Oh my, if that's true you will surely starve. So you were a pig before, I think? Undercover?"

"No. Military."

"Even worse," Phoebe said. "A baby killer. One of Nixon's puppets. And so you are paid for these services? Who do you kill now, soldier?"

Jackson was about to say no one until he remembered he had agreed to kill Cheryl's kidnappers. And he had agreed to kill them for money.

"I was hired to find a girl."

"Here?" Freedom said.

"No. I came here to buy the smack."

"Is that what they call it out there now? Smack?" Freedom said to Phoebe. "I think we have been here too long, dear. Five years and nothing changes in their cities but the slang. Mr. Hurst—"

"Jackson."

"Mr. Hurst. I detect an accent. One of our brothers from the South, perhaps?"

"Charlotte."

"Yes—Charlotte. And so, it must bother you greatly to be asked questions by an uppity nigger. Does it?"

"No, man. It doesn't bother me."

"So, you like our kind?"

"My mother's house is in an all-black neighborhood. Their stuff pawns as good as white folks."

"So you steal from these niggers."

"Sometimes."

"And you seem comfortable with me calling them that. Do you call your neighbors *niggers*?"

"Not very much."

"I see. You know the South Bronx?"

"Heard of it."

"I once killed a man there who called me a nigger and he was a black man, and so, knowing that, Mr. Hurst, do you detest me enough to call me that?"

"No. I like you."

"You do. And why is that?"

"Because you gave me these." Jackson held up the baggies.

Freedom and Phoebe laughed until they cried. Freedom wiped his tears and spread his arms out like a preacher.

"This is our home. Eighty-two of us live and grow and love out here in order to lead a social experiment of organized anarchy. An oxymoron, you think, Mr. Hurst, but no, that is exactly what it is. We are the culmination of the civil rights movement where all—black, white, Hispanic, men, women—all are equal, all are the same. True, communes are dying. The children are leaving for their old homes, but the movement has not failed. The counterculture will one day be *the* culture. The seeds are sown in these children and they will run the world fairly, with compassion and with a new sense of righteousness and concern not only for their brothers and sisters, but for the land, the air, the water. A new dawn, Mr. Hurst. What started as a socialist revolution will one day be the status quo, with the end of capitalism and imperialism, with only small businesses producing and selling to their brothers and sisters in a utopian society."

Freedom stood and raised his hands to the ceiling. "And it started here, in Vermont, in only a hundred communes, but it started—here."

Rain Four leaned over to Jackson's ear and whispered, "He gives this talk to all the new members."

Freedom sat down and wiped his brow, seemingly exhausted.

Phoebe pointed at Jackson. "So, Mr. Hurst. Will you stay for your rehabilitation? Would you like to be free of the devil and work with your hands for the good of all or would you just like to go on caring only about Mr. Hurst?"

It wasn't a bad idea. Maybe he did want to be clean again, but not now, not yet. After he helped Cheryl, maybe he could come back to Red Maple and maybe they could wean him off the stuff as Phoebe promised. He'd pay. He'd have the twenty grand for his work as Aunt Camille's assassin and two thousand a month once he got the P.I. business going.

"I told you I have to find a girl, but when I'm done, I'll come back. It might take a few days to a week."

"O—kay, Hurst. We welcome you. Everyone?"

All thirty spoke as one. "We welcome you."

"Thanks," Jackson said.

Next on the agenda, shoot up, then rest until the smack wore off. He'd still have plenty of time to get to Aunt Camille's and pick up the hundred thousand. What would Phoebe think about that much cash if she was so interested in the thousand? What could he do with that much?

Freedom stood and bellowed. "Sebastian—or Fillmore?"

"What's that?" Jackson asked.

"Your new name when you return for your rehabilitation, Sebastian or Fillmore?"

"What's wrong with Jackson? I like it."

"No. You leave everything when you come to Red Maple." Freedom frowned at Sky Three and Rain Four. "Everything."

"Anything but Fillmore," Jackson said.

"Then—Sebastian."

Chapter 11

A HIPPIE BUYS PROVISIONS

The bitter cold woke him. Freedom and Phoebe had let him shack up in an old barn until he was rested. The usual flashbacks he dredged up from his year in Vietnam had not surfaced, only a dreamless sleep. For the last five years that sleep had brought visions of his sergeant's demise, the chunk of frag jutting from Corporal Riggs's chin, the murder of the whore, and of course the peasant girl. Maybe it was the smack that Freedom had given him, so clean it kept the dreams away. Karen never understood how Jackson could have the same nightmares and always in the same order. He couldn't explain to her or the military shrinks. The next one would be of the girl. He hated that one worst of all and it was the reason he still shot up, wasn't it?

He stumbled out of the barn and made his way to the Jeep. It started hard, but at least it started. How long had he been out? It was still daylight, so he had been asleep for either a few hours or an entire day. When he was juiced, the world stopped.

He slid his watch up the gearshift to read the face. Three twenty. It was an hour drive back to Shrewsbury, but he didn't have to drop off the money until Thursday. He had formulated a plan that might help him identify Cheryl's kidnappers. He'd need some help from Ethan, but then he'd have to tell him about the kidnapping and Aunt Camille would not approve. Before any of that, Jackson needed supplies.

The dope had been fine, but except for the initial feeling of euphoria, it only made him sleepy. Maybe he'd accept Freedom's and Phoebe's invitation for rehab. It seemed like they were more interested in his money than his welfare, but it was also possible they wanted to help him. If the rehab worked, he might stay at the commune for a while. Aunt Camille would pay him whether he worked his new business or not. Things could work out if the moon cooperated.

The mountain road widened at the intersection of the main highway. The Jeep climbed a small snowdrift and then he was on clean pavement.

Jesus, did it ever stop snowing in Vermont? The Jeep ground into fourth gear when he reached fifty.

After an hour of careful driving, he pulled into a Rutland diner to get coffee. He checked a newspaper someone was reading at one of the tables. He was close enough to read the date. Thursday. He had slept over twelve hours. No wonder he looked like shit. He sat at an empty table and gazed through the plate-glass window at a sporting goods store across the street. After gulping down coffee and eggs, he ran across the street through the cold air to the shop.

The Rutland Alpine Sporting Chalet had only one customer besides Jackson and both he and the athletic saleswoman looked up from the ski boots to glare at him. He was used to the look. With his wool coat, three-day shadow, long, dirty-blond hair, blue jeans, and old boots, he guessed it was obvious he wasn't a skier. He didn't care what the saleswoman thought of him. In a few minutes, she'd realize he had money to buy goods and she'd have to treat him like everyone else, despite his sunken cheeks and bloodshot eyes. Jackson was guessing on the last two, since he hadn't dared look in the rearview.

The shop had two floors. Apparel filled the bottom one while mostly skis covered the top loft area. He took off his coat and placed it on a chair. A rank odor emanated from his body. Would the woman let him try on clothes when she smelled him? Not likely. After a few minutes, the customer left.

"Do you carry tents?" Jackson asked.

"Yes," the clerk said, "but they are in back. We mostly sell them in summer months." She had a Scandinavian accent or faked one well. "Today we have a clearance sale on all skis."

"Do you have those small tents that zip up, you know?"

"Yes. In the back. Like I said."

Jackson pulled a wad of bills from his jeans and pretended to count.

"What I need, ma'am, is a small tent, binoculars, warm clothes, snow clothes, like when y'all ice fish."

"*Y'all*," she said, and smiled. That was good. He hadn't seen too many smiles for such a small state. Maybe it wasn't like Charlotte after all, where everyone stuck their noses in other people's business instead of minding their own.

He walked out with ski pants and a ski jacket, both fleece lined, a pup tent with a zipper, a gas heater, binoculars, thick leather boots, galoshes, and a sleeping bag. He'd only need the gear for a few hours, but that would be long enough to identify his prey.

Chapter 12

ENTRENCHED

He waved to Ethan as he drove up to Casa Camille or whatever she called her palace in the sticks. Ethan took a few seconds from warming his hands over the burn barrel to wave back.

Should Jackson talk to him about Cheryl or should he see his aunt first?

He decided on the latter.

Aunt Camille sat across from him, arms crossed, a disapproving look straining her wrinkled skin.

"Do you bathe?" she said.

"I could use a shower and some food."

"The bathrooms are on the second floor and you can fix yourself something in the kitchen. I see you've spent some of my money. Are you planning a ski trip later?"

He pulled his heavy ski coat off and placed it on the sofa.

"I need them for tonight. You can have 'em after that."

"Wouldn't think of it. I assume you found a supplier for your drugs, since you are here and not in a hospital."

"I came back to do what I said I'd do. I'll drop off the money and I'll track down and kill the men who hurt Cheryl. I don't need no more motivation than that. I don't need your damn money. I'll do it for Cheryl."

She lit a cigarette and handed one to Jackson. They both puffed several times before she broke the silence.

"It's after five. There's the money." She pointed with her cigarette at a briefcase.

"A hundred thousand?"

"Yes. I assume that when you eventually kill them, I will get the money back. If you screw up, and it's a certitude you will, then there's a possibility I'll lose my money. I will sacrifice the cash for the safe return of my daughter, regardless. Cheryl is the only thing that matters.

I want her alive, Jackson, and she must not know she wasn't adopted. Bring her home. After that, you can hunt them down and, if you kill them, I'll pay you the bonus. But *only* then. Do you understand?"

Jackson crushed the cigarette in the ashtray.

"I need Ethan to drive me to the drop-off spot in an hour."

"Why?"

"If I'm going to find out who they are I can't be the one to drop off the money on the bridge. Unless they're damn stupid, they'll wait for whoever makes the drop to leave before they retrieve the money. They'll probably have someone follow your Jeep to make sure it's left the area first. I might be able to make a move then, but I have to be entrenched."

"Is this a game to you? *Entrenched.*"

"No. Ethan drops me off. I set up a base, hide, and observe until they come for the money. I done something like it before, south of Khe Sanh. They'll never know I'm there. I can see them and what they're driving, and maybe the plates."

"In the dark?"

"No. In the moonlight."

"In the moonlight."

"Yeah. Out there it'll be like a flashlight."

"I thought in your condition and with your small mental capacity, you couldn't possibly do something even as simple as this. Apparently, I was correct. It's been snowing for the last two weeks and it's not supposed to let up for one more."

"Oh."

"Oh."

"I'm still going to try, but Ethan will have to know about Cheryl."

"No. I forbid you to tell him."

"Then who's going to drop me off and then drop the money later?"

"I will."

Chapter 13

BICKERING

If she kept sucking food through her teeth, he was going to smack her with the pint of vodka he had pulled from his jacket. He took a swig and sloshed it around in his mouth before swallowing. It didn't help his headache.

Aunt Camille disapproved by slamming her foot on the brake. Jackson's head almost hit the windshield.

"Why the hell did you do that?" Jackson said. They were in the middle of the snow-covered highway.

"Is that how you prepare for a job? What kind of private investigator do you plan on being if you're drunk during the investigation?"

"I never said I wanted to be a private eye. You said I was gonna be one. If you paid me two thousand a month and said I was gonna be a ballerina, I'd be a goddamn ballerina."

"Watch your mouth."

"You watch your mouth. You're not my mother." Jackson pointed the bottle at the oncoming traffic. "You gonna get us killed out here."

She shoved the gearshift into first and accelerated. She may have been seventy-five, but she handled the Jeep like a pro. She must have been a real bitch to work for at the syrup factory, a real hard-ass like that bastard Max at the Flynn.

"How far we got to the bridge?" Jackson asked.

"Four miles. What do you expect to discover about these men with you stuck in a tent full of booze?"

"Man, that's my business. I'll find out who they are and when I do, I'll get Cheryl, I'll get your money back, and I'll hunt down and shoot every one of them bastards."

"How will I know that you've killed them?"

"I'll cut their fucking ears off and bring them back to you like we did in 'Nam, if that's what you want."

She seemed to ponder that for a second as she shifted into fourth. Her breasts bounced against the steering wheel as the Jeep traversed each dip in the old highway. She had put on some weight in the last ten years. She rubbed her forehead and smiled.

"That's exactly what I want. They took Cheryl's ear and you will take theirs, and I want you to remove the ears before you kill them, not after. You *will* kill them, won't you, Jackson?"

"I said I would, didn't I? I've killed before. I killed a lot of VC and NVA too. Why do you think I'm so screwed up? You go over there and see how you turn out." He took another swig.

"Is that your excuse?"

"It's a pretty damn good excuse."

"It's a crutch you use to excuse your abominable behavior. Believe me, Jackson, your mother was glad to get rid of you. You're a spoiled, manipulating cretin who uses people until they've had enough of you, like your girl, Karen. I know all about her. I paid that man well to check you out."

"Keep her out of this."

"Why? Because it's too hard for you to—"

He slammed his hand against the dash. "I said, keep her out of this!"

The bitch was quiet for the next mile. He wanted the day to end. He was exhausted from the previous day's sex, the commune, the smack, the booze, and, especially, her.

"So," she said. "Adele doesn't approve of me or the way I raised Cheryl, does she? That's obvious. Jealousy has never been one of your mother's hidden traits."

"She's not jealous. She knows we're poor white trash and won't never amount to much, but she admits it. You're the same as us, except you lucked into money and you won't admit it."

"I ran that plant for twenty years after Edward died. What has Adele done, except raise a loser? A bona fide useless loser. Do you know why I don't mind fronting your so-called investigation business?"

"I know you're gonna tell me whether I give a shit or not."

"Because you'll never make it two years. You'll be lucky to live a year in your condition."

Jackson saluted with the pint of vodka and took a long swig. "You may be right about that, Auntie, and so that twenty grand you're paying me for some dead bodies is gonna make the last six months a blast. Man, what I can do with that."

Let her think what she wanted about him. She'd be surprised if she knew he planned on using some of the money for rehab at the Red Maple. If he were clean, Karen might change her mind about marrying that guy. She *would* change her mind.

His aunt pulled off a side road into a clearing and then onto a small road covered with snow. Ahead was the floating bridge, the narrow stream below it frozen.

She parked a few feet from the bridge. "Now what?" she asked.

Jackson pointed to a clump of firs and birches on a small hill about fifty yards away. "Up there. I'll set up the tent in the trees. They won't see me there."

She floored the Jeep. It spun side to side in the snow as it climbed the hill.

"Won't they see the tracks?" Jackson asked.

"It's going to snow. The moon will be out as you wanted, Jackson. You just won't be able to see it through the three inches of falling snow. Unless you hallucinate it, of course."

"I won't need it. I got another plan."

She threw it in neutral and pulled the emergency brake. "That makes me feel so much better. Get out, and you'd better find out who they are. And let me tell you something, Jackson. And I am absolutely serious."

"What's that?" he said as he opened the door to step out.

"You had better kill them and get my daughter or, I swear to God, I will have you killed. Do you understand?"

Jackson reached in for some of the gear in the back. "You're serious?"

"I am."

"Well, I can't do nothing unless you drop off the money at midnight. You do that and then if I mess up, you can get one of your maple syrup buddies to take me out."

Once he had his gear out, Aunt Camille sped the Jeep down the hill just as it started snowing again.

Chapter 14

WAITING FOR KIDNAPPERS

The snow had covered the Jeep's tracks just as Aunt Camille had predicted. There would be no moonlight, so he'd have to rely on luck and a flashlight for any clues to the identity of Cheryl's kidnappers.

The combination of the enclosed tent, the gas heater, and the vodka kept him warm. If the temperature continued to drop, Jackson would have to get into the sleeping bag until they arrived to pick up their money. He left an opening in the tent to vent the heater exhaust to the outside. He didn't want to kill himself with the carbon monoxide fumes. That would take all the fun away for his aunt if she had to bump him off later.

He had a good view of the bridge with the binoculars, though they'd be useless at night in the overcast conditions. He would have to sneak up on their car and get the numbers off their license plate. Jackson had used his skill for stealthy observation many times in Vietnam, scouting villages or counting the enemy, though never in twenty-degree weather. He needed to stay sharp and aware tonight. He still had six hours until they arrived, which left enough time to rest.

He swallowed the last of the vodka, a faux warmth in his stomach, but better than nothing. He needed a hit and he had two baggies left, but he was determined to show the bitch he could be responsible and lay off the smack until he finished the job.

Jackson slipped into the sleeping bag and rested. No tourists would be visiting the floating bridge this time of year. They'd flock to it later, after the thaw, excited by the wobbly ride as the weight of their cars made the bridge sway on the water. Frozen, it was just another bridge.

Years ago, Jackson had given a speech at his junior high in Charlotte about the famous floating bridge near Brookfield, Vermont, after visiting his aunt's family. Who would have thought that he would return to the site years later to execute his aunt's vengeance for his cousin's kidnapping? He closed his eyes, exhausted. The nightmare would come. He knew and he didn't care. He was too tired to care . . .

His platoon had been in two firefights earlier. The Tet offensive, the name given for the massive strikes against major cities in South Vietnam by the North Vietnamese Army and the Viet Cong, had begun in earnest, and Jackson's platoon was right in the middle of it. They needed to return to Da Nang to defend the city, but Intelligence wanted them to first clear out Lac Ngai, a small village supposedly harboring Viet Cong insurgents. He wanted to get the job done and get the hell back to Da Nang. They had lost Kerry Madison to a sniper in the first firefight and then Eddie Jones stepped on a mine in the second.

Jackson's second lieutenant, Cale Sanders, was a good ol' boy from Macon, but he didn't know shit from Shinola, so the platoon was dependent on Lawrence Becker, Jackson's sergeant and supplier of the heroin Jackson seemed to need more and more of lately.

Becker told Sanders they needed reconnaissance before crossing the Phu Cuu Bridge into the village, but Sanders, who was right out of OCS and didn't have enough goddamn sense to hide his gold bar on his uniform, ignored his veteran sergeant and ordered the men across.

In the middle of the crossing, Sanders's head exploded, blood and brain tissue spraying Corporal Caldwell and PFC Walker. The entire platoon did a right oblique on the bamboo-and-rope bridge and emptied their clips in the direction of the shot.

Rounds whistled overhead as two grunts in front collapsed in a heap. They were taking heavy fire from the huts in the village, orange bursts shooting out of slits and windows.

"Everyone off the fucking bridge—now!" Becker yelled over the gunfire.

The platoon bolted for the village side of the bridge. Jackson and his sergeant dragged two of the wounded across. When they reached the other side, the platoon laid down a volley of fire that splintered the huts. Becker ordered a cease-fire when twenty to thirty villager—old men, women, and children—ran screaming out of the huts and down a dirt road bordered by irrigation ditches.

Becker pointed to them. "Hurst, Caldwell! Round 'em up. Don't let them get to the bush. Go!"

Jackson and Caldwell ran after the villagers, who all seemed to be dressed in black pajamas. Caldwell fired three quick bursts on auto and dropped two in the back of the fleeing group. He yelled for the rest to stop and fired again, this time into the air. They stopped and dropped to their knees, arms up in surrender.

A pregnant woman cried and pressed her hands together as if in prayer.

The firefight in the huts raged on behind them as Becker trotted up to Jackson. He pointed his pistol at the group of villagers and yelled to them, "Get in the damn ditch!" He gestured again with his Colt. They didn't understand but backed into the ditch, anyway, as he threatened them with the gun. He turned to Jackson and Caldwell.

"Take 'em out and then back to the huts. I only have a clip left."

"But, Beck—"

"I said take 'em out, Hurst."

Jackson hesitated then raised his rifle. The women screamed. Caldwell changed the clip in his M16 and stood beside him. Jackson froze when he saw the pregnant woman covering her face with her hands. Could she really be VC? And the old men and the kids?

"Damn it, Hurst," Becker said. He took Jackson's rifle from him and sprayed it like a water hose, mowing down the villagers, the rifle barrel swaying back and forth in its deadly dance. Caldwell joined in as the faces disappeared in blood. Becker threw the empty rifle back to Jackson and handed him his Colt .45.

"Make sure they're dead, you asshole." Becker and Caldwell ran toward the huts. Jackson hesitated for a few seconds, hoping no one in the bloody pile of bodies would move, but then the pregnant woman cried out in pain. Jackson slid down the ditch embankment to her and held the muzzle against her head.

She stared up at him, eyes pleading . . .

Jackson sat up, unzipped the sleeping bag, and slipped out onto the cold floor of the tent. He heard an engine. A car or truck idled near the bridge. He moved the spent heater and unzipped the tent a little more to look out. It was dark. Had he slept so long he'd missed the drop? He grabbed his watch from the pocket of his jacket and looked at the time. Five minutes to midnight.

His arms felt like ice as he held the binoculars up to the slit in the tent. There was a car at the front of the bridge. No, it wasn't a car. It was the Jeep. Aunt Camille opened the driver's-side door and worked her way out of the seat to stand on the icy road. She walked around to the back of the Jeep and lowered the tailgate to remove the briefcase of money. Auntie was punctual if nothing else. As she shut the tailgate, the lights reflected an eerie red glow over her body.

Jackson panned the binoculars, but even if the kidnappers were nearby, he wouldn't be able to see much of them in the dark. He'd have to wait until they retrieved the money to get a close look. If they were smart, they'd park down the road and walk to the bridge. Jackson hoped the cold temperature would make them prefer driving, instead.

She left the briefcase on the bridge about ten steps from the Jeep. She yelled something, but he was too far away to hear what it was. She must have thought the kidnappers were watching her every move.

A few minutes after she left, they drove up in an older four-door sedan. He couldn't tell the make of the car in the dim reflection of their headlights off the snow, but it was boxy and probably inexpensive.

Good. They had driven up to retrieve the money, not walked, so they hadn't thought the plan out well or were new to crime.

If Aunt Camille had called the authorities instead of hiring Jackson, the novice kidnappers would now be in custody, but then they'd live and Aunt Camille wouldn't get her vengeance for her daughter's ear.

Jackson grabbed the flashlight and binoculars, slipped out of the tent, and ran as fast as he could down the small hill. His boots sank in the heavy snow and progress was slow. Why hadn't he bought snowshoes or a damn sled?

No one had exited the car, which Jackson was able to identify as a Ford Falcon or Mercury Comet. It was either blue or green, but it was difficult to tell with only the reflected illumination of the headlights.

He stopped ten yards from the car when a tall, thin black man with an Afro opened the door, lighting the inside. There were two white men in the backseat, both with long brown hair and mustaches. A woman sat between them. A woman. Could he kill a woman after what had happened in that village? Did he have a choice?

The black dude opened the briefcase, smiled when he saw the contents, and held it up to the headlights for his partners to see. Then he shut it and slipped back into the car.

Jackson plodded toward the car through heavy snow, each step a struggle, as he had to pull his legs free of the snow to make any progress.

The car did a three-point turn on the narrow road and sped off toward the main highway.

Jackson jumped from the snowdrift to the road and pulled out the flashlight to shine on the license plate. The flashlight didn't work. It must have broken when he hit the road. The license plate light was dim, a pale yellow that lit up only the right side of the plate: 47B.

Chapter 15

THEY CALL

Jackson spent a restless night in the creaky mansion. Around two thirty in the morning he gave in to his cravings and shot up another one of Freedom's baggies. Aunt Camille had grilled him earlier when she had picked him up at his makeshift hideout near the bridge.

"Who are they?"

"How should I know? They ain't too smart, driving to pick up the money. Three men and a girl."

"Cheryl?"

"No—at least not as far as I could tell. I haven't seen her in ten years, so I'm not sure. Thin, red head, frizzy hair. She didn't go outside the car. A black dude picked up the money and then they bugged out. I got the license plate, or part of it."

"How do you get part of it?"

"A letter and two numbers. I'll go to the DMV and track it down."

"Cut your damn hair, then," she said. "They won't wait on a damn hippie." She swerved but corrected well on the slippery roads. "The letter said they'd call the next day. They promised they'd drop her off somewhere once they had the money. I want you to come with me when I pick her up. We'll get there early so you can follow them after they drop her off. You won't need the DMV. You can take the Jeep and I'll take Cheryl to the hospital in a cab."

He thought about that. "What if they don't drop her off?"

"I don't want to think about it."

"You have to consider calling the cops if they don't. Does it really matter if she knows she wasn't adopted if she's in trouble?"

"Yes, it does. If they don't keep their promise, then you'll have to track them down and make them. That's why I hired you."

The call came at ten that morning.

"Ya did fine, Miss Hebert. The old McGreevy place on Thirty-Seven at noon. She'll be on the side of the road. Cops show up, we shoot her. You understand?"

"Yes," Aunt Camille said. "I understand. And if you don't do as you say, then I will call the FBI. Do you understand?"

There was no reply, just a dial tone. Jackson placed the extension he had been listening on back in its cradle. When he walked into the den, she looked up from the receiver.

"It was the black dude," he said.

"Do you think she's alive?"

"Yeah," he said, but he was lying.

Why would they not kill her? They had the money. It would be stupid to release her unharmed when she could identify them. Well, unharmed, except for the ear. No, she was dead, but why did they bother calling Aunt Camille at all? Was it a cruel trick? He'd find out soon.

They arrived at the old McGreevy farm at eleven, an hour before Cheryl's drop-off. Like before, Jackson hid from sight. After three hours, it was obvious they weren't coming. She was dead. It would be up to him to use his sparse information to track the killers down. He would. For Cheryl.

The four miles back to Shrewsbury seemed endless as his aunt sobbed the entire time, her last vestige of hope for her beloved Cheryl gone. Jackson almost felt sorry for her. Snow fell as she exited the Jeep. She leaned back in. "Kill the girl, too. You hear me?"

Jackson nodded and drove off. He hoped the girl wasn't pregnant.

Chapter 16

GOLDIE HAWN AND THE DMV

There was no Department of Motor Vehicles annex in Rutland, so it was off to Burlington. How much money would he need to offer the clerk to track down the license plate numbers? He still had five hundred. He'd start with a couple of hundred. A clerk would take that, considering they probably made about three dollars an hour. He wondered if real private investigators worked like that.

He pulled the Jeep into a parking place in front of an old brick building that had a severely pitched slate roof. Five-to-six-foot icicles hung from the edge, threatening patrons who rushed into the entrance of the DMV while staring up at the menace, as if one might impale them at any moment. Jackson did the same. If the locals worried about it, so would he.

There were two clerks, an older woman with a stern demeanor and a young girl, maybe his age, with granny glasses, long, blonde hair, and a green body shirt. She wore a bra, which surprised him, but maybe the state required it. Even though the older clerk was available, he waited for the blonde. She would be more likely to help him.

A man in her line finally left and she motioned Jackson over with an index finger.

"Hi," she said.

"Hi, yourself. I've got a problem."

"That's why I'm here. What can I help you with Mr. . . ."

"Jackson."

"Mr. Jackson."

"No. I mean Hurst. First name's Jackson. What's yours?"

She had blue glitter on her eyelids and wore long fake eyelashes. She looked a little like Goldie Hawn. "Melody."

"Cool name. Like a musical or something."

"Yeah, or something. What can I do for you—Jackson?"

"Okay. Here's the deal. I met this guy, a friend, you know, and I let him borrow something and he never returned it, and so I'm looking all over for him, but he never told me his name."

She rolled her eyes. "And he's a friend?"

This wasn't going well. Maybe he should have just offered her money.

"Yeah. Anyway, I need to get in touch with him, but all I have is a letter and two numbers of his license plate. I know you're not supposed to give out addresses, but it's really important. Life or death. And I can pay—a lot."

"Are they at the end of the plate, middle, or the beginning?"

"End."

"I might be able to find it. It won't be easy. I'd have to write a small program and punch out some cards. It's FORTRAN, but it's not too complicated. We share time with the computer at the university. It takes about a half-hour and it's expensive."

"How much?"

"Three dollars." She chuckled. "Oh, and for future queries you might want to know it's not illegal for us to give out license-plate numbers or addresses. And, Jackson?"

"Yeah?"

"I'll help you, but I've got a problem too."

"What's that?"

"I get a lunch break soon and I don't have anybody to smoke a jay with me in my van."

"Sounds good to me, man."

Melody turned out to be adept with computers. After she wrote a simple program, as she said, she placed the cards in a reader connected by phone to an IBM 360 computer mainframe at the college. Apparently, the college handled databases for the state as well as other businesses around the area.

At first, the digits 47B spit out over a hundred possible license plates, but when she modified her program to add blue Mercury Comets or blue Ford Falcons, only one name popped up: Ira Walker. The address was in Brattleboro. After a short break with Melody, he'd check out Mr. Walker to see if he had a young girl with a missing ear tied up in his basement.

Melody was also adept at sex. She didn't mess around once they were in her van, stripping naked as soon as he had closed the side-panel door. She sat cross-legged on the shag rug and lit the joint.

"C'mon, Jackson. Take off your clothes, man. I only have a half hour." She passed him the joint. It was cheap stuff and burned his throat. After some spirited copulation, they lay back against beanbag pillows and shared a warm Boone's Farm wine cooler.

Melody kissed his neck. "There was something else on the printout besides the name and address, Jackson. I didn't want to tell you because you might have freaked and left before we could groove a little, you know?"

"What was it?"

"Well. The guy, Walker? Your friend?"

"Yeah?"

"He reported the car stolen, like two months ago."

Jackson had thought about that earlier but hoped the kidnappers were stupid enough to use their own car.

"I didn't think Ira sounded like a black guy's name, anyway."

"Your friend's black?"

"Yeah. Big afro, too."

"That's Purple Haze," she said, sitting up.

"Who?"

"Purple Haze. That's what we call him. He always has the best acid. He comes to parties at the college. There's one tonight at Chi Omega. Haze will probably be there. The frat boys are out of town, so we use the house. It's out there. You wanna come?"

"Sure. But what's his real name?"

"George something. Wills or Wells, something like that. I bet I know what he has that belongs to you."

She couldn't have known about Cheryl, could she?

"What's that, babe?"

"Acid. The guy's always mooching when he's not selling. He's got a couple of buddies and a girl, Janie something or other. They're all Weathermen wannabes dropping leaflets and wearing the shirts, but nobody believes them."

Jackson couldn't believe his luck. "You sure you're not mixing him up with somebody else?"

"Christ," Melody said, swallowing the last of the sweet wine cooler. "He may be the only black guy in Vermont."

Chapter 17

FRAT PARTY

The Chi Omega house dated back to the nineteenth century, one of many two-and three-story Victorians bordering a park facing the University of Vermont. Large icicles hung from the slate roofs just as they had from the DMV. How many unsuspecting college students had been impaled by the frozen stalactites that seemed to populate every building on the hundred-and-eighty-two-year-old university campus?

The Doors' "LA Woman" blasted through the frigid air as Jackson and Melody stepped into the inviting foyer of the frat house. There were too many partiers to count, none of whom he guessed to be actual fraternity members, the male half with hair as long as or longer than most of the girls. Melody and Jackson both wore their blonde locks to their shoulders and parted it in the middle. They could have passed for siblings.

Purple Haze, aka George, was easy to spot, being the only black guy in the house. He preached to the ten or so rapt partiers who surrounded him near a large couch, a commanding presence, his words booming in sync with his Afro. Jackson grabbed ales for Melody and him and led her to Haze's crowd.

"You think there ain't no fight to be fought no more, don't you?" Purple Haze asked. "Well, there is and it's big, real big. You think Tricky Dick's gonna go down with Agnew and Haldeman and Ehrlichman, that we won one, that the revolution has started and we don't need the SDS or the Weathermen or the Panthers or the BLA no more? Well, bullshit. As long as they got my brothers and your brothers fighting the Man's imperialistic war in Vietnam, our fight ain't over. That war's all about money and making sure Russia and China don't make more than the Rockefellers and Cabots. The Man takes all the brothers and ships 'em out to die so's he can keep his oil. I know. I was there. I saw it all."

Jackson moved to the front by the couch. This was too good to pass up. He bumped a bowl of pills sitting on a coffee table.

"Hey, Johnny Winter," Purple Haze said. "I paid good money for those bennies, you know."

"You were in 'Nam? Where?" Jackson asked.

"All over, man. All over. Don't tell me, you one of them vets who get out and turn hippie and think that's gonna make it all better."

"What division?"

"Hell, man, I had enough of that. They made me go. How 'bout you, 'Nam? You volunteer?"

"Yeah. Marines."

"Marines!"

The crowd had gotten larger.

"Man, so you a baby killer? Old women and babies?"

"Yeah."

"Yeah?"

"Yeah. Babies, women, and old men, but at least I was there."

"So you killed babies? What you think about it now, 'Nam? What you think about the Man's war?" He grabbed Jackson's wrist and flipped it over. "Now you just a junkie, what do you think about it?"

"I don't think we should be there. I think we should get out. You can let go of my arm."

"And what if I don't let go of your arm?"

"I'll make you let go."

"Okay, 'Nam. Make me let go." Purple Haze twisted harder. Jackson grabbed Haze's thumb and bent it to the big man's wrist. Haze howled in pain and went to his knees. Jackson kicked his chest and Haze fell back onto the couch, pissed. The crowd also looked pissed. Jackson was ready to leave anyway. He looked for Melody, but she seemed to have split.

Once outside, he parked the Jeep three cars down from Purple Haze's blue Comet and shut the engine off to wait. Every hour or so he'd start the Jeep to warm the inside. It was two a.m. before Haze, two white guys with long beards, and the redhead with the perm left the party and drove off. Jackson followed their car from far back, since there was little traffic at that hour. A half hour later, they turned down a small snow-covered dirt road into an old farmhouse in Jericho.

Jackson parked off the main road in a spot where he'd have a good view of the farmhouse in the morning. He shut off the engine, bundled up with several blankets, and tried to sleep. The next morning would be the first time he murdered someone illegally.

Chapter 18

A HIGH PI

At dawn, Jackson cooked the smack and held the spoon to his nose. It smelled like sweet syrup, happy nectar. His last baggie, but Freedom and Phoebe might have more at the Red Maple. No matter how hard they professed to damn the smack, they'd sell it just like his pusher in Charlotte had, wouldn't they? People were all the same—pushers were all the same. "God damn the pusher man," he mumbled. As he plunged the needle into his vein, little droplets of blood trickled onto his ski jacket. He didn't like the jacket, anyway.

The heroin was strong, much stronger than the last had been. Was it from the same batch? His arms and legs felt like lead. In and out of sleep, he watched the farmhouse as the morning sun crept over the neglected roof that sagged like a swayback nag.

He rubbed the window to clear enough moisture to see. One of the bearded dudes had come out the front door with just a light jacket on. He was going to freeze his ass off if he stayed out there too long. The guy lit a cigarette and then put his right glove back on and his lighter back in his pocket. He slapped his hands together and walked through snow and around concrete steps to the corner of the farmhouse. He flicked his greasy hair out of his eyes and struggled to twist a huge television antenna fastened to the corner of the farmhouse. He yelled something to someone inside. His breath fogged, shrouding his face. Jackson forced his numb hand on the window crank and turned it slightly to listen.

"How's that?" the dude yelled.

Something indistinguishable bellowed from inside. It sounded like Purple Haze. Jackson could tell by the booming baritone notes. The dude twisted it more.

"That's as far as it turns!" he shouted and ran back inside.

Half an hour. Jackson would rest a half hour and then make his move, if his legs got any feeling back into them and the world stopped spinning. It turned out to be an hour before he felt strong enough to do anything. How long had it been since he'd eaten something? He had shared some food with Melody in her van, but he couldn't remember what it was. Raisins or nuts, maybe.

He took the .38 out of the glove compartment and popped open the cylinder. He spun it slowly. All six rounds were in. He slammed it closed and put a handful of spare bullets in his pocket, but he wouldn't need them. He was a crack shot with a rifle or pistol. He had earned sharpshooter honors with both weapons in the marines, although the pistol he had used then was a clunky Colt .45. Still, he would need only four rounds.

He eased out of the Jeep, slid down an embankment, and toppled into a gully. Snow jammed between his neck and his jacket collar. He pulled it out and let it melt in his mouth. Smack left his mouth dry. He ran to the front of the farmhouse, vomited by the steps, then looked up at the door, but no one had heard him.

It had to be done quickly, though he had to be sure he didn't shoot Cheryl. Three steps up, gun in hand, he twisted the doorknob. The door opened. He slammed into it with his shoulder, startling the four. Bearded dude number one dropped the briefcase of money off his lap. Purple Haze smiled.

"'Nam. What you doing here and with a gun and all?"

Bearded dude number two grabbed a rifle off the dining-room table and leveled it at Jackson. Jackson got a round off, aiming for the torso, but the guy crouched, the bullet slamming into his shoulder, knocking him to the floor.

The redhead screamed, dropped to the floor, and backed away on her ass like a little kid playing on waxed linoleum. Jackson moved over to Purple Haze's side and had the muzzle through the Afro and against the temple.

"Where's Cheryl?"

"What?"

Jackson pulled back the hammer with a loud click. "You heard me, man."

"Hell, 'Nam. What's your problem, man?"

The scream stopped Jackson from pulling the trigger. A tall, thin girl in jeans and a thick jacket stared wide-eyed at him from the hallway. Her hair was light brown, cropped shorter than before, but he knew it was Cheryl from the button nose and dimple.

She had both ears.

"Cheryl?"

She looked around the room at the redhead, the bearded brothers, the spilled money, and then back to him.

"Jackson? Is that you? God, what are you doing?" She pointed at the pistol.

"You got both your ears," Jackson said.

She looked confused and then stared at the blood on bearded guy number two.

"Jesus Christ, you shot Aaron. Why the hell would you do that?"

She pulled Aaron's jacket off and looked under his shirt. It was a small hole below the collarbone. She ran to the kitchen and came back with a wet dishtowel. As she dabbed the blood from the wound, the spent bullet fell out of the shirt to the wooden floor.

"Your mother thinks they cut off your ear so she—"

"Not now, Jackson." She pointed to the redhead. "Janie. Get something to use as a bandage and some peroxide, if they have any. We have to get him to a doctor."

Purple Haze moved toward Jackson. Jackson aimed the gun at him.

"Don't you shoot him, Jackson," Cheryl said. "Put it away. We're not going to do anything."

Jackson gestured with his gun to Aaron. "Dude there was going to try something with that rifle. I want to know what the hell is going on, so everyone just sit down."

No one sat. Jackson fired in the air.

"Now!"

They all sat, Cheryl the last to obey.

"Okay, Cheryl. You tell me what's going on and everybody else shut the fuck up."

"We need to get Aaron to a doctor."

"I may just kill Aaron and then it don't matter, do it? So tell me. Now."

Cheryl lit a cigarette and said nothing until Janie attended the wounded Aaron.

"We needed the money for the cause. You wouldn't understand. My mother definitely wouldn't understand. What do you think she would say if I asked for a hundred thousand to finance Weathermen projects?"

"You faked your own kidnapping? Who the hell's ear is that in the jar at your house, then?"

"That was my idea, 'Nam," Purple Haze said. "Momma ain't gonna give it up for her baby lest we show her we're serious, so we dug up a recently deceased Mrs. Harriet Allen of Bennington, who was beloved by all who knew her, and borrowed an ear she might not be needing. Clever, huh?"

Jackson felt faint, the vertigo coming back. He closed his eyes. When he opened them, the room faded in and out of focus. The smack was screwing with him.

"You tripping, 'Nam?" Purple Haze said. "You come to the rescue on acid? Give me your piece and sit down, dude."

Jackson aimed the barrel at Purple Haze, who backed off, wide-eyed.

"She wants—she wants me to kill 'em," Jackson said.

"Who wants you to kill them?" Cheryl asked.

"Your ma. She wants me to kill all of them."

"My mother said that?"

"Yeah. She doesn't want you to know."

"Know what?"

"So I'm going to kill them and you're not supposed to know."

"Man," Haze said. "This guy's wasted."

"She doesn't want me to know what, Jackson?" Cheryl moved toward him. He aimed at her stomach. No one lives with a stomach wound. She stopped and backed up.

"About you're not being adopted, so I have to kill them and not tell you."

As he passed out, he fired the last three rounds.

Chapter 19

RESURRECTION

The windshield wipers strained under the weight of the falling snow, the repetitive swishing mixing with the static from the car radio. A hand twisted the tuner from one end of the frequency spectrum to the other and then gave up. A woman's hand. Jackson could taste beer. He blinked his eyes to make out her face. Cheryl.

"I think you died three times," she said, then shut off the radio. Warm air blew through vents from the floorboard. "You'd stop breathing for ten or twenty seconds and then start up again with kind of a squeak and a gasp. You freaked me out."

Jackson sat, but with great effort. They weren't moving, though the engine was on.

Cheryl handed him a half-empty beer. It soothed his upset stomach.

"We found your needle in the Jeep. I think you overdosed. Haze said maybe a bad batch."

"Where are they?"

"Who?"

"Haze and your buddies. Where are they?"

"They took the money and left for the commune."

Jackson grabbed the dash and pulled himself up straight. His head hurt worse than his stomach.

"The Red Maple?"

"No. The one we belong to in New Hampshire. I'm not going to tell you the name."

She started to come into focus. Even with the short hair she was beautiful. She looked sixteen. He tried not to imagine her with that freak Aaron.

"Your mother wants you and the money back."

"Well, she can't have either. We need that money and she has enough. She won't miss it." Cheryl wiped something off the side of his mouth with the sleeve of her coat. "Why did she want you to kill my friends?"

"How do you know that?"

"You said it in the house. Right before you shot the sofa three times and passed out."

"Sorry. Your mom thought they cut off your ear and when they didn't drop you off like they promised, she wanted to get back at them. She said she loves you."

"She smothers me. She always has, never letting me have friends over, never letting me visit anyone. That's why we called, to make her think they were going to let me go. I *wanted* to hurt her."

"You did."

"Good. She controlled everything I did. I never want to see her again." Cheryl lit a cigarette.

Jackson reached over and took one out of the pack. He'd let her talk for now. He could go get the money and take her home later.

"What did you mean when you said I'm not adopted?" she asked.

"What?"

"What did you *mean* when you said I wasn't adopted?"

"I said that?"

"Yeah, you said that."

It was out now. Nothing he could do about it but apologize to his aunt later. So much for the Hurst Private Investigation Agency.

"That's why she kept you on a short leash. She saw a young couple float a washtub down Meader Stream. I think that's where she said. You were in the washtub. A newborn, maybe a few days old. She said she had wanted to adopt when my uncle died, but they wouldn't let her and so God brought you to her. She didn't want you to know, so she hired me instead of calling the police; afraid they might find out the truth if they investigated."

"A washtub?"

"Yeah. Your parents dumped you and Aunt Camille saved your life, the way I see it."

"That's why she was upset ten years ago when I wrote the orphanage. I asked them if they could tell me who my parents were and they wrote back saying they had no record of my mother adopting me from there. Mom saw the letter and freaked that I wrote them. She said she adopted me from out of state. I believed her."

"Sorry," Jackson said. "I'm gonna have to go get the money and take you back."

"No. I'm never going back and we're keeping the money. The country needs to change and we'll change it, but it's not cheap."

"She won't pay me if I don't bring her you and the money."

"Probably not, but at least you can tell her I'm alive."

"Yeah. I guess so. Hey, thanks for watching out for me the last few hours."

"That's okay. Thanks for telling me about my real parents. I think I can figure out who they were. I was born around March in '54, according to my mother, so it'd be easy enough to see how many babies were born that month in Rutland General. I imagine they have records."

Jackson nodded. "Or the papers might have announced the birth. Couldn't have been more than five or six babies born that month in Rutland that long ago. I'll check it out. I gotta learn how if I want to be a PI anyway. When I find out, I'll get your real parents' names. I have an office in Burlington. Maybe. Depends on your ma. You can come by. Do you really want to know? I mean, your parents left you for dead."

"I really want to know."

She rolled over into his seat, straddled him, and kissed him hard on the lips. He tried to pull away, but she grabbed the back of his head with surprising strength and held him to her throughout the long kiss.

"I've always wanted to do that, Jackson."

"That ain't right, Cheryl. We're related. I mean, I liked it and all, but it's weird with a cousin, you know."

She pecked him on the lips and slipped back in the driver's seat. "We're not related, Jackson. We never were." She threw the Jeep in gear.

"Where are we going?"

"New Hampshire. You're dropping me off."

Chapter 20
THE SEARCH

Jackson spent the night at the Bent Hill Commune in New Hampshire. Purple Haze gave him three thousand to keep his mouth shut and said he'd kill him if he told anyone where they were. The next morning, Jackson forced down a ham-and-egg breakfast at a roadside diner and then drove to Vermont. He didn't know how long he could go without a hit, but he stopped himself from driving to Red Maple.

He wasn't looking forward to facing Aunt Camille. She would be glad Cheryl was safe and sporting two ears, but would be livid about the fake kidnapping and the loss of the hundred thousand. She'd have his ass on a plane back to Charlotte, but at least he'd have a little money. He wasn't going to tell her Cheryl knew she wasn't adopted.

If Cheryl truly meant it when she said she'd never see her mother again, why tell his aunt he had spilled the beans? She didn't need to know. He still had enough cash to keep high for a few months in Charlotte. And then what? Who knew? Nothing good.

He needed to keep his promise to Cheryl first and find the names of her real parents. He stopped east of Rutland and called the Burlington Library from a payphone.

An older woman answered. "Burlington Public Library. May I help you?"

"Could I have reference?"

"I take care of reference."

"I'm trying to track down a birth announcement from 1954. Do you have copies of newspapers going back that far? And do you have copies of the *Rutland Herald* also?"

"We have them on microfiche. Three papers going back to the 1850s: the *Rutland Herald*, the *Burlington Free Press*, and the *Colchester Review*."

"If I come by today, can I look through them?"

"Yes. Someone will show you how to run the tape on the viewing machine."

Jackson drove through Shrewsbury and kept going to Burlington. Aunt Camille could wait. The only problem he had was how to get the information to Cheryl. Maybe Melody would see Purple Haze at a party and get the news to him. It was a possibility.

He went through a whole month of *Rutland Herald* tapes for March of 1954 and found only two babies announced in the paper, both boys. With no luck there, he decided to look through the *Burlington Free Press* for the same month, in case the baby was born at the Bishop DeGoesbriand Hospital and the parents decided to drive all the way to Rutland to dump Cheryl. Since Burlington was the largest city in Vermont, there would be more births and certainly more girls.

Jackson fed the tape into the machine and turned the knob to advance Monday's paper through the large viewfinder. He slowed it to the section of birth announcements on page six. Two boys were born that day. One to a Mr. and Mrs. John Daley and the other to a Mr. and Mrs. Philip Tatroe. No girls. He advanced the tape to Tuesday's front page. If he found a girl born that day, he'd write down the parents' names and track them down, if they still lived in the area.

Then he saw the headline in two-inch bold letters.

Chapter 21

BREAKING THE BAD NEWS

Jackson stopped at the only phone booth in Shrewsbury to call his mother collect before driving on to his aunt's house. They talked for half an hour. Ten minutes later, he arrived at the mansion. As he parked the Jeep, Ethan met him at the detached garage.

"Miss Camille wants to see you in the den, young man."

"And I want to see her, Ethan."

Ethan looked in the back of the Jeep. "She said you'd be carrying a briefcase of hers."

"No, man, she's mistaken. I can find my own way in, no problem."

Jackson pulled his jacket tight and prepared to run the snow gauntlet to the front door.

"Did you see Miss Cheryl?" Ethan said, his hand on Jackson's bony shoulder.

"Yeah, man. She's cool."

Ethan closed his eyes. "Thank God."

Jackson went in and sat on the couch across from his aunt's chair. Ethan brought him hot tea, although he would have preferred coffee. An antique mantel clock ticked in time with its small pendulum. Was she being fashionably late or was her intent to make him sweat? He had no feeling of anxiety at the moment; unusual for a junkie, he knew.

A whistling sound came into the den from somewhere near the kitchen, followed by a cold wind. Someone had come in from outside. Aunt Camille walked resolutely into the den, dressed in outdoor wear and holding a shotgun split open in the middle. She turned it upside down and shook out the spent shells. From her jacket, she removed two new cartridges, loaded the gun, and slammed it shut.

She leaned the shotgun against the fireplace mantel and removed her snow-soaked jacket and scarf. Underneath, she wore a long-sleeve plaid shirt and blue jeans. She looked masculine with her short hair and tall, broad frame.

Was she trying to send a message to him subliminally? Or maybe not so subliminally. She did threaten to kill him if he failed. He didn't feel like he had failed. She sat in her chair and lit a cigarette.

"I've been having wolf trouble," she said between puffs. "I had never seen a wolf in Vermont in my life until last year. There's one less now, though. I rarely miss with my shotgun."

Jackson sipped his tea and smiled. She gestured to him with her cigarette.

"Correct me if I'm wrong, Jackson, but I don't see my daughter or my briefcase of money and I'm sure Ethan would have mentioned if you had four dead bodies in the back of the Jeep. I hope you're not going to tell me you were sidetracked by something or so stoned you weren't able to follow up on your information. I don't know how I would react if you told me my baby is dead or still missing. I don't think I could control my anger and disappointment. I might even lose my composure and begin shooting wildly with my shotgun. Please tell me, Jackson, none of that has to happen."

Jackson crushed his cigarette into the ashtray.

"Cheryl's all right."

She closed her eyes. "You've seen her?"

"Yeah, and she's got both ears."

Aunt Camille sat up straight in her chair, the ashes dangling on her cigarette. "I don't understand. Why didn't you bring her back? Where's the money? Are they dead? For God's sake, you idiot, say something."

Jackson smiled and leaned back against the couch. "She also knows she ain't adopted."

His aunt stood abruptly. It startled Jackson. "Damn you. I said she wasn't to know! Why did I think a stupid moron could do anything I ask?"

"You wanna hear the story or not?"

"Of course, I want to hear the story. I paid for it."

"You did at that. Now sit down and I'll explain."

Ethan poked his head through the door. She gestured him away. "Everything's fine, Ethan. I'll call you if I need you."

"Yes, ma'am." He closed the door.

"I found them in an old farmhouse in Jericho," Jackson said. "Three guys and one girl, the same group that was at the money drop. George Willis, the black guy, was their leader. He calls himself Purple Haze—"

"What in God's name?"

"Let me keep going. I busted in the farmhouse and shot one of 'em in the arm. They were counting the money. Right before I was about to shoot Purple Haze, Cheryl walked in after listening to us with *both* ears."

"I'm—confused."

"I know. Listen. Cheryl faked her own kidnapping to get a hundred thousand from you. How's that? You understand yet?"

"You're a liar. You kept the money for yourself and never looked for her."

"Not true. She's a member of an underground group, and she's convinced she is bettering the world with your money. She's fine. She's got your money and she's shacked up somewhere out of state."

Aunt Camille stood and walked over to Jackson. She slapped him, her nails drawing blood. "Liar."

Jackson held up his hands. "God's truth. Think about it."

She sat back down and held her head in her hands, sobbing. After a minute, she looked up. "They must have brainwashed her. She wouldn't steal from me unless someone pushed her to do it." She lit another cigarette. "Why did you tell her she wasn't adopted?"

"It slipped out."

"You idiot. You useless idiot junkie. I'll have to hire someone to bring her and my money back. I was insane to think someone my sister bore was worth a damn. I want the thousand I gave you. I'm obviously not going to pay you the bonus and you can forget about the office in Burlington. Go home, Jackson. Go home to my sister and ruin what's left of her life. I don't want to see you again."

Jackson shook his head. "I'm not going anywhere. This is my new home. I *will* open my business in Burlington. You *will* pay me the twenty thousand and you *will* pay me a stipend of two thousand every month until I'm able to build clientele in the business. Also, you won't try to find Cheryl and you won't try to get your money back."

"And why the hell would I do any of that?"

Jackson stood, pulled out a photocopy of the front page of the March 25, 1954, edition of the *Burlington Free Press*, and threw it down on the coffee table in front of her.

She went wide-eyed as she read the headline: *Newborn Abducted from Hospital.*

She opened her mouth but said nothing.

"There was no family or washtub," Jackson said. "You kidnapped someone's baby and hid it here in the mountains until people forgot about the abduction in the big city. You passed Cheryl off as an orphan, but folks around here probably thought some relative left her with you."

"This isn't proof," she said. "There's no way to tie Cheryl to this."

"Maybe. But I'm sure the Burlington police would investigate anyway. Get rid of a twenty-year-old crime. They'll contact the parents and take blood samples. They'll investigate you and they'd find your fake documents. Sooner or later they'll figure it all out and arrest you."

She went slowly over to the fireplace mantel and traced her finger over Cheryl's high school graduation photo.

"They had two children, Jackson. And later, one more. I didn't have anyone. When Edward died, I was alone. Do you know what that's like up here for six months of winter? I had enough money to raise a hundred babies and they wouldn't give me one. Not one!" She backhanded Cheryl's photo off the mantel. The glass shattered on the hard floor. She walked over to the shotgun, placed her hand on the barrels, and glared at Jackson.

"Don't even think about it," he said. "I stopped and called Ma before I came here. She knows everything. If I mysteriously die or go missing, she'll call the Burlington police."

Aunt Camille moved her hand from the shotgun and sat back down.

"And now?" she asked.

"Nothing. Pay me my money. I won't ask for more later. This isn't blackmail."

"That's exactly what it is."

"No, it's not. You promised to pay me a certain amount if I found Cheryl, and I found her. She kept your money, but she's your daughter. At least everyone thinks she's your daughter. I won't tell the police or Cheryl you're a kidnapper. You know what you are and you gotta live with it. I'm going to Bristol to the Red Maple commune to get my head straight, and then when I feel like it, I'll go to Burlington and work. Ma won't say anything about her older sister, the baby stealer, unless something happens to me. I'll grab my stuff and get the hell out of here as soon as I can. You make sure my money goes into an account I can access. If you don't, I'll expose you."

Jackson opened the den door to leave.

"Do you think she'll ever come back?" she asked.

Jackson shrugged. "Maybe. It'll take some time, though."

"I don't have a lot of time left."

"Yeah," he said. "You're right about that."

He shut the door behind him.

Chapter 22

RELUCTANT ANARCHIST

Two Years Later,
North Brook, New York, 1975:

Cheryl dug her nails into the oversized Ford Econoline steering wheel, the odor of old plastic wafting up as she jabbed deeper. Purple Haze leaned in next to her, took a toke from the roach clip, slammed home the magazine into the assault rifle, flipped off the safety, straightened his Afro in the rearview, checked for food in his teeth, and *then* exhaled. He was an arrogant self-centered bastard who had forgotten why he joined the cause in the first place, and the only reason Cheryl hadn't left—he wouldn't let her.

She had wanted to quit the Weathermen since the explosion, the memory still fresh of running naked onto the cobblestone street, her clothes burned from her body, the smell of charred flesh nearly as pungent as the pot smoke Purple Haze now blew through his nostrils.

Two friends had died that day, comrades in arms who, frustrated by the failure of their generation to overthrow the corrupt, imperialist U.S. government, had resorted to violence, to bombs, to death. But the only deaths were their own.

"Move it up closer, baby," Haze ordered Cheryl. She started the van and moved along the curb two spaces closer to the North Brook National Bank, a two-story brick building sandwiched between a McCrory's and a Western Auto. "Brinks takes the fire lane, right, Yardbird?"

"That's right," Yardbird said, without looking up from his shotgun. He shoved shell after shell into the tubular magazine under the barrel. Yardbird got his name from his time at Attica. He was the oldest of the group of five in the stuffy van. The previous week he had led three Black Liberation Army soldiers on their successful break-in at the National

Guard Armory in Plattsburgh, killing two security officers after promising Cheryl there'd be no violence, that they just needed the weapons to rob the armored truck.

"You sure 'bout the fire lane, and you sure there's gonna be a million in that Brinks sucker?" Haze asked Yardbird, who looked up this time.

"How many goddamn armored car robberies you done, Haze? Well, I done two already so maybe I know what I'm talking about when I say the damn truck is going to park in the damn fire lane, and when I say they gonna have a million then they gonna have a million. *Shit.*"

"Okay, cool," Haze said. "I hear you, brother. No doubt you ready. How 'bout you, Aaron? That shoulder still messed up from where 'Nam shot you?"

Aaron was Cheryl's sometime lover. Two years ago, her cousin, Jackson, had wounded him during a botched kidnapping. Sometimes, late at night, after a little acid, she thought about Jackson, and how it felt that time to kiss him and hold him in her arms. They weren't really related since her mother had found her in a washtub as a baby and passed her off as her adopted daughter, but despite that, Cheryl couldn't convince Jackson to go further than a kiss. Still his momma's boy, she guessed.

Aaron held up the M16 in salute. "Arm's fine, Haze. Let's just do this and go home."

"Now that's the kinda attitude I like to hear from you white folks. Maybe you could get your girlfriend here, Miss A-bear, to come around to your thinking. She seems to have a problem following orders lately."

"You're not in charge," Cheryl said.

"I am today, baby. Purple Haze is the fucking man."

Cheryl sneered at him to hide her fear. She was going to be all right. The gang would get the money, change cars, and go home. No one would get hurt as long as no one resisted, and why would they resist when being held up by four gunmen? She needed to shift the subject away from her.

"How'd you get that name, Haze?" she asked. "Don't think you ever told us. You don't look like Hendrix except for the hair."

"Oh, baby, I'll tell ya. You know Jimi wasn't just known for his guitar. No, ma'am. Jimi, the ladies said, was graced by the good Lord with an extra-large member just like myself, and so the ladies that knew that 'bout him started callin' me Purple Haze in honor of the man. You want me to show you?"

"I'll pass."

"We'll see," he said, the smile gone. "What time you got, baby?"

Cheryl checked her watch. "Five."

"Should be arriving anytime. Yardbird? You gonna do the driver, right?"

"Yeah," Yardbird said. He pumped the slide backward and forward to chamber a shell.

"Aaron, you and Comrade Janie check our backs. Anyone tries to be a hero, you stop 'em, dig?"

"We got it, Haze," Janie said. Janie had been with the group since they were SDS back at the University of Vermont. At one time, she and Cheryl had been friends and even lovers, but now Janie had lost sight, like the rest of them had, and she did anything Haze told her to as long as he kept her high and treated her like he did the other soldiers. She pointed her nine-millimeter at Cheryl.

"Haze, she's gonna boogie as soon as we get out of the van. She'll leave her brothers and sister to the pigs. Look at her shaking. Can't trust her, babe. I'm serious. After the townhouse, she told me she was getting out. Maybe I should stay here and watch her."

"Naw," Haze said. He lowered the M16 below the dash and shoved the muzzle against Cheryl's ribs. "Baby, you know what gonna happen if I see this van move one fucking inch while we're out there?"

Cheryl said nothing.

"This van moves, I'll spray it before you get away from the curb. You hear me, sister?"

She nodded.

"Good," he said. He glanced out the windshield then ducked between the bucket seats, sliding into the back of the panel van with the others. The Brinks truck had pulled in front of them and was backing up a few feet. The thick steel doors opened and two guards stepped out, one pulling a hand truck out of the back. Once clear, he slammed the doors and looked around. His gaze met Cheryl's and he nodded. She mouthed the word *help*, but he only smiled at her and followed the other guard into the bank. That was when she saw the patrol car in the side-view mirror.

* * *

Officer Loyal Kendricks liked his job patrolling the streets of North Brook. Most of the six thousand residents of the small community knew him and liked him despite him being the only black officer on the small North Brook police force.

He was still a patrolman after seven years on the force, but that would change in three months when he made sergeant. He knew the chief was taking his time because Loyal was black. It bothered him a little, but not enough to quit and commute fifty damn miles to work for the NYPD like his partner, Dave Brown, the man seated beside him eating his third donut, planned to do.

"You gonna save me one?" Loyal asked.

"I bought 'em," Dave replied.

"Bullshit."

"Okay, so Carol *provided* them with the coffee, but I went inside and got them."

Loyal reached over for the bag. "Gimme one of them jellies without the powder. You'd think the brass would dress us in something other than blue, knowing how messy them powdered ones are."

Loyal took a few bites while steering with his left hand. He turned down Carver Street, the main drag, so he wouldn't have to maneuver and could concentrate on the dollop of jelly about to spill on his uniform, which he'd spent his own damn money on, having it pressed and starched that week.

It was the usual busy afternoon downtown, workers commuting back from the Big Apple to their quiet suburban homes, some stopping to pick up dinner or have drinks at one of the three bars along the strip. If he had a minute before the end of the shift, he'd pick up something from the deli for Yolanda and Loyal Junior, thirteen and taller than Daddy, the boy a terror on the court with colleges already showing interest.

Loyal was coming up on North Brook National. The Brinks truck was blocking the fire lane, as usual. Should be a big load, today being Friday. Millions maybe. A white panel van with tinted windows was parked pretty damn close to the Brinks. The driver's-side window was rolled down.

"What's up with that?" Loyal said to Dave as they came up behind the van. A woman—young girl, maybe—had her arm out the window waving like crazy. The Brinks guards came out of the bank with a hand truck loaded with bags. He drove past. "Gonna double back up here a ways, Dave. Let's see what she wants."

"Get your arm in here, sister," Haze said. "What you doing?"

Cheryl pulled her arm back inside and grabbed the steering wheel. "Nothing," she said.

She realized she had made a huge mistake trying to flag down the patrol car. Haze and the others had no intention to rob the armored car without violence. That was obvious when Yardbird said he was going to "do" the driver. Now, by tipping off the cops, she'd made a bad situation worse. They'd try to stop Haze and there'd be more dead bodies. Maybe she was lucky and they hadn't seen her wave. The patrol car slowed at an intersection two blocks ahead. When the light changed, it made a U-turn. Damn it, she thought. Damn it to Hell.

"Here come the guards," Haze said. He peeked over the seat at the bank entrance. One of the guards was pushing a hand truck with six or seven moneybags on it. The other held the glass door. He had his revolver out by his side.

"This is for the Panthers," Haze said. "This for the BLA and the Weathermen and any of the revolution who would seize funds from the illegitimate to redistribute to the people. Right on?"

"Right on," the group replied.

It was how Cheryl had thought once. She knew someday the revolution would take place as it had in Russia and Cuba and the power would return to the people. The only way that could be achieved was through protest, then defiance, then violence. Hadn't there been violence in all revolutions? But now it was 1975 and the war was over and the protestors and radicals wanted to return to their old lives, to achieve their goals through political, not violent, means. Now there were just leftovers like Purple Haze and Yardbird and Aaron and Janie, common criminals, thugs more interested in money than the cause. Why hadn't she included herself in that list? Wasn't she like them? A psychiatrist once told her she was rebelling against her mother, not society. Maybe he was right. It was moot now. In a few minutes she'd be dead along with the others she had once called comrades.

The three others in the back of the van pulled ski masks over their heads as Purple Haze slid the side door open. He held his fist up in the

Panther salute and stepped out, followed by Yardbird, Aaron, and Janie. Yardbird walked around the van and then sprinted for the front of the Brink's truck. He raised the shotgun at the guard behind the wheel and fired twice, blasting the thick glass inward.

Cheryl screamed at the boom of the shotgun, but couldn't look away. Haze fired three short bursts of the M16 into the guard holding the revolver. Both guards had turned to look at the front of the truck when Yardbird let loose the blasts. Aaron fired on full automatic and the guard pushing the handcart toppled over, his torso nearly split in half.

The North Brook patrol car barreled toward the firefight as the wounded Brinks guard with the pistol rolled on the pavement and fired at Aaron and Janie. The bullets slammed into their protective vests and knocked them to the ground, but they looked unhurt.

Haze fired again at the armed guard, ripping his chest to pieces with the 5.56-millimeter rounds. Janie walked up to the guard lying on the pavement, aimed her pistol, and calmly fired twice into his head.

Yardbird spun around when the patrol car screeched to a halt near the front of the Brinks truck. His shotgun blast blew in the passenger side of the cop's windshield, coloring it red. A huge black cop rolled out of the driver's side, firing all six shots at Yardbird, who only flinched at the impacts on his bulletproof vest. He aimed his shotgun barrel at the big cop, but the gun misfired.

The cop frantically reloaded his revolver as Yardbird fumbled with the shotgun to dislodge the spent shell. He worked the pump until it cleared and then fired at the same time the cop fired three shots back. The cop's left arm took the blast, ripping the sleeve of the uniform to shreds in a spray of blood and bone.

One of the cop's bullets had hit Yardbird in the neck and he was leaning against the Brink's truck, yelling, "Haze! Haze! I'm hit! Haze!"

But Haze was busy helping Aaron and Janie fling the moneybags into the van. After loading six of them, Haze ordered the others into the van and then jumped in himself, sliding the door closed behind him.

"Move this motherfucker!" he yelled to Cheryl, whose hands were frozen to the steering wheel.

"Yardbird's out there, Haze," Aaron said. He slid the door back open. "I'll get him."

"Leave him, and shut the damn door. He's dead. Now shut up and shut the door."

Haze jumped into the passenger seat. He aimed the M16 at Cheryl. "I said go, bitch. Go!"

Cheryl shifted into drive.

"He still alive, Haze," Aaron said.

"Shut the hell up."

"I'm going out," Aaron said. Haze turned and fired a shot that blew off a large chunk of Aaron's forehead. Cheryl cupped her ears.

"Now you'll shut up," Haze said. He shoved the hot muzzle into Cheryl's side.

"Go!"

Cheryl accelerated just as the wounded cop emptied his revolver into the van's windshield. The three rounds missed everyone but fractured the glass, making it impossible to see. Haze used the stock of the M16 to smash out the windshield and Cheryl floored the Econoline, narrowly missing the patrol car.

They had gone over the route a hundred times. She turned right onto Wyatt Road just as four patrol cars raced by on Carver, heading for the robbery. Two left turns and then a right took them into the alley where they had left the Buick. Purple Haze yelled orders to Cheryl and Janie while they threw money and weapons into the trunk. He held his M16 close to him as he slid into the passenger seat. Janie jumped to the back.

Cheryl hesitated outside the Buick. If she ran as hard as she could, she'd be three alleys away before Haze and Janie could react. By that time they'd be ready to leave and would let her go. A nine millimeter pistol protruded from the left rear window.

"Get in, honey," Janie said, almost musically.

Cheryl drove slowly out of town while Haze and Janie crouched down below the windows, holding their weapons on her.

She would drive them to New Hampshire, to the commune where they'd be safe. She wondered what her mother would think when they pasted Cheryl's photograph on the evening news. She wondered what Jackson would think.

Chapter 23

SUPERFLY PI

Fireflies swooped at the flames, risking incineration as they blinked like midnight traffic lights, backing off only when the smoke billowed. Like bothered bees, they hovered a few yards away, gathering courage for their next sortie at Jackson's campfire.

Jackson sniffed the familiar wood smoke that reminded him of his father and their weekly treks through the Carolina woods, sometimes to hunt and sometimes just to be together. He wiped his eyes and blamed it on the smoke.

Dinner was two hotdogs and a baked potato he had cooked in aluminum foil that he removed too early, impatient to get the greasy hotdog taste out of his mouth. He rolled a joint on the sleeping bag after taking care to comb the seeds out of the cheap weed. He had to watch his money. His private investigating firm sometimes took in less than what he owed in rent—and so the cheap weed. It was his only vice, having kicked smack the previous year, though he still smoked cigarettes. Was that a vice? He guessed it was, considering the surgeon general said so.

He checked his watch. Two-thirty. Soon he'd fall asleep. He'd wake up by nine, but just in case he had brought a cheap alarm clock with him. If it was like every Thursday morning at the Burlington Country Club, Marjorie Fitzgerald and Big Bill Cooper would be stopping by the wooded area off the second hole around ten or ten-thirty. But this time Jackson would be there hiding behind a tree or in a gully or someplace where he could click five or six pictures before Margie and Bill caught on.

He held the smoke in his lungs for five heartbeats then blew it out his nostrils. He was getting a pretty good buzz. He took two pictures of the ground with his new Nikon FT2. The 1975 model had come out in January, but his had not arrived at the local photo shop until June. He bought it with what was left of Aunt Camille's money stream that had now run dry. She had promised to foot him for two years only, so now he had to work.

That was why he was camping out on a private golf course at two thirty in the morning. Jerry Fitzgerald, the owner of the local Buick dealership, had hired him to catch his wife and that son-of-a-bitch, Cooper, as Jerry said, *in flagrante delicto*, and Jerry didn't give a damn what it cost him as long as it wasn't more than six hundred dollars.

Jackson negotiated six-fifty from the cheapskate to offset the cost of film, though he hadn't used much in the investigation. Despite following the couple for three weeks, Jackson never saw them together long enough to consummate their illicit affair. They ate dinner and had drinks at the country club and played tennis, but not once had he seen a zipper lowered or a dress lifted.

He thought Jerry Fitzgerald might just be paranoid until one Thursday when he spied the couple from a high hill near the Burlington Country Club with his two-hundred millimeter zoom lens. On the second hole, Bill sliced a driver into a heavily wooded area on the right side of the fairway. The couple looked three-sixty to see they were alone and then drove into the trees to find what Jackson thought was the wayward ball. Twenty minutes later, they drove out of the woods with Margie straightening her hair, golf skirt, and shirt.

Jackson actually said, "Aha."

He opened the manual he had brought along and circled a paragraph. The book was titled *Private Investigation Training* and it had saved his ass several times since he had started taking clients. At first, there hadn't been many, but then he'd bought a short brown wig to hide his long blond hair. That's all it took to get paying clients, mostly small stuff like Jerry Fitzgerald collecting ammo for an impending divorce.

It seemed stupid to camp out overnight on a golf course to catch rutting lovers, but it was a private club and there was no way they'd let Jackson follow the couple during their round, so he had snuck on after dark and hunkered down until morning. No different than Vietnam except there were no mosquitos and no VC trying to blow his head off.

Jackson snuffed out the fire and fell asleep to the loud ticking of the alarm clock and the fireflies' exotic dance. He woke at ten the next morning only because he had to take a wicked piss. Otherwise, Margie and Bill might have discovered a long-haired, skinny bum trespassing on the second hole of the prestigious Burlington Country Club.

He stood and peered through a vee in the pines at the number two tee box. He pissed as he watched, scattering an unlucky praying mantis. Bill Cooper swung mightily with his persimmon driver, knocking the golf ball at least two hundred yards, unfortunately for the eager couple, straight down the fairway. Undaunted, he hit another that rattled over Jackson's head before dropping near his sleeping bag and the damn clock he had forgotten to turn on the alarm.

Jackson gathered the sleeping bag, camera, and clock, then hid behind a large maple near a gully that still had a little snow at the bottom—not unusual, he had found out from the locals. Snow sometimes made it through June if the gully was deep enough.

Margie had hit her tee shot and they were barreling down the sloped fairway. After the usual surveillance to make sure no one saw them, Bill and Margie drove over pine needles and wet maple leaves into the tree shelter to find Bill's ball.

Bill wasted no time, massaging Margie's right breast like he was kneading dough. Margie responded with a French kiss, though the golf cart hadn't yet come to a full stop. Jackson leaned out from behind the tree and raised his Nikon.

Bill Cooper was a sixty-five-year-old millionaire who owned most of the Burlington docks, fitting for a guy built like a stevedore. He didn't look sixty-five. Margie, on the other hand, was forty-five, attractive, and kept herself thin by chain smoking and never experiencing the joy of giving birth. She was also quite athletic. She lifted her skirt, pulled off her panties, and mounted Bill before Bill had his Sansabelts to his ankles. Jackson rattled off shot after shot, the lovers lost in lust, unaware of him or his clicking camera.

He had a good view of the carnal action through the viewfinder and understood completely why Mr. Cooper went by the moniker "Big Bill." Jackson wondered how the jilted Mr. Fitzgerald would react to the photos of Margie enjoying herself.

He let them finish, as if he had a choice. Margie rolled off Bill and squealed when her bare bottom hit the cold golf cart seat. Jackson accidentally stepped on the alarm clock. Margie had a cigarette out and nearly lit when she looked up at the sound and her eyes met Jackson's.

"Who the fuck are you?" she asked.

Was this the same Margie who rolled her eyes at the restaurant table when a fellow diner said, "Damn"? Jackson gave a little wave and clicked a few more pictures.

"Answer the lady," Bill roared. He slid out of the cart, waddled like a penguin, and then, after pulling his pants all the way off, strode over toward Jackson. "What the hell do you think you're doing?"

His dick was limp but still hung prodigiously. Jackson smiled, unable to take his eyes off it.

"Seriously, man," Jackson said. "You gotta do porn."

Bill did not see the humor in that. He charged Jackson, who let the big guy have it with a roundhouse kick to the solar plexus. Margie screamed as Bill doubled over, out of breath, and fell to his knees. Margie came at Jackson swinging. He held her off with an outstretched arm until she gave up and went back to Bill.

"Is Jerry paying you to take those?" she asked, pointing at the camera.

Jackson shrugged. "He needs proof for the divorce, Margie. He knew Bill here was dicking you but he didn't have the goods." Jackson bowed slightly. "Jackson Hurst of Hurst Investigations, three blocks off Williston on South Hero. Sorry about the intrusion, but I gotta make a living." He looked over at Bill. "Hey, man, you okay?"

"What do you care, asshole?" Bill wheezed.

"Just checking. Say, what are you, like, John Holmes's father or something?"

"Stinking hippie," Margie replied for her man.

"Hey, I'd like to stay," Jackson said, "but I've gotta develop these and stop by the Buick dealership. Y'all have a nice day, ya hear?" Jackson grabbed the sleeping bag and clock and tucked them under his arm.

"How much is he paying you?" Bill asked.

"Jerry?"

"Just tell me, damn it." Bill had caught his breath enough to slowly step into his underwear and was working on the pants.

"A thousand," Jackson lied. What the hell? Shoot for the moon.

Margie walked over and thumped Jackson's chest with her index finger. "You tell that son-of-a-bitch he can have his divorce and I hope he gets run over by one of his shitty cars. And I hope you do too, you prick."

Jackson could think of no retort. He wished he had his PI manual to tell him how to handle the irate spouse.

Big Bill, now zipped up, reached into his pants pocket and took out a money clip. He removed several bills from it and counted them to himself, licking his finger on the fifth and sixth. He offered them to Jackson.

"I'll give you two thousand for that camera, son."

Jackson looked at the three five-hundred-dollar bills and the five hundreds and whistled. "Jesus. You keep that much in your pocket?"

"Never know when it'll come in handy. So, you agree? I get the camera and you tell Jerry Fitzgerald to go screw himself. What do you say?"

Jackson thought about it. There was nothing in the manual about it but, man, he had to pay the rent. "I'll keep the camera, give you the film, and then I'll tell Jerry to go screw himself."

Bill proffered his hand. Jackson shook it.

"Deal," Bill said.

Jackson pulled the film out and handed it to Bill.

"Maybe I'll develop it, anyway," Bill said. "What do you think, baby?" He slapped Margie's ass.

"I think we'll burn it," she replied.

Jackson gave a half-salute and headed toward a hill that led to Williston Road and off the property. "You folks have a nice day and enjoy the rest of your round. Been nice doin' business with you."

"Up yours, asshole," Margie said.

Chapter 24

SOLITUDE

It wasn't the isolation that frightened her. It was the darkness.

Cheryl had driven Purple Haze and Janie into what had been their home for the last two years, the Bent Hill Commune—once a thriving community, now a ghost town in disarray. The families who had lived in the New Hampshire commune since 1967 had all left, some from frustration, some forced out by more radical members, and some because they were just tired of the lifestyle. Most of those who had quit the communes stayed local, though, filtering into the small towns and cities of New Hampshire and Vermont, hoping to make a difference after failing to change the nation. Perhaps more could be accomplished on school boards and city councils than by killing cops and bystanders. Cheryl wanted to believe that. It was something she desired, something she'd never have now as a prisoner in the commune she had once roamed freely with like-minded revolutionaries.

Her prison was an attic room with only a double bed and two end tables, the ceilings pitched so severely she hit her head pacing the floor, wondering if the FBI would track them here. If they did, it might be a better fate than the one she imagined Janie and Haze had for her. They had boarded up the only window in the room and removed all the light bulbs from the lamps.

Cheryl had taken a bath in the small, attached bathroom as soon as they had locked her up for real and imaginary crimes against the cause. She wanted to wash off the stink of Aaron's blood. It had permeated every pore of her body on the chaotic ride from the North Brook Bank to the second car.

She lay on the bed listening to Haze, Janie, and Lester Wester, the owner of Bent Hill, discussing plans. Plans about her. Muffled voices rose and fell in volume and pitch. After an hour of this, they went silent except for footfalls as they climbed the seventy-year-old staircase to the attic. The bright light stung her eyes when the door opened.

"Haze?" she called out.

She saw his face in the dim light of the stairwell. He said nothing. Janie and Lester were with him. He flipped a coin. Lester called heads. It was tails. Haze smiled. They walked in. Janie held three light bulbs. She screwed them into the lamps around the room. A dull yellow light cast long shadows on the walls and pitched ceilings.

Like automatons, Janie and Haze removed Cheryl's clothes while Lester watched, sweat beading on the tip of his nose. He shoved his long tongue out and licked his nose like some freak in a sideshow.

"C'mon, Haze," Cheryl said. "It doesn't have to be like this, baby. Let's drop a little acid, the right way, slow, and let it happen."

"This ain't supposed to be fun." Haze dropped his pants and pulled off his T-shirt as another bead of sweat fell from Lester's nose onto the floor. "This is payment, girl."

He spread her legs. Janie knelt by the bed and squeezed Cheryl's breasts. She was high, her pupils dilated.

"For what?" Cheryl said.

"For you waving down the pigs. You think we didn't see that?"

Haze mounted her, his eyes bulging with a yellow tint, the veins around the pupils like red bolts of lightning. Mescaline, probably, his drug of choice lately. He wrapped his large hands around her throat while he thrust into her.

Janie smiled, her pretty face inches from Cheryl's. "That's what happens to rats, baby."

Haze cut off her circulation first, then her oxygen, creating a feeling of euphoria, then nausea, as she kicked her legs hard against the bed, trying to knock the incredibly strong man off her, his moans barely audible as she blacked out. When she woke, Haze had been replaced by Lester, the aged owner whom the residents had not so affectionately called Lester the Molester behind his back. The sweat that earlier had been collecting around his curved nose now covered his face. He choked Cheryl with great effort, slipping out of her a few times to catch his balance, the strain of the strangulation and rape obviously too much for the old man.

This time Cheryl hallucinated before she lost consciousness, Lester, Haze, and Janie floating above her, holding hands and singing one of the hundred tunes her fellow residents and their children used to sing around bonfires, all the adults drunk or stoned.

When she awoke, yellow light burned her eyes, though it seemed as if a huge weight had been lifted off her chest. Janie leaned over and kissed Cheryl hard on the mouth. Then she licked one of Cheryl's nipples so tenderly, Cheryl might have hugged her if Haze hadn't pinned her arms over her head.

Janie sat upright, let out a banshee wail, and then pounced on Cheryl, squeezing her neck with much less force than the men had used. Whatever the three of them were on it seemed to be compelling them to kill her. Janie finally tired when she was unable to black out Cheryl as the men had.

The three of them dressed and shared a bottle of wine. Cheryl stared at them from the soiled bed, too weak to sit, her throat dry, her neck sore and raw. Haze left the room and then came back a few minutes later with a camera. The bed smelled of urine, the mattress soaked beneath her.

"Sit the bitch up, Lester," Haze ordered. Lester tried but couldn't lift Cheryl until Janie came over and helped him. They sat her up against the metal headboard.

"Give her some wine," Haze said to Janie.

Janie handed the bottle to Cheryl, who choked when she drank it too fast. The wine dripped over her breasts onto the sheet to join the urine stain between her legs.

Haze aimed his camera and took two quick pictures of Cheryl. "Nah, that ain't good," he said. "Lester, hold the nine to her head." Lester put the muzzle of the pistol against Cheryl's temple while Haze took another picture, closer this time. Her three assailants disappeared in the blinding flash, reemerging slowly as the black dot dissolved.

"That's good," Haze said. "You know, Miss Hebert, the brothers came by and took their deserving share, leaving me, Lester, and Comrade Janie there with only two hundred thou. I was supposed to get four hundred, babe, but 'cause of you waving down them pigs, I didn't have time for more bags. So you know what you gonna do for Purple Haze now?"

Cheryl still couldn't speak, emitting only a squeak.

"What's that?" he said. "I'm sorry, babe, couldn't understand what it is you saying. I think you were saying, 'Anything you want, Haze.' Right?"

Cheryl nodded.

"That's right. Okay, so here it is. You owe me two hundred thousand. Your mama paid once, so she'll pay again, but this time she ain't gonna go for that fake ear no more, so Purple Haze gonna send her a before-and-after photo of her little girl." Haze pulled a box cutter from his pocket and pushed the razor blade out with his thumb. "Already got me some before photos, so let's work on an after."

Cheryl screamed as Haze sliced off her right earlobe.

Chapter 25

WAKING STATE

Jackson was near the state of inner peace in his exercise. He found he could transcend more easily from dream to inner peace and finally to the waking state if he used the sukhasana pose, sitting legs crossed, spine straight, with his hands resting on his knees. He chanted "Ommmm" in rhythm with sitar music coming from his stereo in the back of his small office.

Most in the yoga class he attended every Tuesday night at the Burlington Auditorium used the exercise and mantra to slow down their nervous systems and calm their minds, thus improving their health. Jackson, on the other hand, used it to take his mind off his incredible craving for a fix. He'd been clean a year, thanks to Freedom and Phoebe, the leaders of the now-defunct Red Maple Commune outside Bristol, but like an alcoholic, a junkie was always a junkie.

He'd had to do the exercise twice a day since Big Bill Cooper bought his photos and silence with two thousand dollars. The minute Jackson had the money, he felt the loneliness and solitude of his small apartment off Pine Street, wondering how many hits of smack he could score with what was left over from paying his overdue office rent.

He fought the urge with yoga. The ashtanga method seemed to work best not only to stem the cravings, but also to stop, or at least limit, the nightmares that had followed him back from the Vietnam jungles.

One thing the yoga did not help with was his concern for Cheryl. She had gone too far this time and now three men were dead because of her good intentions. He shared her desire to change the world, though not that way. Gandhi and Martin Luther King created more positive change with protest than any anarchist did with violence. Cheryl was on the FBI's top-ten most wanted list along with Purple Haze and Janie Anderson. Their pictures were on the national newscasts and in all the papers. It was only a matter of time before they were caught. Jackson knew where they were hiding, though he wouldn't turn them in. He didn't know Cheryl that well, having seen her for only that short time during her fake kidnapping, but he knew she was incapable of killing anyone.

A few more chants and he'd leave inner peace and go on to waking.

"Ommmm. Ommmm. Ommmm."

He opened his eyes. Two well-dressed men stood in front of him. He probably shouldn't have done today's exercise naked, and he probably shouldn't have left his office door unlocked. They wore black suits, white shirts, and black ties. The short hair and the bulges in their jackets screamed FBI or marshals. The man directly in front of him was about forty, the younger one to his right maybe ten years younger. He wore a smirk as he stared at Jackson's erection. Jackson stared at it himself.

"Sorry 'bout that, man. Happens sometimes when the individual spirit goes through the veil and beyond thinking. You get liberated from the three states in order to achieve enlightenment, and then sometimes—bam—boner. Know what I'm sayin'?"

The older guy did the talking. "Public nudity is against the law in this city. I can recite the statute if you want."

"It ain't public, man. I'm in the privacy of my own home."

"You live here?"

"Today I do." Jackson stood and folded the blanket he had been sitting on. His erection subsided as he sat behind his desk. The talker handed him two business cards.

"I'm Special Agent in Charge, Andrew Postlewait, and this is Special Agent, Daniel Baker. We're from the Albany division."

"New York?"

"Burlington is part of our jurisdiction. You know why we're here, Hurst. We'd like to talk to you about your cousin, after you dress."

"I'm okay," Jackson said. "This is the way I come outta my mamma and the way God meant us."

"We're not okay. Do you mind?"

"Sure, man."

Jackson went to the back room to dress. The city was filled with uptight dudes like Postlewait. When Jackson was in rehab at the Red Maple, he'd sometimes gone days without clothes. He slipped on his blue jeans and a tie-dyed shirt. When he returned to the front office, the agents were sitting in front of his cluttered desk.

"We'll try not to keep you long," Postlewait said. "When was the last time you saw Cheryl Hebert?"

"I don't know, when I was twelve or thirteen in Charlotte. They were visiting."

"You expect us to believe that?"

Jackson pulled his long blond hair out of his eyes. He hadn't cut it in a while and it was beginning to be a pain in the ass. He had grown a mustache, also blond, that the young ladies at UVM seemed to like. "Believe what you want."

Postlewait turned to face the taciturn Baker. Baker pulled a file out of a briefcase and read aloud.

"You spent one year in Forsyth for drug smuggling, been arrested six times in the Charlotte area for possession, burglary, and public drunkenness. You were dishonorably discharged in 1969 from the Marine Corps. In December 1973, you moved to Burlington to set up a private investigating business despite being a convicted felon. You spent the whole of 1974 alternating between the Red Maple commune in Bristol and the Medical Center Hospital in Burlington, apparently in rehabilitation for heroin addiction. In January of this year, you officially began working as a private investigator. Since then you have had a total of four clients."

Jackson lit a cigarette. "I could use you guys on some of my cases."

"Thanks, Dan," Postlewait said. "Okay, Hurst. Sound right to you?"

"Far out."

"So you obtain a get-out-of-jail-free card in Charlotte and your aunt pays for you to come to Burlington and set up a business and it has nothing to do with Cheryl Hebert?"

"Yeah. They didn't get along too well. Cheryl was adopted and didn't see eye to eye with her momma, I guess 'cause she ain't her real daughter."

"She's not adopted," Postlewait said.

He stared into Jackson's eyes, maybe waiting to see his reaction. Jackson was surprised Postlewait knew and he probably showed it.

"What's that?" Jackson said.

"You heard me. We checked with the St. Joseph orphanage in Rutland and they have no record of Cheryl's adoption by Camille Hebert. In fact, no orphanage within a thousand miles has a record of her adoption. Apparently, Mrs. Hebert had papers forged. We tried to talk with your aunt yesterday, but because of her recent stroke she's unable to communicate with us or she's pretending she doesn't understand. So, what about you? Did you know she wasn't adopted?"

Jackson crushed the stub in the ashtray. "News to me, man."

"I think you're lying."

"Whatever."

"Maybe you don't understand the seriousness of the charges against your cousin. Accessory to murder, bank robbery, illegal possession of firearms, illegal flight, and about six other crimes. At the least, it's thirty years. At worst, life. If you've heard from her, you can tell us now and you won't be prosecuted."

"I haven't heard from her."

"Do you know George Willis?"

"Who?"

"Your cousin's associate, Purple Haze. Do you know him?"

"No, not that I can recall." Jackson sat up and then cursed himself for reacting. The agent obviously noticed.

"So you've never met him?"

"Don't think so."

The agent nodded to Baker. Baker spoke.

"Three days ago we interviewed a Miss Melody Minter of the Burlington Vermont Department of Motor Vehicles."

"Hold it a second, Dan," Postlewait said. "Mr. Hurst, do you know Miss Minter?"

"We date once in a while, off and on."

"Do you want Agent Baker to keep going or do you want to talk about your relationship with Mr. Willis?"

Jackson said nothing. How much did they know about his involvement with Cheryl's fake kidnapping? Maybe they were guessing. He'd let them tell him what they knew. They'd already caught him in one lie. Postlewait nodded to Baker, who continued.

"She said you came to her to try to determine the identity of the owner of a 1970 Mercury Comet. You had only three digits of the license plate. After identifying the owner, she determined it had been stolen by George Willis. Later that night, you went with her to a party where he was in attendance, and you accosted him."

Postlewait took over.

"Miss Minter said you told her Mr. Willis had something of yours.

She said she left the party when you fought with him. You still deny you know him?"

"I might have seen him that one time. He had something of mine, that's all. You know I had a problem—with smack. I gave the guy some money a few days before and he was supposed to get me a few baggies. I tracked him down, that's it."

"And he just happens to be the same guy who spent the last five years with your cousin, both involved with the SDS, the Panthers, and the Weather Underground? You just happened to randomly buy drugs from Willis?"

"Yeah."

"That's too much of a coincidence, Hurst. Okay, here's the deal: we want to monitor your phone here and at your apartment in case your cousin tries to contact you. Do you have any objection to that?"

"Hey, man, you're the FBI. If J. Edgar wants to tap my phones, what the hell can I say? You'll do it whether I care or not."

"Mr. Hoover has been dead for four years, but I'm glad we understand each other. I assume you'll contact us if she tries to get in touch with you."

"Yeah. Sure. But you need to know something about her."

"What's that, Mr. Hurst?"

"Listen, man. I know Cheryl's caught up in this, but I know her. When we were kids she used to cry when I shot dragonflies with a BB gun. She wouldn't kill anybody. You're making a mistake. She might have been driving the van, but she wouldn't hurt a fly. I'm serious."

Postlewait stood. Baker did likewise.

"Let me give you some background, Hurst," Postlewait said. "Officer Dave Brown was a seven-year veteran of the North Brook Police Department. He had recently accepted a position with the NYPD with a pay increase of six dollars an hour. To celebrate his new job, his wife Cyndi and his six-year-old daughter, Kathleen, planned to throw him a party on Wednesday. Unfortunately for him, Harold Jackson blew off half his head with a shotgun stolen from a Plattsburgh National Guard Armory a week earlier.

"These were the guns used to kill him and three Brink's guards during a robbery by Mr. Jackson, Aaron Watson, George Willis, and Janie Anderson. Two of the assailants escaped in a van driven by your cousin, Cheryl Hebert, a devout member of the Weather Underground and an associate of the BLA. This is the same Cheryl Hebert who a year earlier had her clothes burned off in an explosion of a townhouse in Greenwich Village, a known bomb factory of the Weathermen. She and Janie Anderson were given medical attention for their burns by a neighbor, who also dressed them in her clothing so they wouldn't have to ride in the ambulance naked, except Cheryl, Janie, and an unidentified associate, took off, leaving their bomb-making compatriots dead in the burned-out building.

"Oh, and back to Officer Dave Brown of the North Brook Police. His daughter, Kathleen, saved up a year's allowance to buy him a reel for his fishing rod that he wanted. Instead, she used the money to buy flowers for his grave. So don't tell *me* your cousin is innocent and wouldn't hurt a damn fly. You tell that to Kathleen Brown."

As the agents were walking out of the office, Postlewait turned and said, "We're watching you, Hurst. If she contacts you—you call us. You understand?"

Jackson nodded, but that wasn't going to happen.

The phone rang four times before Jackson lifted the receiver off the cradle.

"Hurst Investigations."

"Jackson?"

"Yeah."

"This is Ethan."

"Hey, Ethan. How the hell are ya?"

"Good, sir. It's Miss Camille. She wants to see you. It's urgent."

Chapter 26

CAMILLE SPEAKS, SORT OF

The drive up the mountain to his aunt's large house during the summer was different than it had been in the winter. Majestic poplars now towered over the three-story Victorian, their jade canopies shading it from the morning sun.

Aunt Camille owned forty acres in Shrewsbury that ran down the mountainside to the outskirts of Rutland. A large portion of the acreage had long rows of corn stalks that seemed to grow smaller the farther Jackson gazed down the slope. Contoured furrows filled the rest of the farmland, plowed to mimic the moguls and peaks so the soil wouldn't erode in the summer rainstorms.

Ethan Pembroke, Aunt Camille's caretaker, saluted Jackson from the seat of his John Deere tractor. There were about twenty fresh rows of plowed dirt, so Jackson, knowing nothing of farming other than what Ethan had told him, guessed it was the time of year to plant.

Ethan labored up the mountainside, the tractor's giant rubber wheels flinging topsoil. The low sun reflected a bright orange ball off Lake George, a body of water so narrow you could seemingly fling a rock across it to New York State.

Just visible to the north, a small ferry crossed from Charlotte to Essex. Jackson liked riding the Lake Champlain ferries. The crossings helped him forget Karen, Vietnam, and the heroin. During those trips, he forced himself to think only of pleasant things as the cold lake water sprayed against the sides of the sturdy boats.

Other times he thought of Cheryl. He wondered what it might have been like if she had been his girlfriend instead of Karen. He thought of that long kiss they shared the day he tried to rescue her from her supposed kidnappers.

Now summoned to his aunt's house, he figured she wanted him to go after Cheryl again. He could find her. He had an advantage over the

Feds because he had a good idea where she might be hiding. The question, though, was whether he wanted to find her.

Ethan slid off the tractor, a bull of a man, still sporting a huge white beard. Ethan proffered his hand. Jackson's fingers hurt when they shook.

"Thank you for coming. How long's it been?" Ethan said.

"About three months since I seen you, but a year and a half since your boss could stand me being around."

"Yes, yes. That's the way she is, son. Always has been."

"How is she?"

"Not good. She'll tell you about it when you see her. Been a month since the stroke and she hardly leaves the house. She doesn't like me to help her, but I do what I can since the paralysis."

Jackson lit a cigarette. Ethan joined him with one of his own.

"The Feds came by to see me today," Jackson said.

"They were here, too, yesterday."

"Yeah, they told me. Said she can't talk no more. Mind's all addled. How'd you know she wanted to see me?"

Ethan chuckled as smoke floated out his nostrils and filtered through his yellow-stained mustache. "She can talk. Not fast and it's hard to figure what she's saying, but her mind's still sharp. She put on that charade for the FBI so they'd leave her be. She's upset enough that Cheryl's involved in killing those men and that robbery, and now something else has happened that she wants to talk to you about. That's why she called, though she says she can barely tolerate you."

"Feeling's mutual."

"Well, what is, is. Let's go in so I can tell her you're here. She wants to speak to you alone. One thing though, Jackson."

"What's that?"

"Whatever you decide to do for Miss Camille, I want to talk to you afterward. It's important."

"That's cool, man. You're 'bout my only friend now that I've alienated half of Burlington with my investigations into their lurid lives and all."

They stepped onto the porch. Ethan opened the front door. "How's that going, son?"

"Not bad. Got enough money to buy one of those new calculators. If you click in 7734 and hold it upside down it spells hell."

"I'm happy for you, Jackson. Go on in and I'll bring coffee. She's in the den. And don't stare at her."

Aunt Camille sat in a large rocker near the fireplace. The den seemed brighter in the summer light, the hundreds of books lining the high walls less menacing than they had been the first time they met when she had assessed her useless nephew with her condescending scrutiny. He shifted on the sofa to get a better look at her. It was bad, her entire left side drooping and lifeless, one eye lower than the other, something you might pay fifty cents to see in a freak show.

She puffed on a cigarette clamped firmly in the right side of bluish lips. Spittle dribbled out the drooped side of her mouth whenever she sucked in the smoke that escaped out her nose. She pulled the cigarette out and held it over the ashtray. "I—" she began, straining to speak. "I—don't care for you—Jackson." The words were slurred and slow to come out.

"Yeah. Ethan reminded me of that outside. Well, I don't give a damn if you like me or not." That shut her up for the moment. "What do you want?"

"Have—have." She stopped to take a deep breath. It was hard not to feel sorry for her. There but for the grace of God, and all that. "Have you—have you told any—anyone?"

He jerked back his hair and rubbed his chin. "Do you mean have I told anyone you kidnapped a baby from the Fitzpatrick family in 1954? That what you're saying?"

She nodded.

"No. Except Ma, but you know that already. Your secret's safe, though the FBI knows, sure as hell, you didn't adopt her. Sooner or later they'll figure it out and reserve you a room in the big house. I think it's life now, but I ain't sure."

She pointed to a manila envelope on the coffee table. Jackson snuffed out his cigarette in the ashtray and picked it up. It was addressed to her.

"Cheryl," she said, speaking softer.

"You want me to go and fetch her, I know. You think I know where she is. Well, I do. I got a pretty good idea, anyway, but why should I? She's gonna get caught sooner or later and, if they catch her after I trotted all the way up to get her, they'll put my ass in the can for accessory. So why bother?"

She kept pointing at the envelope. He opened it. It had a Polaroid of Cheryl, blood dripping off the bottom of her right ear, those beautiful eyes, sunken, dark, filled with fright. He read the note. Purple Haze wanted two hundred thousand this time and there was no fake ear enclosed.

"Jesus Christ," he said.

Aunt Camille's eyes welled with tears. "She didn't—She wouldn't—k—kill."

"Yeah, I don't believe it either. She might have been along for the ride but she wouldn't kill anyone, even a cop."

"Where?"

"New Hampshire, I guess. Only one way to find out. They're holding her for two hundred grand, so she's not there because she wants to be. No messing around this time. They're dead soon as I find 'em and then I'll get Cheryl fixed up so she can turn herself in. I can't—"

"No." Aunt Camille said.

"What do you want me to do? If she doesn't turn herself in, they'll lock her up for life. The TV said she waved at a cop. That tells you she didn't want any part of it. I'm gonna have her give herself up."

"No—" His aunt took shallow breaths. She held her hand out as if stopping traffic. "No—I'm—I'm—"

"The devil incarnate?" Jackson regretted saying it almost immediately when she closed her eyes and sighed.

"I'm—dying." She kept her hand out to silence him. "A month—maybe."

"From the stroke?" Jackson asked. "They can be that accurate?"

She tried to shake her head, drool dribbling onto her shirt. "Cancer," she said. "Lungs—a month. Bring her home—please. My Cheryl—my baby—please."

She let her head flop back against the rocker.

Jackson put the photo and the note back in the envelope and stood. "I'll get her. I'll bring her back." He stood in the den doorway. "But she ain't *your* baby."

Jackson almost drove away in his beat-up Fairlane before he remembered he had promised to see Ethan. He shut the car off and loped around the barn to where Ethan was hosing down the tractor wheels.

"Sorry, man. Almost forgot."

"Did she show you the picture?" Ethan asked.

"You know about that?"

"Yes. I know about that and about the fake kidnapping two years ago and everything else."

"Well, that's something. Why'd she tell the help about her personal stuff?"

"Because, Jackson, I've shared Miss Camille's bed for the last seventeen years."

Jackson flinched. "You? And her? You mean you two—"

"Yes. When she hired me to take care of her property, she was a lonely single mother. She's a harsh woman, always has been, but she could be loving, and she was not unattractive. We were both lonely, so it was only natural. She and I have no secrets. I know she found Cheryl in the stream, that Cheryl's not adopted."

"Well, maybe she didn't tell you everything."

"What do you mean?"

"Nothin'. Okay, so you know they got her and cut her. I think I know where she's at and I'm going to get her so she can say goodbye to Momma before Momma dies, but then she has to turn herself in."

"Are you in love with her?"

That stunned him. What was it with these backwoods New Englanders, always trying to shock you with their words?

"What makes you think that?"

"Miss Camille says you are."

"Well—she's wrong. I like Cheryl. A lot. We both think alike. We both think something can be done to fix this country, but I don't love her. Jesus, man, she's my cousin."

Ethan rolled up the hose on a metal stand. "Technically, no, but I see your point, son. I'm very fond of Miss Cheryl myself. I'd like to think I helped raise her. I should have been stronger with Camille and not have let her be so protective of her daughter, but it's like you said, I was hired help." He placed his huge hand on Jackson's shoulder. "Son, I want to go with you. These are bad people and I can help. I fought in the war."

"Jesus, Ethan. Which war? The Civil? What are you, like eighty?"

"I'm seventy-seven and I could break your neck before you could laugh at that. And it was World War One."

Jackson shook his head. "I'm going alone, man. Somebody's got to take care of Aunt Camille, anyway. Better you than me. I'll get Cheryl.

Don't worry about it. It's like in *The Godfather*, I'll make the dude an offer he can't refuse."

"Do you have a gun?" Ethan asked.

"I'm a PI, man. What do you think?"

"Go with God then, son."

"Let's hope so," Jackson said. He slipped into the car and sped off down the narrow mountain road.

Chapter 27

BENT HILL

Jackson had hoped to arrive at the Bent Hill Commune in New Hampshire before dark, if the Fairlane cooperated. It didn't, barely reaching the speed limit during the long drive. The commune was built on the Wester Ranch in 1967 when the owner, Lester Wester, used his inheritance to attract the young and beautiful to, as Leary said, turn on, tune in, and drop out.

According to Cheryl, Wester's motivation was not to enlighten but to surround himself with young men and women who had no inhibitions. He provided the land, the drugs, and the tools for farming. At one time they had more than a hundred self-supporting idealists working together to change the world. Wester looked the other way when members of radical organizations like the Weather Underground and the Panthers needed a place to hide out. Jackson hoped Cheryl, Purple Haze, and Janie Anderson had taken advantage of Wester's hospitality.

Once Jackson had turned off the main highway, the dirt road to the commune ran for about a half mile alongside a utility right-of-way until it came to a locked gate. Rather than try to bust the hardened lock and chain, he barreled the eight-year-old Ford through the barbed wire alongside it. It was just a few hundred yards from there to a road made of small river rocks.

He drove through an arched entryway with a plywood sign nailed to it that read, "Wester Ranch." So it wasn't the Bent Hill anymore; deserted like all the other communes in New England.

He shut off the headlights and slowed the car to a crawl, rocks crunching beneath the tires. The only other sound was an owl in the distance screeching at its night prey. Jackson rolled the driver's-side window down halfway. That's as far as it traveled anyway, the forty-dollar price tag too high for him to have it fixed.

He stopped the car and listened. The owl hunted in the distance. A stream rushed nearby, behind the large two-story farmhouse. The last time Jackson had been there, Wester had used the farmhouse for his family, whoever his family was that week.

Lights were on in the first floor only. Jackson removed the revolver from the glove compartment and placed it next to his right thigh. He decided he'd circle around the back of the house to see if it were just the three of them and Cheryl so he could get the jump on them. A flashlight beam on his left lit up the front seat of the Fairlane. It blinded his vision when he turned to face it.

"You lost, son?"

Jackson rested his right hand on his revolver. "Looking for Bent Hill. Trying to find a Mr. Lester Wester."

"You found him. I know your voice, don't I?"

"I was here a few years ago. I dropped off my cousin, Cheryl, and then I stayed a day. Jackson Hurst."

"I remember you. Haze talks about you. That why you're here? To get the reward money? You figure they're here hiding out, don't you?"

"That ain't why I'm here. I came to help them, that's all, Lester." Jackson slid his index finger against the trigger. Something poked the left side of his head. Out the corner of his eye, he could just see the muzzle of Wester's pistol illuminated by the flashlight beam.

"Now just hand me that gun, son. Take it by the barrel and ease it through the window to me. You'd be dead already if I didn't think Haze wanted to talk to you. That's right—gently."

Jackson did as he was told. Wester took the revolver and flung it somewhere between him and the house in the high grass. "Now shut the engine off and come out of the car, slow as can be, hands first."

Jackson stalled to give himself time to recall chapter seven of the twenty-year-old private investigator training manual. That chapter had been a little more interesting than the others had, specifically because it went over in detail how to escape a gunman who had the drop on you, whether it was from behind, in front, or, as in this case, with a gun barrel against the side of your head. What he remembered was that a gun to the head was the best of all scenarios.

If the gunman was four feet in front of you, and you dove for cover, it was easy for him to follow your movement with his arm and you were done for, but if the gun muzzle was against your head, you could duck down faster than the assailant can get a round off.

So he did just that. He ducked forward while rolling the window up, hoping to limit Wester's movement. There were four brilliant flashes in quick succession that blinded Jackson worse than the flashlight had.

His ears rang from the loud explosions, yet he still heard Wester scream as Jackson floored the old Fairlane with Wester still wedged in the drivers-side window. Wester got off two more shots that blew out the back window before his weight was too much for his glass bear trap and he, the gun, and the busted window fell hard to the rock road.

The left rear of the Fairlane rose as it rolled over Wester. Jackson stopped the car and threw it into reverse as another round took out the side mirror.

Wester screamed again as Jackson backed over his human speed bump. That quieted him but, to be sure, Jackson threw it back into drive. Amidst the quiet of the night, the sickening sound of cracking bones assured him that Lester Wester was no longer a threat.

Jackson turned off the ignition. If Haze and Janie were there they would have heard the gunshots and come to Wester's rescue. Maybe he'd get lucky and find Cheryl alone.

He picked up Wester's flashlight and illuminated the old commune owner's corpse. An eyeball had popped out from where the skull had cracked nearly in half, the now mostly flattened head oozing blood and brain matter into the river rock.

He found Wester's pistol. How many times had the man fired? Six? Seven? Jackson wasn't familiar with the brand so he had to guess the clip held ten to fifteen rounds. It was such an odd pistol, he was afraid to eject the magazine, fearing he couldn't get it back in.

He worked his way over to the house, scanning and listening for others. The front door of the two-story farmhouse squeaked as it opened. He did a quick check of the first floor and then the second. From the clutter, it was obvious there were others beside Wester living there. He called out in an even voice, holding the pistol out in front of him.

"Cheryl?"

A muffled sound came from the attic. Jackson climbed the ten, carpeted stairs to a large door and then crouched before opening it. The room's lone occupant was a naked girl on a small bed, her left arm tied to the bedpost with rope. She had bruises on her arms and legs. Dried blood gathered under her nose. She had close-cropped black hair, messily cut, as if she had done it herself. He wasn't sure it was Cheryl until he saw the chopped earlobe, the area around it red and swollen.

She stared at him with those expressive eyes. "Jackson?" she said in a hoarse whisper.

Jackson sat on the side of the bed and placed Wester's gun atop the soiled mattress near her breast.

"To the rescue," he said. "Now hush, cousin. Let's get you outta here."

"Haze," she said. "He's—"

"I said hush. He ain't here. Lester's dead. Now I'm gonna move you up a little to ease the tension on the rope."

She moaned as he put his hands under her arms and lifted her higher on the pillow. The rope went slack. It took him more than a minute to untie her hand, the hemp slippery from her blood where it had rubbed her wrist. She sighed loudly and passed out for a few seconds when he lowered her arm to her side.

"I'm sorry," she said.

He pushed her greasy hair back off her forehead. "You should be. You're a pain in the ass and so's your mother. Now, c'mon, let's get you up and dressed. You can clean later."

She smiled through blistered lips, most of her teeth black with blood. She was about to say something until she flinched. She was looking over his shoulder. He shoved the pistol beneath her.

"'Nam. Damn it. Is that you, 'Nam?"

He knew the voice. Purple Haze. Jackson turned to face him. Standing beside Haze was Janie Anderson. She had a pistol aimed at Jackson. Haze held an M16 in front of him, though at ease. Jackson slipped his hand under Cheryl for the hidden pistol.

Haze raised the M16, muzzle forward and hip high.

"Get those hands up, 'Nam. I might got me something in mind for you if you don't mess up and get yourself shot. We seen what you did to poor Lester down there and we know that pervert always packed something. Where you got it, 'Nam? Five seconds or Comrade Janie will eliminate our bourgeois prisoner here. Five—four—three—"

Jackson gestured toward Cheryl with his head. "There," he said.

"Well, get it, then. Slow. Hand it to my compatriot in arms."

Jackson retrieved the pistol by the barrel and gave it to Janie, who still had her gun trained on him. He couldn't remember anything in the manual that covered this scenario. Maybe they had a kiss-your-ass-goodbye section somewhere he'd missed.

"That's good," Haze said. "Now get up and strip down to the tighty-whities. Watch him, baby," he said to Janie. "He knows that Bruce Lee, Kung Fu shit and is thinking 'bout chopping Mr. Haze and his white chick. Thinking he's gonna rescue the cuz and be the hero again. Hey, boy, I gotta admit you look a hell of a lot better than the last time I seen you. That was right here, wasn't it? Dropping off the bitch and remembering where this place is. Pretty smart for a redneck. You call the Feds?"

"Man, I just came to help. Get you guys and Cheryl out of here, ya know? He stuck his damn gun in my face when I drove up. What'd you want me to do, let him kill me?"

Haze laughed. "Well, I know ain't none of that true." He waved the gun at Jackson. "Clothes off. Make sure you ain't got no guns or knives taped to ya like in Vietnam."

Jackson stripped down to his underwear.

"Sit down, honky." Haze gestured toward the bed. Janie gave Lester's pistol to Haze, who pocketed it. "Okay. We got everything under control, don't we? Now, 'Nam, I figure we got three options. I will go over them if that is acceptable to you and Miss Hebert."

"Whatever, man," Jackson said. He had no options he could think of with an M16 and a pistol aimed at him.

Janie's eyes were glassy and she looked at any moment like she might topple over. Acid probably, a hallucinogenic, for sure, and it was a miracle she hadn't accidentally fired her gun. She was attractive in her blue jeans, long-sleeved CPO shirt, and leather vest. The black beret must have been to show support for the Panthers or maybe she liked the way it looked on her.

Jackson needed to convince Haze he could help him escape. Even isolated in the New Hampshire mountains, sooner or later someone would wonder why Wester hadn't made his way back into town.

"Option one," Haze said. "We kill you and cousin, pick up Momma's ransom money, and head for—" He turned to Janie. "What's that place, baby?"

"Manzanillo."

"Yeah, whatever. Few friends there to take care of Haze. You know what I'm saying, 'Nam? They say they can pass me off as a dark Mexican. That's something, right, Cher?"

"Sure, Haze," Cheryl whispered. "We'll all go, 'kay?"

"Naw—naw. You're way ahead of me. Option two. Janie here does her thing to Cheryl and we take 'Nam with us and have him get Momma Hebert's two hundred thou. Less exposure for Purple and Janie that way. Then three, and I think you gonna like this one. We take both you kids with us and keep Cheryl alive in case she have to convince Momma."

"Listen, Haze," Jackson said. "I'll get the money and bring it back here."

"There ain't no option four, 'Nam, so it's time to vote. Raise your right hand for your choice. Option one?"

Only Janie raised her hand.

"You can vote too, you know," Haze said to Jackson. "Bitch, too." He aimed the M16 at Cheryl, who closed her eyes. "Still a democracy until my brothers run the country, far as I know. No hands? Okay. Option two?"

Haze raised his hand.

"Hmm," he said. "I think I know where this is going. Option three?"

Jackson raised his hand over his head, but Cheryl could only lift hers to her waist.

Haze smiled. "Two to one to one. Hey, girl. You tell 'em the other rule?"

"What other rule?" Janie slurred.

"The rule that say 'Nam and the bitch can vote, but the votes don't count. So it's either Janie's option one or my option two. We seem to have a dilemma. Only one thing to do. Flip a coin."

Jackson tensed, ready to jump at either one of them if they took their eyes off him. Maybe he could take a gun away. He had to do something. The coin flipped through the air. Janie called heads. Haze kept his gun and gaze on Jackson. He must have seen something in his mannerisms that made him alert. As it turned out, Haze didn't need to look at the coin.

Janie yelled, "Heads!"

"Oh, man," Haze said smiling. "Bad luck for you two, 'Nam. Now you get your ass up off the bed and let my little revolutionary chiquita have some room."

Janie placed her gun in her body holster and pulled a hunting knife from a sheath tied to her boot.

"She don't like guns," Haze said. Janie palmed the knife from hand to hand until she was standing next to the bed. She passed the blade near Cheryl's mouth, the tip touching her lips. Cheryl jerked her head back.

Janie waved the knife over Cheryl's head. "Like I said, baby. This is what we do to rats."

Cheryl screamed as blood splattered against Jackson's face and chest just as there was a deafening boom. Janie toppled over onto the bed, her head a bloody mass attached to her neck only by the thinnest of red sinew.

A huge man with a yellow-stained beard stood in the doorway, his shotgun pointed at Purple Haze.

Ethan.

He had followed Jackson there. Before Jackson could get up to help, Haze had dropped to the floor, rolled over, and come up in a crouch, his M16 aimed at Ethan's chest. They both fired at the same time, the shotgun blast again spraying Jackson with blood.

Ethan stood for a few heartbeats and then dropped to his knees. Blood pooled from the multiple shots he took across his chest. Jackson caught him before he toppled over and laid him down on the floor.

"Miss Cheryl?" Ethan said, blood bubbles forming at his mouth.

Jackson looked around to find her. He had no idea if she was hurt or not after all hell had broken loose. She wasn't on the bed. He started to panic until he felt her hand on his shoulder. She knelt and placed her head against Ethan's bloody chest.

"Uncle Ethan. God, I'm so sorry."

He folded his huge arms around her and whispered, "Miss Cheryl?"

She lifted herself off him and wiped her eyes.

"Yes, Ethan?"

"Miss Cheryl. She—she loves you. She wants you to—" He blew out one last breath and closed his eyes.

Cheryl leaned over and placed her cheek against his. "I know, Ethan. I know."

Chapter 28

STEPPING OVER CORPSES

Except for the wound on her ear and a few cuts and bruises around her legs and arms, Cheryl was in good physical shape. Mentally, though, she was fucked-up. Vietnam had desensitized him enough that seeing Purple Haze and Janie lying like ragdolls, their heads nearly blown off, didn't affect his mind or his stomach, not like Cheryl's. After she vomited twice, Jackson led her downstairs to the large bathroom. He asked her repeatedly if she was all right, but she only shook her head and pulled her knees to her chin as she sat naked on the cold floor.

Jackson needed a shower to wash off the blood. His appearance probably freaked Cheryl out as much as the corpses upstairs had. First, though, he'd have to wash her. Her ear was swollen, red, and possibly infected. It was unlikely as hell that Wester kept penicillin around. Just in case, though, Jackson would check cabinets while Cheryl soaked the caked blood off herself.

He lowered her gently into the tub of warm water, as she had little strength of her own. She obviously hadn't washed in days and smelled rank, probably from the blood. He washed her as carefully as he could and apologized as he cleaned the sore ear. She said nothing and stared ahead, flinching only when he washed an injured part. He'd often thought late at night in his small apartment what it would feel like to touch Cheryl, to gently squeeze her breasts, to feel her mound. Now he knew and yet he felt nothing sexual at all. It was hard to have erotic thoughts with three dead bodies in the attic.

They'd have to leave soon. He needed to get her to her mother and then he needed to convince her to turn herself in. Hell, he was probably in more trouble than Cheryl for helping her. With his record, he'd definitely be visiting a northern prison in the future. They couldn't be as bad as the one in South Carolina. At least he hoped not.

Cheryl touched his hand as he cleaned beneath one of her eyes with a washcloth. "We can't leave him there," she said.

"We can't take him with us."

"Really? Jesus, Jackson, I never would have guessed that. I'm not going anywhere until we bury him."

"Listen. I came here to help you. If it weren't for you and your damn—"

"Go ahead and say it. If it wasn't for me and my damn causes, Ethan would be alive. You don't think I know that?"

"That's not what I meant, exactly. Just seems you'd be more grateful that me and Ethan came up here because of you. He told me he'd stay home with your mother 'cause she's dying and all. I didn't know he'd follow me."

"She's dying?"

"That's right. You didn't know that yet, did you? She had a stroke but that's not what's killing her. She's got cancer in the lungs and asked me to come get you. She saw Haze's ransom letter with all the pictures and whatnot and sent me to clean up your mess, again. After you go home and say goodbye you can turn yourself in."

"After I go home and say goodbye, I'm going to Mexico."

"What the hell's wrong with you? You can't—you know what, just forget about it. I'm tired. We'll talk about it later—at the motel. Now, get out. I need a shower. Get some clothes on and we'll go."

She shook her head. "Not until we bury Ethan."

"Oh, for God's sake. It's dark, he weighs three hundred pounds, and he's in the attic. We leave him there the cops will know he shot it out with Haze. We bury him, they'll blame it on you and me."

"I don't care. I'll do it myself. Hand me a towel."

He helped her out of the tub. She wrapped the towel around her and hugged him. "I'm sorry," she said. "You were stupid to come, but thank you."

He touched her hair lightly. Her warm tears wet his shoulder.

"Okay, you win. I'd better bury him before I clean up. I'd just have to wash again."

It took all his strength to drag Ethan down the three flights of stairs and then outside across the road to a gully. The ground was soft there and easy to dig with a shovel Cheryl had found in the barn.

After Jackson showered and dressed, he helped Cheryl pack a suitcase of clothes, some hers, some Janie's. Wester apparently was a hypochondriac or was concerned enough about his and his followers' health to stock up on enough medical supplies for an army, including plenty of penicillin pills. Jackson filled four paper bags full of supplies and groceries and put them in the trunk of the Fairlane.

Cheryl finished her coffee and went into the living room. Jackson followed her. She pulled a large satchel from a desk drawer and opened it. There was more cash in it than Jackson had ever seen in his life. The bills were still wrapped in bank bands. She stood over it for a few moments and looked as if she were going to reach in for a couple of bundles but, instead, closed it back and walked outside to the car.

Jackson rubbed his chin. They'd need money for the trip and he had spent a lot of the two thousand Cooper had paid him, but a guy with a record didn't need to make it any worse by spending stolen money.

Cheryl shifted to the passenger side of the Fairlane when she saw him. The fresh air was a relief from the tangy smell of Haze's and Janie's blood that had dripped through the cracks of the old attic floor.

He slid in behind the wheel. "It'll be a while before someone comes to check on Lester," he said.

Cheryl mumbled "bastard" and stared out into the dark through the bullet-ridden windshield. Wester's body was about ten feet away and, thankfully, downwind.

"We'll stop somewhere, then head for your place in the morning," Jackson said. "You take the pills?" She nodded. "Okay. The Feds are gonna be watching your place. We might not be able to get in to see your mom. That's the case, then maybe you just better turn yourself in. They might let you see her anyway, her dying and such."

She turned to face him. "I said I'm not turning myself in. How many times do I have to tell you? They're not going to believe me if I say I was forced to drive the van. Jesus, they'll say I joined the Underground willingly and they're right. I did. I'm going to Mexico, to the safe house Haze talked about. I know where it is. You can drive me there or bail. It's up to you."

Jackson turned the ignition key. The starter gave a loud snap, black smoke wafting up from under the car.

"It's dead," he said. "We can't take this anywhere."

"Good. We wouldn't be able to see out the front or back anyway. How'd he miss you?"

He didn't answer, lost in thought. The only other vehicle was Aunt Camille's Jeep, which Ethan had driven there. He hoped the keys weren't buried with him.

"Does Haze have a car?"

She shook her head. "No, but Lester does. Haze and Janie were probably driving it. I don't know where he keeps it."

It seemed that Ethan did have the keys in his pocket, since they weren't in the ignition. It took ten minutes before they found Wester's red-and-white GMC Jimmy in an old barn. Cheryl moved the supplies and luggage into it while Jackson searched the house for Wester's keys. He was about to give up and exhume Ethan when he saw them hanging on a keyboard in the kitchen wall.

Cheryl loaded the last of the bags into the Jimmy. He couldn't blame her for being scared of prison. It was possible she could start a new life in Mexico—not likely, but possible.

He covered his nose with a dishtowel from the kitchen and walked up the stairs to the attic. Janie's blood-red eyes stared at him from her nearly decapitated head. The rag didn't help and despite his earlier affirmation of an iron stomach, he vomited onto Haze's corpse. Jackson placed the satchel of money next to Haze then rushed downstairs to wash his mouth out with some cider from the refrigerator. Then he headed for the barn. Life had seemed a lot easier when he was hooked on smack.

Chapter 29

MOTELING

Cheryl didn't say much until they reached the main highway.

At one point, he touched her shoulder and asked how she was doing. She flinched.

"Do we even know where we're going?" she said. Her ear looked better, less red. Wester's penicillin seemed to be fighting the infection. She had a cute turned-up nose, something he hadn't noticed since they were kids. She spoke with the confidence of the affluent. "Jackson?"

"What?"

"I asked you where we're going."

"I told you. Your house, but I don't know how the hell we're gonna get in with the Feds watching it. I promised your ma, though it might be too late. She didn't look so good. Anyway, it's about two hundred to Rutland and I'm wasted. Let's stop and crash somewhere when we get past the state line. It will be a while before anybody checks on Lester, so we should be okay as long as nobody recognizes you."

"Why would they recognize me?"

"You don't watch much TV, do you? Your picture's on all three networks and in every post office. You, Haze, and Janie made the top-ten most wanted."

"Me?"

"Yeah. God. You didn't know?"

"I don't understand. Why me? I didn't kill anybody. I didn't even shoot a gun."

"Guilt by association. Besides, you drove the getaway car. Remember?"

They drove over a steep hill. Jackson pumped the brakes and downshifted, still getting used to the Jimmy's temperamental idiosyncrasies. There seemed to be endless rows of maples along the side of the interstate highway, the light from the GMC illuminating the canopies when he shifted lanes.

He drove another fifty miles and then exited at White River Junction. The lone billboard off the exit wasn't lit, but he made out the gist of it from his headlights: *Easy Off/On—White River Junction Best Western.* A large arrow pointed east on State Road Four. The easy off/on turned out to be two miles away. The motel was hidden halfway up a large hill by maples and poplars in full bloom. He pulled into the dirt and gravel parking lot.

Cheryl had fallen asleep. The crimson light from the motel's sign washed over her face. Jackson pulled her watch cap off, exposing her short black bob. She looked a little like Audrey Hepburn and just as pretty. When he laid her down on the seat to let her sleep, she woke.

"We're at a motel in Vermont," he said.

"How far to the house?" Her voice cracked, still raw from her captivity.

"Fifty or so, I guess. Listen. I'll go in and get a room. You stay here—and keep down. If the cops find those bodies at Lester's, they'll be looking for us."

"Why would they be looking for you? They didn't know you came after me."

"My car, Einstein. It's ten feet from Lester. It's in my name."

She rubbed his arm. "I'm sorry, Jackson. Really."

He held her gaze until she gave a Mona Lisa smile. She moved her hand away, brushing his gently, her fingernails smooth, manicured. Even revolutionaries liked to look good.

"That's all right," he said. "Think of a way to get in your mother's house without the Feds seeing us. I'll go out later and get some hair coloring for you, blonde maybe."

Cheryl sat up to light a cigarette.

"They're going to see you," Jackson said.

"Oh—they are not. Let me think." After a few puffs, she continued. "If we take Four through the Coolidge State Forest we can come up on the house the back way. The road stops about a hundred yards or so before our place, but we can walk from there. Do you think they'd watch the backyard? There's only one road to the house and that's up the mountain to the front."

"We can try. If we can't get in, then what?" He hoped she'd say she'd turn herself in but he also hoped she'd say Mexico.

"I'm not going to jail. I'd die in there."

Jackson slid out of the car and quickly shut the door to kill the dome light. "Stay down."

"Do you have any money?" she asked.

"About a thousand. And it's mine. I didn't touch the cash in Lester's house."

"I didn't say you did."

"All right. I'll be back."

The clerk, an older woman, narrowed her eyes at him when he said he was by himself, though she took the eighteen dollars for the room anyway.

"The pool's not been cleaned since the snow, so I wouldn't risk it if I were you. You need anything, it's zero on the phone until 11:30 and then it's a recording."

Jackson gave his name as Jim Alexander and thanked her. He asked for an eight o'clock wake-up call.

He parked in front of the room, looking around before leading Cheryl into number twelve. There was only a king-sized bed in the middle of the room. Cheryl was about to lie on it when Jackson stopped her.

"Let's clean the ear first."

Cheryl sighed and then winced as he pulled off the tape and Band-Aid. She went to the vanity mirror to look at it.

"I'll have to grow my hair out."

He dabbed at it with a washcloth. Once it had dried, he warned her not to cry out and then poured hydrogen peroxide on it. He finished with salve and a bandage. Before she could lie down again, he made her take some more penicillin.

She stretched out on the bed and closed her eyes. "You should have been my mother," she said then fell asleep.

Jackson took off his wig, peed, brushed his teeth, shut out the lights, and then lay beside her, Cheryl's quiet snoring lulling him to sleep. Sometime in the middle of the night he woke to his name. Cheryl's voice was a lovely alto with an actress's tenor and cadence, almost as if she were singing.

"Jackson, are you awake?" She nudged his shoulder with hers. "Jackson?"

"Hmm," he said. He needed a cigarette. "You want a smoke?"

"Yeah."

"Camel okay? I've got some weed in one of the bags if you'd rather have some of that."

"Camel's fine. I just need to talk," she said.

He lit two cigarettes and handed one to her. "About what?"

"Did you ever find out who my real parents were?"

He sucked on the cigarette, the red glow of the tip the only light in the room. "Yeah, the next day, after I dropped you off."

Smoke lifted above them and then settled in the corner of the room, blown there by the rickety air conditioner that he had left on low.

"So for two years you've known and didn't tell me?"

"You didn't exactly leave a forwarding address. The commune said you split after a week."

She took another puff and turned to face him. Her breath was warm, with a hint of tobacco. "Tell me now. Tell me they're crooks or bums or trash who live near the dump and hated each other and their kids if they have any. Tell me they're murderers who would gladly watch a baby die in the river rather than take care of her. Tell me they're in jail, Jackson."

He blew smoke out his nostrils and sighed. Should he tell her the truth, that her adopted mother lied about Cheryl being abandoned? Should he tell her the respectable owner of timber and maple syrup factories, Mrs. Camille Hebert, abducted her from Bishop DeGoesbriand Hospital in 1954?

"They live in South Burlington."

"Really?"

"Really."

"Do they have a name?"

"No. It's a family of bears."

She slapped his arm hard. It hurt like hell.

"Tell me."

"They're the Dennis Fitzpatrick family. They live at Twelve, Woodland Road in Mayfair Park. It's a two-story house with a detached garage and a swimming pool in the backyard. It's a family of five—well, six, including you. Dennis is forty-eight. Linda is forty-seven. Danny is twenty-five and attending Holy Cross. Jeff is twenty-three and works as a fire ranger out in Williston, and Emily's twelve."

"Shit," Cheryl said.

"Yeah. I guess so."

"So why would they dump their first girl in the river and then keep another one when it came along?"

"Who the hell knows? Maybe they were broke. Maybe they saw your mother on the riverbank. Who knows?"

He should tell her the truth, but God knew how she'd react. She wouldn't want to see her mother if she knew and he had promised he'd bring her back to Aunt Camille before it was too late. He'd tell her the truth after his aunt died.

"I want to see them."

"That's a good idea. They probably haven't seen your picture the thousand times they've shown it on TV. Local girl makes national news and the respectable Fitzpatricks of South Burlington stayed ignorant as hell. Why don't we worry about seeing your ma and forget about them."

"No. I'll see my mother and then I'll see my real parents and I'll ask them why they did what they did. I'm sorry to be obdurate, but I am going to see them."

Jackson snuffed out the cigarette in the ashtray near the phone. "I have no idea what that means, but I do know you're stubborn as hell."

"Exactly," she said.

Chapter 30

THE EDUCATED MR. POSTLEWAIT

Afetid odor hung in the confined attic, seemingly made smaller by the three evidence assistants, two FBI special agents, and the corpses of the reprobates, Janie Anderson and George Willis, aka Purple Haze. Special Agent in Charge Andrew Postlewait believed, with what he thought appropriate zeal, that the two debauched anarchists received their due.

The bloated bodies seemed phantasmal, frozen in their death poses, Willis's face unrecognizable, the once-pretty Miss Anderson, a near headless torso, no longer capable of murdering law-abiding Brinks guards and North Brook police officers. God had dealt his retribution as God always had. If there was one thing Postlewait had learned in his fifteen years in the Bureau, it was that criminals never went unpunished; whether at the hand of the authorities or by their fellow criminals.

The surgeon's mask was hot and uncomfortable, yet necessary to reduce the overwhelming stench. Postlewait examined Willis's corpse while Agent Baker went outside to supervise the recovery of the large man they had found buried in a snow-lined gully. That body played an important part in Postlewait's hypothesis. He felt he had a handle on the sequence of events and—except for a few unexplained anomalies, such as who shot whom—believed he had a lucid picture of the scene as it had played out.

Postlewait rolled Willis's body slightly to check for any other wounds beside the shotgun blast to the face. Agent Baker had returned from his duty and stood next to him patiently, taciturn as always. He was a good man.

"Sir?"

Postlewait didn't answer, concentrating on the prostrate corpse. Blood had pooled in the black man's arms. Rigor mortis had been in earnest and was now gone. The criminal had been dead at least twenty-four to forty-eight hours. He closely examined the back for any other wounds they might have missed. "What is it, Dan?"

"We've identified the body. The one in the ditch."

"Ethan Pembroke."

"Well, yes, sir. How did you know?"

"Deputy Wendell checked the registration and license plate of the Jeep and informed me earlier that it belonged to the mother, Mrs. Camille Hebert. I assumed that, since she is in no condition to go anywhere, it would have to have been her caretaker who came, the large bearded gent we interviewed."

The agents had been ordered to the grizzly scene by the Albany office when Deputy Sheriff Joseph Wendell had called in three dead at the Wester Ranch. The deputy could identify only one of the victims, Lester Wester, a man the officer had known for years and had arrested many times for both misdemeanors and felonies.

The deputy often made his rounds out near the utility right of way, the area a frequent stomping grounds for vandals and poachers. The gate leading to Wester's ranch was intact, but the observant officer saw that someone had mowed down the barbed-wire fence alongside it. Although he expected some kind of trouble on the ranch, a burglar or aggressive bear hunters, he hadn't expected to find the owner, Lester Wester, lying in blood near a beat-up Ford, his skull flattened and crushed.

"So tell me, Dan," Postlewait said. "Have you assimilated the data into a logical hypothesis?"

Agent Baker raised his eyebrows at the question. Postlewait would sometimes have to remind himself that he was one of only a few agents in the Bureau with both English and law-enforcement degrees.

Baker adjusted his white mask to speak. "I could make a guess, sir, but it would be a bad one."

"Then I'll present mine and we'll see what you think."

Baker again adjusted the mask, as his sweat had soaked it out of shape. "Do you think we could go downstairs or outside? The smell—"

"We have the scene, the scenario, in front of us, Dan. It's not going to get any worse. After the technicians finish what little they have left, they'll transport them to the morgue."

"Think there's a morgue around here?"

"No. Rutland or Manchester would be the closest. All right, let's go over what we know." Postlewait pointed to Janie Anderson. One technician was helping another lift her torso onto a stretcher. They'd have to carry her down, the staircase too steep for a rolling gurney. Almost as an afterthought, the technician lifted her nearly decapitated head onto the stretcher, and covered both it and the body with a sheet.

A newspaper photographer had already arrived and was outside.

"Both Miss Anderson and Willis were shot with that." Postlewait pointed at a shotgun, tinted gray with fingerprint dust. "You agree?"

"Makes sense," Baker said. "We won't know for sure until forensics."

"True, but we know it's probably only one shooter, according to the technician's initial analysis of the prints. So—who was the shooter? Cheryl Hebert? Jackson Hurst? Or the late Mr. Ethan Pembroke?"

"Could be any one of them. Or someone else."

"Maybe. From our interview with Hurst, he didn't seem like the shotgun type, do you think?"

"No, sir. He seemed to me to be just a whacked-out hippie."

"Precisely," Postlewait said. He frowned. He was starting to sound more and more like Sherlock Holmes. He'd have to watch himself. Hopefully, Baker didn't notice. "The shotgun would most likely belong to a woodsman like Pembroke."

Baker nodded. "Like I said, sir, forensics will figure it out. Pembroke had three chest shots. Had to be from the M16 near Willis. So you think Pembroke shot Anderson and Willis. But a shot in the face like that—" He pointed at Willis. "—you'd think might throw Willis's aim off."

"Willis could have fired first," Postlewait said, "then Pembroke let loose with the shotgun. More likely, they shot at the same time."

"So where does that leave Hurst and Cheryl Hebert, sir? Where were they when this was going on?"

Postlewait handed a Polaroid picture to Baker. It showed a frightened Cheryl Hebert tied to the bed, her right ear bleeding profusely from the bottom. "We found this in a dresser drawer while you were outside digging up Pembroke. Hebert was tied to the bed. There's blood on the rope. Hurst may have come to pick up or rescue his cousin and Willis and Anderson may have gotten the jump on him, I'm not sure. We know one of them is alive, since someone had to drag the body to the ditch. They cared enough about the old man not to leave him up here to rot. My guess is Hurst dragged him down the stairs and buried him. It had to be Hurst since Pembroke has to weigh about three hundred pounds. So it looks like Pembroke shot Anderson and Willis and Willis shot Pembroke. By the pattern of the holes in the wall, Willis definitely shot him here."

Baker picked up a pistol by the muzzle. "Whose gun is this, then?"

Postlewait shook his head. "That's a conundrum. So, Dan, where do *you* think Mr. Hurst and Miss Hebert are?"

"Long gone."

"Long gone. But why? If she tried to flag down those police officers in North Brook and was obviously held captive here against her will, why flee?"

"She's a hippie like Hurst, sir. Who knows what they're thinking half the time?"

Postlewait ignored him. Investigations were no place for opinions. Facts only. Well, facts and instinct. "The Ford belongs to Hurst and the Jeep belongs to Camille Hebert, so *how* did they leave?"

"I can answer that, sir."

Postlewait smiled. He already knew how the fugitives left, but why not let Baker tell him? He was new, though learning quickly.

"The deputy said Wester has a new GMC. A red one with a white top. They took it and left after burying the old man."

"Why didn't they take one of the other cars?"

Baker shrugged. "The Ford's shot up, but the Jeep's in decent shape. Can't say."

Postlewait gestured with his head to the satchel beside Willis. It was tagged and dusted. "Two hundred thousand. Why did Hurst and Hebert leave it here? What do you think?"

Baker shrugged. "Who the hell knows? Pardon my French, sir."

Postlewait frowned. "Get an APB on the GMC."

"Did it a half hour ago, sir. There's only a couple of roads they could have taken. We'll have them in a day."

"Call Jones and Millikan at the Hebert house. Tell him to keep watch for the GMC."

"That's the last place they'd go."

Postlewait nodded. "Call them anyway."

Chapter 31

CHERYL GETS PANCAKES, BUTTER—AND MADE

They weren't able to sneak out of the motel as he had hoped. Cheryl, obviously exhausted from her trauma of the previous day, had slept until almost eleven. Now the manager watched, hands on her hips, as Cheryl sleepily entered the GMC. Jackson figured the nosy woman was pissed at him for lying to her about how many were in the room. He hoped she wouldn't call the cops for a lousy three dollars.

Despite the violence and gore they had experienced the previous day, they were both hungry. Neither had eaten in a couple of days and, though it was around noon, he wanted breakfast. He had just about given up finding a place to eat on the highway when he saw the Maple Inn, a small diner attached to the front of a farmhouse. Did every business outside Burlington have the word *maple* somewhere in its name? He slowed and flipped up the turn signal.

"Why are you stopping?" Cheryl said.

"Hey, there. Didn't know you were awake." Jackson shoved the gearshift into neutral and adjusted his wig. He handed her his sunglasses. "Wear these and stay in the car. I'll see if I can get us some chow to go."

"Chow?"

"Sorry. Old habit from the war."

"Do you still have the nightmares?"

"I don't remember telling you about those."

"You were stoned all the way to the commune after you shot Aaron and—"

She sighed quietly and put on the sunglasses. He had forgotten Cheryl and Aaron had been lovers, or maybe he didn't want to think of her with someone else.

"You want anything special? Has to be breakfast, though."

She smiled. They were kids again, back in Charlotte, shooting dragonflies with BB guns, blushing at an innocent kiss. "Pancakes and butter."

Three farmers sat on stools leaning over their food like the mama and papa sans used to in the villages outside Da Nang, as if they hadn't eaten in a year. At least he thought they were farmers. All three wearing ball caps, boots, and bib-and-brace dungarees. A short woman, about forty, with premature gray hair and wearing a filthy apron, smiled at Jackson. "I'll be right with you, sir."

"Thank you, ma'am."

"Ma'am. Oh my. I knew you weren't from here, but *ma'am*. Harry, come out and listen to this young man talk. It's like *Gone With the Wind*." She leaned over the counter and whispered, "Harry's a good cook but a lousy husband, if you know what I mean."

"Yes, ma'am. I was wondering if I could order some breakfast to go."

"That your wife out in the truck?"

Jackson turned to look out the large windows. Cheryl not only wasn't keeping her head down, she had her nose pressed against the passenger-side window staring at the restaurant.

"Yes, ma'am. She—she hurt her leg bad up a ways in the mountains—in a stream. The slippery rocks and all, so I'll bring her the food if you don't mind fixing it."

"You mean vittles. Isn't that what folks from the South call it?"

"No, just food—if you don't mind."

"What part of the South are you from, dear?"

"Georgia."

"That's what I thought. He's from Georgia, Harry."

Harry slicked back the greasy hair on his balding head and continued cooking, looking up only to knock the ashes off his cigarette.

"I've been to Atlanta," one of the farmers said. "Didn't care for it."

The one in the middle looked up from his food. "Son, you've got something hanging from the back of your head."

Jackson felt the back of his neck. Some of his long hair underneath the wig had fallen out. He shoved it back in. So much for anonymity.

The woman took out her pad to take his order. "Fell on the rocks, huh? Poor thing. My little brother—Joey, that's his name. Anyway, one time we were at the Pothole. Do you know where that is?"

"No, ma'am."

"It's about fifteen miles north, in Bolton. A natural brook and water-fall, the water cold as a witch's tit, and you can jump off a cliff into a pool where it collects before heading down the mountain. Once you're in the pool, you swim straight down ten feet deep or so and go under a little cave and come out on the bank."

"Yes, ma'am."

She looked at him, then at Harry, and then thought about something for a moment with eyebrows raised. "Harry, what was I going to tell him?"

"Your stupid brother," Harry said between puffs.

"That's right. Anyway, he came up on the riverbed and slipped on the rocks. Broke his leg, just like your wife."

"She didn't break it, ma'am. Just a sprain."

"I bet you don't have the cold water we have here. Not in the South. Where were you from again?"

"Mobile."

"Isn't that in Alabama? You said you were from Georgia, didn't you?"

He needed to get his lies straight. He had been better at it when he was hooked on the smack. "Mobile, Georgia. It's a small town. Barely a town."

"Okay, dear. Now what can I do you for?"

"Do you have biscuits and gravy?"

She chewed on her pencil. "We have biscuits and we have gravy, but not at the same time."

"I meant sausage gravy you pour over the biscuits."

"Oh, God no. Sorry."

Jackson settled for biscuits, egg sandwiches, some bacon, and of course Cheryl's pancakes and butter with "real maple syrup," as the woman said, "not the Aunt Jemima kind." It took only ten minutes before he had the food in a small box.

He thanked the woman and as he walked out one of the farmers said, "Don't think I've ever seen a young man in a wig. Don't seem right around here."

Jackson ignored him and headed for the GMC.

Cheryl took off the sunglasses and smiled when she saw him. Was it for him or the food? After she had inhaled a pancake, he figured it was the latter.

They rolled the windows down to let some of the cool mountain air in. Both looked up from their pancakes when they heard a tapping on the roof.

Framed in Cheryl's window was the woman from the restaurant. She smiled and held up a small paper bag. "You forgot your biscuits, dear." She handed them to Cheryl.

The woman's eyes went wide as she quietly said, "Oh my. Um—anyway—no gravy. There you go. Have a nice trip."

She turned and rushed back to the diner. It was difficult to see her through the reflected sunlight on the restaurant glass, but she was unmistakably pointing out Jackson and Cheryl to the once-disinterested Harry, who suddenly looked very interested.

"She made you," Jackson said.

"She what?" Cheryl adked, wiping syrup from her cheek.

"Made you. She recognized you. We gotta go and we gotta get rid of Lester's Jimmy."

"Do you think she'll call the police?"

"Hell, yeah. She's freaking."

As they drove away, Cheryl took a bite of biscuit. "Made you. Where'd you come up with that one, Jackson?"

"It's in the manual. I'll never say it again, Mother."

"God, I hope not. Man, you're a trip."

Chapter 32

OLD-MAN PREBOR DON'T CARE

Cheryl knew the roads they needed to take to stay off the main highway. They kicked up very little dirt with the Jimmy's snow tires because of the hard-packed clay. The Feds wouldn't think of looking on the back roads, but the Vermont cops might. Both of them. He chuckled at his little joke.

"What's so funny?" Cheryl said.

"I was thinking the Vermont cops might think of looking for us on the back roads. Both of them." He chuckled again.

"You misplaced your modifier. You make it sound like there are two roads, not two cops."

Jackson flicked his spent cigarette out the window. "You sure you ain't related to Aunt Camille?"

Maybe that was the wrong thing to say or maybe she took it the wrong way. Regardless, it was ten minutes and four more potholed roads before she spoke again.

"You were talking in your sleep last night."

"Me?" He couldn't see her face, but he knew she had rolled her eyes. "I didn't have any dreams so can't imagine what I had to say." He was lying. Though, it wasn't a dream. It was a nightmare. The nightmare.

"You kept saying, 'I'm sorry, ma'am. Really, I'm sorry.' and, 'It won't hurt. You won't feel nothing. I'm sorry.' Was that Vietnam? I thought you were going to jump out of your bed. It was scary as hell."

"Don't know. Can't think why I said that. Maybe a bad dream. Half the time I can't remember." He'd tell Cheryl about the village girl, someday, but not now. "Hey—roll a joint. In the glove compartment. There's a lid and some papers."

She rolled two joints, neither one very well. Attractive girls usually had someone else supply and roll their weed. He had always rolled Karen's. Cheryl shoved one all the way in her mouth to wet it thoroughly. When it dried, she lit up. He didn't so much want to get high as to share it with her. Anyway, the pot would take the edge off the steep inclines and holes in the road that rattled his bones.

She closed her eyes and blew out smoke that caught in the slipstream of a narrow opening in her window. "What am I going to say to her, Jackson? Thank you for lying to me. Thank you for keeping me locked up and alone in our huge house with no friends, no school, no life."

Jackson grabbed the joint from her. "You won't have to say anything to her if we don't get rid of this car. We've been driving by too many houses not to have somebody notice us."

He took a couple of tokes and handed it back to her. Their fingers touched and he could feel his face flush. She was kind enough not to say anything, but she smiled a little and gave him a sweet raise of her brow.

"I know where we can get an old pickup," she said. "Take the next right and follow the path down the hill. It's the Prebor farm. We used to borrow it all the time and go on joyrides."

"Who's we?"

"It was when I was in junior high. Mom and Ethan taught me at home until I was thirteen, and then she let me go to a parochial school. I'd sneak out late at night and meet some of the other kids. That's when I had my first smoke and first drink. It was fun, but it didn't last long, the sheriff putting a quick stop to it. When Mother found out, she pulled me from the school and never let me attend another until college, and only then when I threatened to run away if she didn't let me enroll. We compromised on UVM. She's the reason I'm in this mess in the first place, at least according to my shrink. Anyway, the truck should be at Prebor's. He leaves the keys in it. I doubt he'd call the cops if we leave him the GMC."

"Your ma forced you to join those groups?"

"What's that supposed to mean? From what we heard about you, you weren't exactly a Boy Scout—burglary, prison, and weren't you hooked on heroin, or did I imagine seeing you so strung out when you came in, blasting Aaron like some kind of cowboy?"

"Okay, I'll give you that. I guess what I'm saying is, maybe you ought to stop blaming your ma for all that trouble you got yourself in. She might have screwed you up, but she didn't stop you from quitting them groups when they started shooting people and blowing them to hell."

"Words of wisdom from a baby killer." She shrugged. "I'm sorry. That was cruel of me. Turn here. The farm's at the end of the road."

She lit the other joint and said nothing until they were at the bottom of the road. Prebor's farm had seen better days. Most of the barn's roof had collapsed into itself, gully-like. The pickup looked to be forty years old and was all one color. Rust. Jackson shut off the GMC.

"I tried to quit the Weathermen," she said. "Haze said he'd kill me if I did and he meant it. I still believe what we were trying to accomplish was right. You see what the establishment is like. Look at Watergate. If we let up, there will be a hundred Vietnams. You know that. What? You support the bastards now that you're out?"

He blew out the smoke he had held in for ten beats. He was getting a good buzz, considering the weed was a little old and stale. "No. A lot of vets like me were against the war, except I'm not sure I can call myself a vet since they kicked me out. But like you, I blamed my problems on everything else but me—Vietnam, my pa's death, my girlfriend. I had rehab at the Red Maple for a year and one thing Freedom and Phoebe—they ran the commune—the one thing they beat into me was that I gotta stop blaming other things and other people for my problems."

"So you don't think I should blame my mother."

"That's right."

"You don't know her like I do."

"I know she's a mean bitch. Well, guess what? You ain't the first kid to have a mean bitch for a momma."

"So when we see her you want me to kiss her and hug her and ask forgiveness, the prodigal daughter come home, head down?"

"She's dying. How about you pretend?"

She took a hit on the joint, massaged her temples, then flicked the roach out the window, and pointed to the bags of supplies Jackson had taken from Wester's ranch. "We'll see when we get there. Help me move this stuff into the truck."

"Won't the guy come out when he sees us heisting his truck?"

She shook her head. "He's ninety. He never gets out of the chair anymore, according to Eth—"

She took a deep breath as tears welled in her eyes.

"You okay?"

"Yeah," she said, but she didn't look okay.

They moved everything from the Jimmy to the old pickup. The keys were in the ignition, as Cheryl had promised. Jackson ground the gearshift into first. Old man Prebor was just visible though the screen door. He turned his head from the TV to look at them, stared for a few seconds, and then went back to watching his show.

Despite never getting the piece of junk out of second, they arrived at a wooded knoll behind Cheryl's house thirty minutes later. You could just see the backyard through the trees. An FBI agent sat on the back porch, or at least a man dressed like an FBI agent sat there. The black coat, black pants, white shirt, and skinny tie gave him away. They had been notified of the fiasco at the Maple Inn and were waiting for the fugitive to come and visit her mother. That was obvious.

"That's it, then," Jackson said. "Unless you know another way in."

Before Cheryl could answer, the man stood, flicked his cigarette into the backyard, walked down the porch steps, and then turned the corner to greet a black car that had pulled up to the side of the house. The agent in the car held out a bag, probably lunch.

"Let's go," Jackson said.

He stood and grabbed Cheryl by the arm. They sped toward the back of the house. The door was unlocked. They hurried inside and had just closed the door when the agent returned to his watch, grinder in hand.

Cheryl knew the house better than he did so he let her lead. They walked down a narrow hallway, passing the kitchen where a woman dressed in a nurse's uniform smoked a cigarette and drank coffee while she read a newspaper. Her back was to them.

"You think your ma's in her bedroom, being sick and all?" Jackson whispered.

"Probably not." Cheryl continued her slow walk down the hallway. "She never leaves the den if she can help it."

Jackson had been to the house only once since he had accused his aunt of kidnapping Cheryl when she was a newborn. Aunt Camille had forbidden him from ever seeing or contacting her again, though he'd called her a couple of times to remind her to send him the monthly check she had promised him. She might already be dead, though the nurse in the kitchen hinted otherwise. They approached the den doors.

"I got a feeling getting in is easier than getting out," he said.

Cheryl grabbed the doorknob. "You're full of optimism. If she's not here, we'll go upstairs, and quickly. I'll say goodbye and good riddance and we'll split."

"Such a nice girl."

"Oh, Christ. Shut up."

When Jackson saw his aunt in a recliner that dwarfed her, he knew it was too late. Her mouth was wide open, the left side of her face shiny of drool. The eyes were open, but her chest was still, the skin the color of the patches of snow that still dotted the brown lawn outside. Her entire left side drooped horribly.

Cheryl walked to her and whispered, "Mother?"

Jackson gently touched Cheryl's shoulder. "She's gone. Let's go."

Aunt Camille had a cup with a straw in her right hand that was seconds from dropping to the hardwood floor. He tried to take it from her.

"Jackson?" Aunt Camille said it in a whisper that made him jump back. "Jackson—come here."

The slurred words were nearly unintelligible. He leaned over near her face. Her breath smelled like rotten fruit.

"What?"

"Grow up—asshole."

He stood back and smiled. "Ya ain't changed a bit, Auntie."

She said something, but he couldn't understand her, the words barely audible. He leaned in again.

"Cut—cut your god—goddamn—" She gave up and closed her eyes.

"Hair?" he said.

She nodded.

Cheryl knelt in front of her mother and held her hand. Aunt Camille turned to face her. "My—baby."

Cheryl smiled. "Yes, Mother, your baby, and Mother, your baby's in trouble. We can't stay. Jackson's helping me. He's going to take me somewhere safe."

Jackson didn't recall agreeing to that.

"Mother," Cheryl continued, lovingly massaging her mother's hand, the blue veins rolling with each caress. "Mother—I know you didn't adopt me. I know that family left me in that washbin at the stream, and you found me, and raised me, and loved me. I wanted to say thank you before you—anyway, I love you. I'm sorry for hurting you, for leaving you, but you wouldn't let me—you wouldn't let me go and be like everybody else. You see? I still love you. I do."

She rested her head on her mother's lap.

The only reaction from her mother was to drool a glob of saliva out the left side of her mouth. Cheryl stood and turned away to cry. Aunt Camille hooked a crooked finger toward Jackson. He held his breath to block the stink and leaned back in.

"You—you—"

"You what?" he said.

"You didn't—tell her."

He shook his head.

It almost looked like she was going to say, "Thank you," but caught herself.

Even in death's grip she wouldn't give in. She began to shake and gasp for air. Cheryl held Jackson's arm until her mother stopped her mini-seizure or whatever it was. As if a secret alarm were attached to her body, the door of the den opened. The nurse stuck her head in and said, "Are you all right, Mrs. Hebert?" When she noticed Jackson and Cheryl were also in the room, she said, "Who—" and then, like the woman in the restaurant, her eyes went wide as her gaze met Cheryl's. The door shut quicker than it had opened.

"Damn it," Jackson said. "We either have to run for it or give ourselves up." He walked over to the bay window to view the front lawn. The nurse ran to the agent and then pointed at the house. "It's up to you," he said to Cheryl.

She looked resigned to her fate. "There's no way out, Jackson. I'll go first." She turned to her mother, who was breathing shallow, rapid breaths. With great effort, his aunt pointed to the fireplace. "What, Mother?"

Just then the agent's voice boomed from outside. "Cheryl Hebert! Jackson Hurst! This is the FBI. Come out without weapons and with your hands up!"

Aunt Camille continued to point.

"What?" Cheryl said again.

Her mother whispered, "Jackson—" He leaned in. "Push—push—"

"Push what?"

"Push it—the brick."

The whole fireplace was made of brick from the firebox to the ceiling. He walked over to it and pushed one that stuck out slightly below the mantel.

Nothing happened.

Aunt Camille shook her head slowly. "Above," she whispered.

"She must mean above the mantel," Cheryl said.

Jackson pushed another brick and it moved a few inches with a click. The entire bottom half of the fireplace swiveled in. "Damn," he said. "That's handy."

Aunt Camille whispered something to Cheryl, who repeated it for Jackson. "She said it was for bootleggers. The house must have been a speakeasy. Let's go." She kissed her mother. "I'm sorry, Mother. Thank you for everything. I love you."

Footsteps came up the hallway. Jackson pulled Cheryl into the dark tunnel and had just shut the fireplace when he heard men's voices in the den.

Chapter 33

THE GREAT ESCAPE

It was a tunnel of sorts, the only light visible a thin line of yellow between the fireplace door and the den wall. Muffled voices floated into the black abyss—likely two or three FBI men, and another, a woman's, probably the nurse. Was she also an agent?

Cheryl held Jackson's hand tightly.

He pried her nails from his palm and whispered, "Ease off, you're killing me."

She loosened her grip and shuddered.

It was an odd mix of smells, a combination of mildew, ammonia, and the one odor he was worried about, rotten eggs.

Cheryl spoke softly in his ear. "I can't see a thing," she said, the minty smell of her breath a welcome respite.

She had a way of stating the obvious. She might have been a revolutionary soldier capable of shooting cops and blowing up the establishment, but to him she was just a girl, albeit an intelligent and attractive one, despite her half earlobe and multiple bruises.

"There might be flammable gases in here," he said. "Hydrogen sulfide, maybe. You had to know all the smells in Vietnam when it was your turn as a tunnel rat. Light a match and we could blow out both ends of this tunnel and us with it. There's not much air in here, so we'd better get moving."

He removed his belt. It was all leather except for the buckle. He had bought it on Church Street in downtown Burlington at a leather shop because he liked the fifteen peace symbols burned into its entire length. He handed one end to Cheryl. "Hold this and I'll work my way to the exit, wherever that is. You know anything about this?"

"She didn't even tell me I wasn't adopted. Why the hell would she tell me about an old bootlegger's tunnel? How far do you think we have to go?"

"Won't know till we get there. Wasn't that a Partridge Family song or something?"

"I listened to the Stones. Don't go so fast."

He worked his way down the tunnel, and it was *down*, with a slope that tested his footing, the ground wet and soft, lined with a slick layer of mud or algae. The roof was about six feet, though it narrowed at parts, his head bumping on the hard granite ceiling. It must have taken a year to cut through the rock—probably worth it during Prohibition, with even conservative Vermonters caught up in the nationwide booze orgy.

Cheryl screamed and the belt went slack. She grabbed his waist and nearly squeezed the breath out of him. He reached for his pistol, but it was back at the ranch where the late Lester Wester had thrown it in the high grass.

"Something crawled over my foot," she said, still hugging him. "I think it was a snake."

He took the opportunity to smell her hair and enjoy the sensation of her firm breasts against his chest. "Whatever it was it doesn't matter, since they probably know we're in here now. Did you have to scream?"

"I reacted. I'm sorry."

"Okay. Maybe we got lucky. We're far enough away from the den by now. Listen, there's only one type of poisonous snake in Vermont, a timber rattlesnake, and it's a million to one there'd be one in here. Probably a garter. Don't worry about it. Hang on a sec, I'll try the lighter. The air smells better here."

He lit his Zippo and they weren't blown to hell, so the concentration of gas wasn't high enough to ignite. He held it near the floor of the tunnel and was greeted by the black eyes and red tongue of, surprisingly enough, a timber rattlesnake. He nudged Cheryl around it and farther down the tunnel.

"See," he said. "Just a garter. Let's keep going. I think I see something ahead."

The something was five streaks of light at the end of the tunnel. He figured he and Cheryl must have walked about a hundred yards. A hell of a lot of rock excavation for 1920 or thereabouts, but folks needed their liquor. The streaks of light were the slits between several planks, possibly one by sixes, strapped together into a door about four feet above the floor of the tunnel. There must have been some stairs there at one time to help the bootleggers climb out. Jackson put the lighter in front of him and held up his hand to keep Cheryl from speaking. They stayed in that position until he was sure no one was outside.

He accidentally dropped the lighter when the flame licked a finger. Cheryl leaned down to retrieve it and toppled over, planting her face in Jackson's shoe. He grabbed her by the back of her collar and lifted her to him. She came to almost immediately.

"What happened?" she said. "I remember leaning over and—that's it."

"It's the gas. Must still be some down there, near our feet. It's heavier than air. Robs you of your oxygen and you're out like a light. You okay?"

"Yes. You can let go of me."

"Sorry."

He and Cheryl pushed out on the door, but it wouldn't budge.

"Do you think it's locked?" she said.

He peered through one of the slits. "No. It looks like the grass and sod grew over the edges. No way in hell it's gonna open, even if there were ten of us."

"I don't like the dark, Jackson. It reminds me of the attic room. They blocked the window and took the bulbs—"

"We can talk about it later, okay?"

She apparently wanted to talk about it now. "I offered to make it a party, but that wasn't what they wanted, what he wanted. They tied me up and took turns. It wasn't sex, at least not to me. They wanted to hurt me. Janie wanted to kill me. Maybe she was still angry because we broke up."

"Broke up? You mean you and her?"

"Is that a problem?"

"I guess not. I'm just trying to imagine the two of you."

"Pig."

"Karen said that a few times."

"She your girlfriend?"

"Yeah." He waited for her to say something else, but she let it drop.

"Should we head back to the fireplace?" she asked.

Jackson pushed on the door again. "The slats look old. If they aren't hardwood like oak or something, they might break."

"Break with what?" she said. "We don't have anything to break it with."

He moved her to the side of the tunnel.

"I spent thirty bucks a month for the karate classes and haven't had much of a chance to use the lessons. I'll try to kick it. If I fall after the kick and pass out near the ground like you did, lift my head up. Cool?"

"Yeah, okay."

He stepped back a few feet, went into a crouch, and then jumped up, whipping his leg into a modified roundhouse kick. His foot landed squarely on the middle of one of the boards, cracking it in half. A few seconds later he was in Cheryl's arms.

"You passed out when you hit the floor," she said. "You all right?"

"Yeah, in a minute."

"You weigh a ton. You've gained a lot of weight since you cleaned up, haven't you?"

"Smack kills the appetite, but pot brings it back. Okay—one more board."

He again put a powerful kick on the adjacent board and once again woke up in Cheryl's arms. He could get used to that.

Once they had pulled the broken boards out of the way, there was enough room for them to get out. Cheryl was easy, Jackson having only to boost her through. He had the worst of it, barely able to pull himself out of the tunnel using every bit of his arm strength. It reminded him of Parris Island and the million chin-ups he had to do to pass basic training so as not be set-back with the lazy and overweight. Apparently his DI was right when he said he'd thank him someday for the hell he'd put him through.

Cheryl recognized the area. "That's Elger's Pond, so the truck should be up that path and on the other side of a patch of birch trees at the end of the road." She pulled out an envelope she had stashed in the ass of her jeans. Like their clothes, it was stained with mud and algae.

"What's that?" Jackson asked.

"While you were at the fireplace, Mother gave it to me, or she pointed it out on the coffee table, anyway."

Cheryl opened it. Inside were stacks of hundred and fifty dollar bills. Jackson flipped through them.

"At least seven thousand," he said. "Maybe more."

She shoved the envelope back in her jeans. "We'll need it in Manzanillo. They take dollars and Hector and Maritza will want rent to hide us out."

She seemed sure he would take her to Mexico. It would have been nice if she had asked.

"I haven't said I'm going."

"Think about it, Jackson. If we turn ourselves in, what's the best we could expect? Five, ten years? You must have known that when you came to get me."

She was right. Accessory after the fact. The manual spelled it out plainly and warned its future investigators to never harbor a criminal. It was the only advice from the book he hadn't followed.

"Okay. But what are we gonna do when we get there? How long do we stay?"

She thought for a moment. She had only one dimple, on the right side of her face and, oddly, only when she frowned. "I thought I might hide out a few years and then move back to the States, maybe Colorado or Oregon. Start a new life someplace where I could blend in."

"And me?"

"I'm sorry, I got you into this. I really am."

They were at the truck. He'd lost track of the time while they were talking. "We have to get out of these clothes," he said. "Mine are soaked with whatever that crap was on the ground."

Cheryl changed on one side of the truck while Jackson did the same on the other. When he was naked, he turned his head to get a look at Cheryl. She was also naked and had turned her head to get a look at him. They both blushed. Odd, he thought, considering he had washed every inch of her body at the ranch house. This felt different, though. Neither one spoke about it while they sat in Prebor's truck smoking cigarettes.

"I'm ready to see my parents," she said.

The dimple had disappeared. He missed it already.

"That's not a good idea. The Feds will find the tunnel soon enough and figure out we dumped the GMC. We'll head south and cross our fingers. We can boost a car every once in a while to throw 'em off."

She finished her cigarette and threw it out on the dirt road. "No, I want to see them. I want them to explain to me why they abandoned me."

"They'll turn us in."

"Then we'll kill them." She waited a few heartbeats and then smiled. "I'm joking. God, you should have seen your face. They won't turn us in. They essentially tried to murder me in '54. They left me in a lake in a small tub. They'll go to jail if they turn us in."

It was time to tell her. His aunt was probably dead, or would die soon, so it didn't matter anymore. "Ya know, I wasn't being entirely truthful when I said your ma found you in that pond."

The dimple reappeared. "What part of it wasn't true?"

"None of it."

"By none of it, do you mean all of it?"

"Yeah. Whatever. You know what I meant to say. Your mother lied to me about it and I kept the truth from you because I didn't want to hurt you. It's hard to explain."

She pulled the cigarette from his mouth and threw it out the window. "What is the truth, Jackson?"

"Well."

"Well what, for Christ's sake?"

"Well, I wasn't lying about your parents. You are the Fitzpatricks' daughter and all, but it turns out your ma—well—"

"If I had a knife, I'd stab you. Now, what?"

"Turns out your ma kidnapped you from the hospital the day you were born."

Cheryl looked like she wanted to say something. She opened and shut her mouth three or four times, though nothing came out. She seemed angry at first and then just tired and sad. Tears cascaded down her bruised cheeks and onto her blouse. She put her arms around his neck, resting her head on his shoulder. Her tears wet his shirt near the collar. It was comforting. It reminded him of Karen when she said it was over.

"I told her I loved her, Jackson."

Chapter 34

THE PERFECT FAMILY

Jackson thought he had made a good case against visiting Cheryl's real parents for almost the entire eighty miles from Aunt Camille's house to South Burlington. He would have gotten better results talking to his hand. Cheryl was adamant. She would not go anywhere until she had spoken to them. Mexico could wait.

His argument that there was a possibility her parents might not welcome her with open arms, that they might agree with the US Government that killing soldiers, guards, and cops were crimes deserving of punishment, landed on deaf ears, one of which lacked an earlobe.

They drove the entire way without incident. Apparently, the Feds, cops, and every conscientious Vermont citizen seeking the $100,000 reward, were not looking for a 1940 rusted pickup truck struggling on back roads. The FBI had not discovered they had stolen Prebor's truck, or maybe Prebor conveniently didn't tell them, happy with the exchange.

Cheryl said little on the long drive and stayed busy alternating between smoking and biting her nails. As nervous as she was, Jackson felt an unusual calm, as if he had reached level three of the ashtanga transcendental state, the cool air filling his nostrils, the bright sun lighting the way to the waking state.

He should be worried about what might happen to him, what probably would happen to him. He had been in prison and had survived, and would survive again, but he hadn't felt this good in years. Maybe it was the traveling or the excitement of the chase, or even the danger, each day different and memorable. Maybe it was just hanging out with Cheryl. Jackson and Cheryl against the world.

He maneuvered his way through a busy Williston Road, his mouth watering as they drove by Al's French Frys, his favorite dive for burgers and fries, but they couldn't stop for fear of being recognized. Every mother, brother, and uncle was looking for him, and eventually someone would recognize the hippy private investigator despite his wig, which needed a good cleaning, having survived blood, mud, and algae. The turnoff to Mayfair Park was less than a mile. Good. Cheryl fidgeted like she had to pee.

"Calm down," he said.

"I'm going to be seeing my parents for the first time in my life and all you can say is 'calm down'?"

"They're not gonna know you and they're not gonna believe you, anyway. They'll think you look familiar, then they'll remember they saw your face on the news and at the post office and on TV and every other damn place and then they'll either shoot you or call the cops."

"Well, aren't you just Mr. Positive."

Jackson pulled into a cul-de-sac of empty lots in the development and tried to shut off the old Ford. It motored like it had the croup, before it mercifully died.

"Why'd you stop here?" Cheryl asked.

"We're a block away. It's best we not drive up in this piece of crap. Neighbors would wonder what's up with the Fitzpatricks. They'd also be less inclined to snoop if we held hands." He took her hand as they strolled side by side like two young lovers out for a walk. "It's in the manual."

"Where is this mysterious manual?"

"Back in the Fairlane. I guess I forgot to get it out after I rolled the tires over Lester's head."

"Lovely," she said.

The house hadn't changed much in the two years since Jackson had driven by during his investigation of Cheryl's abduction. It was a dull green, though he thought it might have been gray before, but he had been strung out at the time, so who knew? It could have been paisley.

They stood on the stoop of the two-story Cape Cod and rang the doorbell. The Gold Medallion Badge near the bell boasted an All-Electric House. Jackson would not have been surprised if Ward Cleaver had answered. Instead, it was Emily, the twelve-year-old. If she had been eight years older, Cheryl could have been looking in a mirror. Emily shot them that same smirk Cheryl had down to a science.

"My mother doesn't buy anything from anybody at the door. She says she'd rather go to Gaines and pick out what she wants and spend less money on it."

Cheryl tried to interrupt, but the motor mouth kept on trucking.

"If you're Jehovah's or Hare Krishna, she'll just say she's a practicing Catholic, but that's not true since we only go to church on Christmas and Easter, but you're not Hare Krishna 'cause you'd be bald." She pointed at Jackson. "Why is he wearing a wig? Is he really bald? What's wrong with your ear?"

Cheryl smiled. "You must be Emily."

Emily seemed surprised when she heard her name. She turned and bellowed. That was the only way you could describe it. A bellow. "Mom! Somebody's at the door!"

"Who is it?" the distant voice came back.

"I dunno!"

Cheryl squeezed Jackson's arm. "I'm so nervous."

He wanted to hold her, reassure her, and tell her that they'll accept her unconditionally right before they turned the both of them over to the FBI. Maybe he'd leave the last part out.

An older version of Cheryl walked through the foyer smiling as if she had known them all their lives. "I apologize for Emily," she said. "She's twelve going on thirty. What can I do for you?"

Cheryl stuttered and sputtered, giving her best impression of Prebor's old pickup before taking a deep breath. "Hello, Mother."

Mrs. Fitzpatrick seemed about to say, "What?" then stopped herself. She stared down at Emily, then looked up at Cheryl and narrowed her eyes as if to say, "Could it be?" She looked again at Emily, then once more at Cheryl. Tears tumbled down her cheeks. If crying was genetic, there was no doubt the two were related.

She embraced Cheryl. "Oh, dear Jesus. Abigail. Oh, Abigail. Dear Jesus. I knew you were alive."

They held each other like that for an interminable amount of time, alternating sobs and whimpers. Jackson caught Emily's gaze, who shrugged.

"Oh, my God, come in," Linda Fitzpatrick said. "Dennis! Dennis! Come here! Quickly!"

A million thoughts must have raced through Dennis's mind, wondering what horrific sights awaited: fire, Emily dead, a nuclear explosion. He stumbled into the living room out of breath. "What is it?"

Linda turned Cheryl's shoulders to face him like a mother displaying her small child to relatives. "It's Abigail, Dennis. I told you. You didn't believe me." Dennis mimicked Linda's first reaction, comparing his long-lost daughter's face to his wife's and other daughter's. "Oh, for Christ's sake, Dennis. Hug her."

He did, and Jackson fought his own tears. He had dealt with tragedy and depression, but this was a first for jealousy. He had tolerated Karen's new man without a thought, but Cheryl had gone from no parents to an entire family in a moment. How could he not be jealous?

The two of them sat across from Dennis and Linda, a coffee table separating them. Emily wedged herself on the edge of it and squinted at Jackson. The twelve-year-old was making him uncomfortable. Dennis spoke first, holding his hand up to Linda. It wasn't a mean gesture. He just wanted to speak first.

"I think it's obvious you are who you say you are, miss, but we have to be sure. Could you tell us your name—your story? When our baby— when *you* were kidnapped, it nearly destroyed us, so you can see, I don't want my family hurt any more than they already are."

"I know who they are," Emily said.

"What?" Dennis said.

"I know who they are. They're the ones on TV, the ones the police are looking for. The kissing cousins, I can't remember their names." Emily ran to the kitchen and came back with a newspaper. Dennis and Linda leaned in to see where she was pointing.

"Kissing cousins?" Jackson said. "Where'd they come up with that?"

Emily turned the paper around for Jackson and Cheryl to see. The headline read: "Kissing Cousins Spotted near Bolton." Emily had her finger on a paragraph. "The lady at the restaurant said he saw her kiss your cheek." She pointed at Cheryl.

Jackson felt his face flush. Cheryl followed suit.

"You're Cheryl Hebert?" Linda said.

Cheryl nodded. "This is Jackson Hurst. He was my cousin at one time, but it's a long story, Mom."

The "Mom" did it. Cheryl could have told Linda anything at that point and Linda would have believed her.

For the next hour, she told her story starting with her kidnapping at the hospital by Camille Hebert, her isolation at the Shrewsbury mansion, the SDS, the Weathermen, the BLA, and Panthers. She included all the details of the National Guard armory hold-up, her fake kidnapping, and the Brinks robbery. When she got to the parts of her imprisonment at Bent Hill, the deaths of Haze, Janie, Lester Wester, and her Uncle Ethan, she asked Emily to leave the room. She left out the explosion in the New York City townhouse.

"That explains your ear, honey," Linda said. "Are you okay?"

"Yes. Jackson took care of me."

Jackson smiled and added his story, from Charlotte to his search for his cousin, to his PI business, and latest caper with Cheryl. It wasn't necessary, but he explained that if they got caught, both would go to prison.

Cheryl wrapped it up. "And if they find out you helped us, sheltered us, you'll be charged. You know that."

"Where will you go?" Linda said.

"Mexico," Cheryl said. "For a while, until I can get back to the States."

"If you haven't committed the crimes you're charged with," Dennis said, "why not turn yourself in? We could help with the attorneys."

"I'm sorry. I'm not as innocent as you think. I stood by while people were killed and buildings were bombed. I'm afraid of prison, of the isolation. I can't go there. I'm sorry."

Linda stood and then sat down on the table in front of Cheryl. "You're not going to prison, honey. You're going to Mexico and we're going to help you. Right, Dennis?" She turned her head to face him. He shrugged. She held Cheryl's hands. "Listen. You two can stay here tonight. I'll go out and get some hair color. We can dye his hair and he can shave his mustache."

Jackson took off his wig. His long blonde hair fell past his shoulders. He held some of it out. "I'll need a heap of color for this."

"We'll cut it short," Linda said. Jackson held up a finger to protest, but she ignored him. "I won't call you Abigail anymore if it makes you uncomfortable."

"I'm used to Cheryl. I didn't mention it, but the FBI was at my moth . . ." She trailed off.

"I don't mind if you call her that," Linda said.

"My mother's house. They don't know what type of vehicle we're driving. It's parked in the cul-de-sac."

Dennis stood. "Give me the keys. I'll move my car out and put yours in the garage." Jackson gave him the keys to the pickup.

"Okay, then," Linda said. "You'll eat dinner with us and stay the night. Then you can go in the morning. And after you leave Mexico, you'll visit us once in a while. Your brothers will be surprised to see they have another sister."

Emily slid next to her mother. "My brothers didn't want me, anyway. Do you play games? Monopoly, Life?"

"A little," Jackson said.

Emily pointed to Cheryl. "I meant her."

Cheryl held her arms out and Emily rested her head on her shoulder as they hugged.

"I'll play any game you want, Sis."

Emily closed her eyes and whispered, "Sis."

Linda rubbed Emily's hair. "You can play after they eat and change their appearance, Em. But right now, you and I are headed to Gracey's to get what we need."

Jackson wasn't sure if it was the right word, but when Linda and Cheryl cut and colored his hair, he felt emasculated. With what little was left on his head now colored brown and his mustache gone, he looked like a square. Cheryl put some Butch hair wax in the front to give him a flattop.

"You look like one of the Kingston Trio."

"Groovy. What about you? You ain't got enough hair to cut as it is."

"Linda's giving me a wig. Redhead or blonde?" She tried them both on. She looked better as a blonde, but she was trying to flee the police, not enter a beauty pageant.

"Redhead," he said.

After dinner, Cheryl and Emily played Monopoly for hours. Dennis and Linda watched them like proud parents. Cheryl only left her sister alone once and that was to ask Jackson where the eight-thousand dollars was.

"In the glove compartment."

"I need a thousand."

"What for? I thought you said Hector would want rent money."

"It's for Emily. She's in the band and they're collecting money to go to New York for the Macy's Parade."

"She flying by a private plane?"

"Just get the money."

He did and he didn't feel all that bad about it.

While everyone else was busy, he watched the news. The reporter interviewed Special Agent in Charge Mark Postlewait, still diligently tracking the kissing cousins. Jackson could only wish the kissing part was true. Postlewait told of their escape and how the FBI had set a dragnet and would soon have them. The reporter asked why he thought they returned to the Hebert house.

"I assume Cheryl Hebert wanted to see her mother before she died. When we entered the house, Mrs. Hebert was already dead. We don't think the daughter had anything to do with that. Mrs. Hebert died of natural causes."

Jackson glanced over at Cheryl, who was pretending to choke Emily, as apparently Emily owned Boardwalk or Park Place or both. They both laughed. He'd tell her tonight, not now. She may have been kidnapped by the woman, but she had also been her daughter for more than twenty years.

Aunt Camille was cruel and heartless to him, but she'd loved Cheryl.

Chapter 35

NEW MOM AND DAD TO THE RESCUE

Daylight shone in from the window in streaks, the large maple outside blocking all light except for what filtered through the mighty leaves. Jackson had slept in Danny's room since he was away, working on his master's from Holy Cross. The photo of him with his family leaned precariously against a table lamp, the college boy too lazy to hang it on a wall.

Danny had long black hair parted in the middle, which would have meant little to Jackson, except for his own Eagle Scout cut. He frowned as he inspected himself in the mirror. He supposed Linda and Dennis were right, shearing his long hair like he was a bleating sheep. They hadn't done it to help him escape. They had done it to help Cheryl escape.

He sighed and flipped up the tuft of brown hair in the front. Somewhere in his head he heard Crosby, Stills, and Nash singing "Almost Cut My Hair."

Cheryl had been assigned Jeff's room, but after ten minutes of continuous whining, Cheryl agreed to sleep in Emily's room. For twenty-one years Cheryl had been an only child. For twenty-five years Jackson had been an only child. He had a right to be jealous. He would have loved to have had a brother or sister. After witnessing this warm family reunion, he had his first epiphany. Many in his platoon had epiphanies after firefights, but not Jackson. Now he had his and realized he had a mother who loved him, despite all the crap he'd thrown at her since his father died. He'd never thought about her loss, only his own. She'd stood by him, defended him, took care of him, and he'd repaid her by getting in all kinds of shit and making her life miserable. He sat down and wrote a letter. It wasn't enough, but it was a start.

After a shower, they had a breakfast of eggs, bacon, and, of course, pancakes with lots of butter for Cheryl that her mom made special just for her. Linda and Dennis had filled four paper bags with food, beer, medical supplies, and anything else they thought their daughter would need on her twenty-five-hundred-mile trek to Mexico. They'd need every bit of the supplies, limiting stops to bathroom breaks and gas stations.

Jackson wouldn't take any chances with Prebor's truck. He'd get rid of it and find something else at the first opportunity.

"I have a gun you can take," Dennis said over coffee. He was in a suit, ready to start a normal day at the office without worrying about who was searching for who. "Either a rifle or a .45 Colt I used in Korea."

Jackson shook his head. He felt naked without his long hair. "We'll get by without it. Thanks, though."

"Will you write us?" Linda asked Cheryl. "When you get a chance, once you're settled."

Cheryl wiped her mouth of maple syrup. Four pancakes in about the same number of minutes. She had to weigh maybe a hundred and twenty pounds, though she ate like a lumberjack. She was oddly attractive in her auburn wig.

"Every week if you want me to." She pulled Emily to her. "And you too. But you can't write us until we're back in the States."

Us. That was the first time she had mentioned the two of them as *us*. Did she want him to live with her in Mexico or did she misspeak?

After breakfast, they loaded the truck. Dennis left first for his work, and after Emily scouted the street, Jackson and Cheryl got in the truck as Linda opened the garage. Linda stood by the passenger door with Emily. She kissed Cheryl. Emily did the same, and touched Cheryl's wounded ear.

"Does it hurt?"

Cheryl shrugged. "A little. No worse than getting it pierced, though."

Emily smiled and spoke softly. "I put some games in the bag for you and Jackson to play at night. Can I visit you?"

Cheryl nodded. "Of course, Em. It'll be a while, and not until I move back here."

She pulled Emily's hand to her and kissed it. Linda brushed Cheryl's hair out of her eyes, and stealthily checked Cheryl's ear for the umpteenth time.

"I hate Camille Hebert for taking you, honey. Every day I wondered who would steal a baby, my baby. At night, before sleep, I'd think about you. Were you playing with other children? Were you a good student? Did you love your parents? Did you look anything like Emily? I don't know if you believe in God, but I can't help but think someone answered my prayers. You'll get over this trouble and, when you do, we'll be here." Linda leaned in and hugged her neck. "I love you."

"I love you too, Mom. And you, Emily. Practice your Monopoly. I'll be back sooner than you think."

"Take care of her, Jackson," Linda said.

"I will, ma'am." Jackson got the clunker started after only three tries. When Emily gave the okay, they drove out of Mayfair Park and on to Williston Road. Just before the I-89 cloverleaf, a car coming in the opposite direction made Jackson look twice.

"That's funny," he said.

"What's that?"

"I swear I saw some big kid driving Lester's Jimmy. Red and white, right?"

"I guess. Did you smoke some of that weed this morning?"

"Yeah, during breakfast. You didn't see me through your pile of pancakes?"

"Screw you. How long will we drive?"

"All day—until dark, anyway. We should get through New York, maybe into Pennsylvania. You're the navigator. Dennis put a map in the glove compartment."

"Great," she said. "That's where I put the pot. Dad must think the world of his long-lost daughter."

"Yeah—I think he does."

She attempted a smile and then lit a cigarette for both of them. They stopped for lunch at a rest area, running in to use the bathroom when it emptied of fellow travelers. They'd had no incidents except when a cop passed them and Jackson shoved Cheryl into his lap to hide her, getting a jab in the ribs for his trouble.

When night fell, they stopped in Breezewood, Pennsylvania, at a cheap motel on a road that paralleled the interstate. It was clean, but had only one bed. It came with a small efficiency, which surprised Jackson, considering it cost only ten bucks a night. They could cook in the room and not worry about being seen during dinner.

The shower felt good, cleaning off layers of exhaust that had filtered into the pickup's cab from the lousy muffler. Cheryl came out of the bathroom with just a towel on. It looked like a cheap miniskirt from the sixties. God, he missed miniskirts. He turned away while she dressed in jeans and a T-shirt.

"What a gentleman," she said. "How long will it take us?"

Jackson stared as she zipped up the front of her jeans. "To do what?"

"Get your head out of the gutter. To get to Mexico."

"Four days, I guess. We'll dump the clunker in the morning and find something else. You hungry?"

She shook her head. "Maybe later."

She turned on the TV. It picked up one station and the picture faded in and out. She shut it off.

"Any ice in the fridge?" she asked. She didn't bother waiting and looked for herself. She dumped an ice tray in the sink and put three or four cubes in glasses, then poured warm beer over them. She handed one to Jackson. The beer cooled almost instantly. They both sat on the bed cross-legged.

Jackson clinked his glass with hers. "To Mexico. You want me to teach you some yoga?"

"How 'bout some weed, instead? I'll get it."

"You think that's a smart thing to do? Go outside with half the country looking for you?"

"It's night. I don't glow in the dark."

She came back from the pickup with a baggie. There was enough left for two or three joints. She spread it out on a plate and did a better job rolling them this time.

"I'm getting good at this," she said. When she had three built, she lit one, took a few tokes, and passed it to him. "How 'bout Monopoly. I kicked my sister's ass. I can kick yours."

Without the wig, she looked her age. The bruises had turned a brownish purple and the ear was just slightly red on the bottom where Haze had sliced it. Surprisingly, her nipples didn't poke out of the tight T-shirt like they usually did. She had a bra on. Linda must have given her a pile of clothes like she had with him. Danny would be surprised when he returned from college to find most of his clothes gone.

After two joints, two beers, and a half-assed game of Monopoly, they both were seriously high. Jackson had the radio on a pop station, and the songs seemed to stretch out forever. Cheryl leaned over and steadied herself on his thighs. He almost swallowed his spit.

"What now?" she said. "We've got Sorry and Chutes and Ladders. What's wrong with my sister? Putting in Chutes and Ladders? That sounds good, huh, Jackson? Sister."

Jackson looked in the paper bag and found a deck of cards. "Here we go. Penny a point."

"Get me another beer first," she said.

And he thought *he* had an addictive personality. The beer was cold from being in the fridge. A haze of pot smoke hung in the air. He lit the last joint. Why spoil the fun? She spoke close to his ear. Her breath was warm and boozy.

"How about—" She dropped her voice to a whisper, "strip poker."

Jackson couldn't think of anything to say. The two times she had leaned on his thighs had made him forget she'd ever been a cousin. "Jackson?" She knocked on his head. "You there?"

He passed her the joint. "You're the boss," he said, sounding as stupid as a teenager.

"That's right. Okay, I've got four items of clothing on, shirt, bra, panties, and—jeans. Now you, sir."

He thought for a second. "Three."

"Okay, so put on one sock and we're even."

He grabbed his sock off the floor. Cheryl took a sip of beer and then had a toke. She held it forever and then blew it into his face. He won the first hand with a pair of sixes and a pair of queens. She moved closer to him and looked up at him with dreamy eyes. "What first, Jackson? Shirt? Pants?"

"I'll leave it to you," he said.

Off came the shirt. The bra was ivory and a little large. He stared at her cleavage and felt he had the largest erection he had ever had in his life. Karen was sexy and a great lover, but he'd never felt as aroused with her as he did now.

In the second hand, he had three jacks. Pretty soon she'd be undressed and he'd be close to busting his zipper. She looked at her cards.

"I only have two pairs. A pair of fours. And another pair of fours. You lose. Off with the pants."

He turned away from her and unzipped. She laughed and said, "Shy Southern boys." When he turned back she stared at his bulge.

"We are excited, aren't we?"

He lost the next hand and his shirt. The sock was long gone and forgotten. Cheryl's breaths quickened and matched his when their toes touched. She lost the next hand under suspect circumstances, throwing the cards down, saying she had nothing. When Jackson tried to look at the discards, she mixed them with the others. As tight as her bellbottom blue jeans were, she had them off with one pull. She threw them at him and had another sip of beer.

He won the next hand fair and square. She turned her back to him. "Help me, would you?" He fumbled with the snap. When it released, she leaned back to give him an accidental feel. Her breasts were amazingly firm and upright. There was very little tan line, her skin olive with a slight sheen.

"Where's this going, Cheryl?"

"I dunno, Jackson. Where is this going? Two more hands and we're through, I guess. Hey. Open your mouth."

"What?"

"Open your damn mouth. I'll be your bong."

Cheryl took a large toke and again leaned on his thighs, her hands near an erupting Vesuvius if she moved them any closer. He opened as ordered and she blew smoke into his mouth. He nearly choked, but when she didn't move away he exhaled out his nostrils and kissed the softest lips he had ever kissed in his life. She fell on top of him, knocking him flat on the bed, grinding her hips into him with a fervor. Her breasts flattened on his chest as he pulled her against him by her buttocks. They kissed as if both starved for the sensation.

"Jackson, I love you. Did you know that? I've always loved you."

He felt his face flush as he tasted the sweet mixture of weed and beer on her tongue. He rolled her on to her back and pulled off her panties, struggling to get them past her knees. She moved his hand away and wriggled out of them the rest of the way, then knelt to take off his underwear. As she threw them to the orange-carpeted floor, he pulled her back to him and gently stroked her mound. He rolled her under him, entering her as if they had been lovers all their lives. They moved with little effort, moaning rhythmically to the squeals of the bedsprings, their bodies shuddering, their faces pinned to each other, gasping for air.

"Tell me you love me, Jackson."

He kissed her wounded earlobe. "I always have, babe."

When they had finished, he rolled over and held her as he fell asleep.

Chapter 36

MR. JOSHUA ROBERT PREBOR

The twin barrels of the shotgun looked like the dead eyes of an enormous snake. A sudden blast of light woke Jackson, interrupting his dream, a sexual one as it turned out—appropriate, considering the previous night's acrobatics with Cheryl. She breathed baby breaths, her nose poking against his chin stubble. She had the warmest body of any girl he'd ever slept with. He elbowed her breast.

"What?" she slurred.

He gestured with his head toward the large man in front of them. The man or boy—it was difficult to tell in the opaque light—sat on the ground level air conditioner. The sheer white curtains were closed, but their intruder must have drawn open the heavy, dark drapes.

Cheryl squealed, pulled the sheet over her breasts, and said, "Who the hell are you?"

The intruder gave a wry grin and pulled back the hammers on an old shotgun. He was twice the weight he should have been and had a black mole the size of a dime just over the bridge of his nose. He had bowl-shaped, greasy hair that Jackson swore he could smell from the bed. His eyes, nose, and mouth lacked any sense of symmetry, as if God had played Mr. Potato Head while drunk.

"Well, Miss Hebert, I am Joshua Robert Prebor. Good morning. You know the papers can't call you the kissing cousins anymore." He put his hand over his mouth and giggled. Not laughed—giggled. "They have to call you the fucking cousins now."

Jackson sat up in the bed. Joshua Robert Prebor aimed the barrels at his head.

"Easy, man," Jackson said. "How'd you get in here? That door's steel and got a lock, deadbolt, and chain."

Prebor waved the gun at him in little circles. "Don't you try anything, Mr. Hurst. You just don't try anything. I'll kill you and her, too.

You hear what I'm saying? Doesn't matter to the federal authorities if you're dead or alive."

"What do you want?" Cheryl said.

"Two things, miss. Two things."

Jackson and Cheryl waited for what seemed an interminable amount of time.

"And, they are?" Cheryl said.

"One. A hundred thousand dollars. My reward for bringing in one of the FBI's ten most wanted. Do you know what I can do with a hundred thousand? I can buy a '76 Camaro before it even hits the showroom. I can live in the city and move out of the farmhouse. That's what the hero Joshua Robert Prebor can do. You know what I'm saying?"

"I asked you how you got in," Jackson said.

The farmer's son ignored him. He had to be a farmer's son, the bib-and-braces denim overalls struggling to keep all of him in.

"And two. I want to see your titties. And I mean right now." He adjusted his aim toward Cheryl. "Drop that sheet, Miss Hebert."

"C'mon, man," Jackson said. "Leave her alone. Take what we got and get out."

The swinging shotgun repositioned on Jackson. It was like watching a damn tennis match.

"Mr. Vietnam Veteran, big private investigator. Go ahead. Make my day. That's right, I saw the movie. Now you tell your cousin to drop that sheet or you'll be eating lead."

"Eating lead?" Cheryl said.

"That's right. Let's see them titties, Miss Hebert. Count of three or boom. One—"

Cheryl dropped the sheet. Mr. Potato Head's eyes popped out of their sockets. He moved off the air conditioner and waddled over to her side of the bed, the barrel never moving off Jackson.

"Oh my God," Prebor said as he squeezed her left breast, tweaking the nipple until she cried out. "Oh my God, they're the most beautiful titties I've ever seen. You know what I'm saying?"

Jackson tacitly agreed. Prebor backed up to the AC and sat down. The metal vent bent under the strain.

"How'd you get in, man?" Jackson said again.

Prebor jerked his thumb to the left, his eyes, the gun, and that god-awful mole still directed on Jackson. "The adjoining door, sir. I explained to the manager that number fourteen is my most favorite number in the whole world, and if she'd be so kind as to let me have that room—and she said of course I could. I had to wait all night for you two to fall asleep. It seemed like every time I thought you were finished, you'd start up again. Unh, unh, unh."

Prebor stood and thrust out his portly pelvis to demonstrate. "Finally, after you were through and my hand and dick were sore, I let myself in. I'm good at locks. Let myself in to neighbors' places all the time."

"Are you related to Mr. Prebor in Shrewsbury?" Cheryl asked.

Prebor didn't reply until he admired Cheryl's titties once again. "I am, indeed. I am his grandson. When I went over to his farm to borrow ten dollars, I saw someone had replaced Grandpa's truck with a new GMC Jimmy, just like the one the papers said might be in the possession of the wanted Cheryl Hebert and Jackson Hurst. When I saw you were not there I surmised you exchanged vehicles and fled the authorities. I saw a great opportunity and borrowed the GMC to hunt you down. Successfully." He rubbed his crotch as if to add an exclamation. "Ooh. Still sore."

"Okay, man," Jackson said, shifting his feet near the edge of the bed. One distraction and he could grab the gun. Keep him talking, just like the manual said. "This is Pennsylvania. How'd you find us?"

"Accidentally, Mr. Hurst. I drove the Jimmy to Burlington thinking you might hide out in your office. I knew about your office from the papers, of course." The mole danced as he spoke. It was like *Sing Along with Mitch*. "You weren't there so I drove along Williston Road to check the motels. You drove right by me. Hard to miss you in Grandpa's truck."

"That was you, huh?"

"That was me. From there, I followed you here. I could have turned you in anytime, but the police know about me and some of the trouble I've been in and would have found a way to screw me out of the money. You know what I'm saying? No, Mr. Hurst and Miss Hebert, I am going to take you myself to the nearest FBI office and get my promise of the reward money. In writing."

"I gotta pee," Jackson said. He swung his legs off the bed.

"Pee in the bed," Prebor said.

Jackson stood. "Oh, c'mon, man."

"My finger is one quarter inch from the trigger, Mr. Hurst. One quarter inch. Get in that bed now and pee where you sit. Don't make me shoot you."

Jackson reached for his underwear on the floor. Prebor pulled the triggers. There were two loud clicks.

Prebor looked at the shotgun and said, "Oh, my." He broke the breach and fumbled in his shirt pocket for the two shotgun shells that he had apparently forgotten to load into his gun. "Oh my, oh my," he repeated.

He had just gotten one cartridge in when Jackson chopped the boy's neck with the heel of his left hand. Joshua Robert Prebor's eyes rolled into the back of his head as he toppled off the air conditioner, planting his odd face in the orange pile carpet.

"My God, Jackson," Cheryl said. "How'd you do that?"

He smiled at his sprite. He was the hero this time. "My sensei beat it into me until I knew exactly where to hit somebody. Nothin' special. A knife strike, the Japanese call it. You hit the brachial plexus, a bunch of nerves down the neck, and they're out, but not for long. Let's get him on the bed. There's some old rope in the truck. Get it, and we'll tie him up."

Prebor came to as Jackson finished tying him to the bed. "Mr. Prebor, since we're being so formal like and all, I'll address you as Mr. Prebor. Anyway, we are gonna leave you here a while. Maid will come soon enough." Jackson covered up Prebor's mouth with some first aid tape and made sure he could breathe through his nose. "Don't catch a cold now, brother. That funny nose of yours is all you got to breathe outta. You know what I'm saying?"

Cheryl waited in the pickup while Jackson went to the manager's office. He paid the lady for three days in advance and told her they didn't need a maid until then since they were newlyweds and didn't want to be disturbed. They drove twenty miles before Jackson pulled into a grocery store parking lot.

"Stay here. I saw a car for sale out in front of that house."

He pointed down the street to an old craftsman. A late model Pontiac had a "For Sale" sign in the window. He took five hundred dollars out of the glove compartment of the pickup. Half an hour later he and Cheryl were moving everything over to the '68 Lemans.

"It's got air conditioning," Jackson said as they drove away. "We'll need it in Texas."

Cheryl lit a cigarette. "He'll tell them about us."

"Who? Mr. Joshua Robert Prebor? It'll be awhile. By that time, we're in Mexico if we can get across the border."

Cheryl blew smoke out the window. "I'll call Maritza—the day before we get to Laredo. We can walk across the Rio Grande there. I know a spot. Hector can pick us up there on the other side. How much is left?"

"About six thousand."

"Hope it's enough," she said. She slid over to him and squeezed his knee. "Did you mean it?"

"Last night?"

"No. A year ago. Yes, last night."

He kissed her a quick one on the lips. "I'd never lie to you, babe."

Chapter 37

POSTLEWAIT SETS A TRAP

Special Agent Baker rang the doorbell. Postlewait had earlier gone over the role Baker was to play in the interrogation. His partner could be dimwitted at times, though he made up for it with his loyalty and skills, including his marksmanship—far above average.

It was an admirable house. The Fitzpatricks either purchased it in a depressed market or perhaps Dennis Fitzpatrick made more of a salary than the records indicated. Still, a very nice house. Too bad they'd have to sell it to pay for attorney fees and the inevitable liabilities they'd incur while spending the next few years in prison. *Que sera*. Criminals must be punished if they commit crimes. Otherwise, anarchy would reign.

Linda Fitzpatrick and her daughter Emily answered the door. He'd talk first, then Baker, if Baker remembered the earlier briefing.

"Good morning," Postlewait said. "Are you Mrs. Dennis Fitzpatrick?"

"Yes. How may I help you?" She was quite attractive, her beauty diminished somewhat by an elaborate hairdo and a petticoat dress. Odd attire for the times and yet—seductive. An erudite pixy. Charming.

"I'm Special Agent in Charge Andrew Postlewait and this is my associate, Special Agent Dan Baker. We're from the Albany division of the Bureau."

"The FBI?"

"Yes. Excuse me. The FBI. I was wondering if we could come in for a few minutes to talk with you and your husband, if he's home?"

"He's home. What's this about?"

It was Baker's turn to talk. If his associate had forgotten his cue, Postlewait would need to extemporize. Fortunately, the young agent did remember. It was Postlewait's job to watch her eyes, gauge her reaction.

"It's about Cheryl Hebert, Mrs. Fitzpatrick," Baker said.

The eyes did react, only slightly, but he saw it, a minute flicker of recognition. From that point on he would consider any response otherwise a lie.

"The girl they're looking for? What would we have to do with her?"

This time Emily also reacted. Tears welled in her eyes. She wiped them stealthily with her sleeve. If he failed to get the parents to confess, he would have no trouble getting this young sprite to tell all.

"Just a few questions, if you don't mind."

"No, of course not. Come in." Then she held her hands out suddenly to stop them. "I'm sorry, would you mind showing me your identification and badges?"

They did and she led them to a large living room. He sat on a long sofa near Baker.

"Your husband?" Baker said.

He walked in on cue, wiping his hands on a dishtowel. There was grease under his fingernails and a smudge he had missed on his forehead. Had he been listening to their conversation at the door? Of course, he had, and the towel and grease had been hastily acquired. Did they think FBI agents hadn't seen it all? Well, perhaps not Baker but, indeed, Postlewait had seen it all and if he wrote it down, it would be a bestseller.

"What's this about?" Dennis said.

"They're with the FBI, Dennis," Linda said. "They want to talk about Cheryl Hebert."

"That girl?"

"Yes, sir," Postlewait said.

The pre-teen began chewing her nails. Perhaps he'd just question her to save time. He squinted at her. She started crying, little sobs that little girls with something to hide always seemed to emanate under duress.

Linda took her hand. "Go upstairs, Emily. We can handle this."

Emily stood.

"I'd rather she stay, Mrs. Fitzpatrick," Postlewait said. "I believe she can singularly help us in our investigation. Please sit, young lady. It won't be long, I assure you. Let me fill you folks in on what has occurred in the last few days, if you don't mind. As you know, Cheryl Hebert is wanted in connection with the murders of three Brinks guards as well as a North Brook, New York, policeman. She, George Willis, and a Miss Janie Anderson escaped. Mr. Willis, Miss Anderson, Mr. Lester

Wester, and a Mr. Ethan Pembroke were later found shot to death at Mr. Wester's ranch in New Hampshire.

"Miss Hebert and her accomplice, a Mr. Jackson Hurst, fled the scene and are on the run. I'm sure you know all this, since it is on the television and in the papers. What you may not know is that we don't believe Miss Hebert or Jackson Hurst shot any of the victims. Nonetheless, we are still pursuing them."

Linda interrupted. "Would you gentlemen like something to drink? Tea? Lemonade?"

"Yes," Baker said. "Coffee, if you have some."

Postlewait frowned but sat stoically until she returned with two cups. The coffee smelled delicious.

He accepted the cup and continued. "Yesterday, in a motel in Breezewood, Pennsylvania, the maid found a Mr. Joshua Prebor bound and gagged in a room Jackson Hurst had paid for in advance. Two days earlier, Mr. Prebor had tried to hold Miss Hebert and Mr. Jackson in order to turn them over for the reward. He failed. If he had called the authorities, instead of taking matters into his own hands, we would have the two in custody. As it is now, they have had a two-day head start to an unknown destination. Mr. and Mrs. Fitzpatrick, do you have any idea what vehicle the perpetrators drove away in?"

Dennis held his hands out. "No idea."

Postlewait took a moment to sip his coffee. Emily continued to whimper. Let them sweat. "It was a 1946 Ford pickup, the same truck a neighbor of yours spotted in the cul-de-sac just a few doors down from here."

"I'm sorry," Linda said. "I still don't know what this has to do with us."

"I'll tell you." Watch for her reaction, he told himself. "When your neighbor reported he had seen a vehicle like the one shown on the television news—by the way, it was found abandoned outside Breezewood—we did background research on you and your neighbors. Nothing popped up other than some information on an investigation that occurred in 1954. Your child, I believe. Abigail."

"Yes," Dennis said. "The FBI was involved in the case."

"We were, indeed," Postlewait said. "And we've come to the conclusion that Cheryl Hebert is Abigail."

He watched Linda's reaction. It was there but delayed, as he thought it would be. She knew already.

"That can't be." Linda squeezed Dennis's hand. "Can it?"

"We believe so. Camille Hebert kidnapped your daughter and passed her off as her adopted child for the last twenty-one years. Cheryl was here, wasn't she, she and that Hurst fellow?"

"Are you out of your mind?" Dennis said. "We never saw either of them or that truck. If that is our daughter and she had come here, we would have talked her into turning herself in or we would have turned her in ourselves."

Emily was near frantic, shaking badly. Postlewait calmly took another sip. "Oh, she was here, Mr. Fitzpatrick. We're sure of it, just as we're sure you helped them. That, sir, is accessory after the fact. Do you have any idea of the consequences of your actions?"

"It's not true," Linda said.

"It's true," Postlewait said. "I will have fingerprint technicians out here scouring this place within an hour if you don't come to your senses. Are you telling me they won't find Hurst's and Hebert's fingerprints in this house? Do you really want a team of investigators tearing this place apart?"

Emily burst out crying. "Stop. Stop. Please." She turned to face her parents. "I'm so sorry, Mom. I'm so sorry. I thought it'd be better if I didn't say anything. I'm sorry."

Postlewait put down his coffee. Ah—the easy confession from the mouth of a babe, a child who would have to wait several years for her parents' release from prison.

"What are you saying, young lady?" Postlewait asked.

"It's true," she said.

Agent Baker smiled at Postlewait.

"They did come by here," Emily continued. "I answered the door and she—Cheryl—she said she was my sister, Abigail. They wanted to see Mom and Dad, but I told them my parents were out. They went shopping and they said they might go to a movie or dinner."

Postlewait stopped her. "Are you saying your parents weren't home when she was here? Did they see them later?"

"No. That's what I'm saying. My parents didn't know I let them in the house. The two ate something and used the bathrooms. I didn't tell my mom and dad because I was scared. Mom talks about Abigail all the time and I—" She cried in her mother's lap.

"It's okay, baby. Tell the truth," Linda said.

Emily sniffed. "Okay. Anyway, they said they couldn't stay. I was afraid if I told Mom and she called the police, I'd be in trouble."

She broke down into an incoherent babbling. The kid was either the best actress in the world or the best liar.

Of course, there was the possibility she was telling the truth.

Regardless, he could do nothing about it. The truth would come later, in the trial. If there was one. There was always the chance it could end up a standoff in some old farmhouse or barn. He didn't relish the possibility. Hebert and Hurst were criminals. but apparently not of the same level as their dead compatriots. Still, he would get them. He always got them. That was why he was a special agent in charge, because he always got them.

Chapter 38

LAREDO

The sun was large, orange, and nearly set as Jackson and Cheryl arrived at the narrowest part of the Rio Grande on the outskirts of Laredo. Hector Acevedo sat in a rusty, white Volkswagen Beetle about fifty feet away on the other side. He waved a cigarette out the passenger window to acknowledge them. Cheryl waved back.

The VW was too small for the big Puerto Rican, his shoulders hunched forward to keep his head below a torn headliner.

"You believe me now?" Cheryl said, flipping her own cigarette onto the parched riverbank. "I said he'd be here, him or Maritza. He's a pig, always has been. I don't understand why she stays with him. She's so sweet and helpful. Last year she hid Janie and me until the townhouse fiasco blew over." Cheryl's dimple popped in and out as she spoke. They had stayed at two more non-descript motels since that night in Vermont. "Do you love me, Jackson? Tell me you love me."

She'd repeated the mantra the last two nights, the excitement of the passionate words dulled by their repetition.

"Yeah, I love you." And he did love her and always would. She just needed to stop asking him.

Despite the obvious drought, the Rio Grande sped by at a serious clip.

"How we supposed to get across?" he said. "I can swim, but not against that son-of-a-bitch. It'll knock our legs straight out, babe."

She kissed him and opened the passenger door. "I've done this before. It's at most, three feet deep here. It just looks like more. Get everything you can carry and we'll head across."

"Why doesn't Pedro come over here and help us? We're giving him six grand."

"Don't call him Pedro. He has a temper."

"Well, why won't he help?"

"It's his way. I can't explain. Just get the stuff and let's go. It's getting dark."

"What about the LeMans?"

Before Cheryl could answer, two Mexicans drove up in a pickup. One of them held his hands out for the keys.

"Hector's men," Cheryl said. "Give him the keys. It's part of the price."

The man smiled when Jackson handed them over, the dude obviously thrilled with the Pontiac, rubbing his hand over the sleek roof like it was a stripper's ass.

Jackson followed Cheryl, who despite three brown bags cradled in her arms, strode confidently across the Rio Grande, leaving the US of A and entering Mexico. So much for the border patrol.

Cheryl sat in the front, giving Hector a polite kiss on the cheek.

"*Corazon de Melon*," he said to her. "How is our little anarchist?" Hector's bucket seat was positioned all the way back to give him legroom, so Jackson sat behind Cheryl. The huge man gestured with his thumb, "Who's the Boy Scout?" He narrowed his eyes at Jackson. "*Si*, a Boy Scout."

"Jackson Hurst. Hector Acevedo," Cheryl said. Jackson proffered his hand between the seats. Hector ignored it. "The keesing cousins," Hector said, driving with one hand, smoking with the other. "Maybe more than keesing, I think." The torn fabric of the headliner flapped behind Hector's neck, which was the same width as his head. "Hang on." He reached for a CB microphone. He spoke rapid Spanish to someone who said little other than "*Si*." Hector started and ended with what sounded like "Blooble." He hung the mic in its cradle and finished the cigarette. "Idiot never drove no automatic. He likes the color, though. Nice of you gringos to donate to the cause."

"Our pleasure," Jackson said. "Hey man, what's a blooble?"

"That's my handle. Blooble," Hector said.

"Spell it, dude."

"Blooble, blooble." The man's face flushed. "B-l-u-e-b-u-l-l. Blooble."

"Oh—got it. Blue Bull."

Hector grinned and stared at Jackson in the rearview. "Used to be the name of my trucking company in Queens. Thirteen trucks—moving vans. Best money I ever made until the IRS caught on. It's why Maritza and me came here, the Feds after me for a few tax mistakes, and her for blowing up things."

"Things?" Jackson said.

"Things—things. Tell him, sister. You know what things. You been here before for things."

Cheryl lit one of Hector's cigarettes.

"Jackson and I will talk about it later."

"Oh, man, that's why I love this girl. 'Jackson and I.' She thinks she's a millionaire like her mommy. She's a damn fine chiquita though, man. Hey— Maritza wants to talk about Haze. About how you two messed him up."

Cheryl blew smoke out the window. "We were there. My uncle shot them."

"That's not what the paper says."

"Paper's wrong," Jackson said.

Blue Bull got back on the CB and rattled off a million words for the next ten minutes.

"I told the guy to call Maritza," Hector said. "I tell her fifteen hours, maybe more, before we get there. You'll dig Manzanillo, man. You'll really dig it. Like old times, Cher. Old times."

Not much more was said for the rest of the trip in the bumpy Beetle, the Mexican countryside hidden under the blackest shroud Jackson had ever seen, nothing but occasional light from small *casitas* and a few *haciendas*. Cheryl drifted in and out of sleep, interrupted by the rough road and lousy shock absorbers. By the time they reached the Pacific, it was morning.

Maritza's fugitive bed-and-breakfast was a small, white stucco house about a half mile from the beach. It had four tiny bedrooms and a kidney-shaped pool. Maritza had coffee for them at the kitchen table. The room smelled of peppers and humidity. A dip in the pool would have been nice.

She was nearly six feet tall with a child's face of smooth brown skin. Jet-black hair fell just below her shoulders. She wore men's tan slacks, army boots, and a white sleeveless T-shirt stained slightly yellow under her arms. Her smile seemed indelible, even with her mouth closed. She held her arms out to Cheryl.

"Oh, my baby, you are in so much trouble. What am I going to do with you, my *nena*? *Te amo mucho, mi amor.*"

They embraced, then kissed, mouth to mouth, lingering. Cheryl could have backed away, though Maritza held her tightly. There was no reluctance from Cheryl that Jackson could see. Seconds crawled by until the girls separated and then embraced again. It had to be a Mexican custom.

The four of them sat around the table, sipping coffee, a strong, thick brew that coated the inside of Jackson's mouth. Hector looked as tired as the two of them, yawning as the girls caught up.

"So," Maritza said, "welcome back to *Casa Jimenez*. Unless Hector is fortunate tonight with his dealings you two may be my last guests. Two months ago, an Irishman left without paying and now the money is due our landlord. Tell me, *nena,* that you brought the Brinks cash."

Jackson spoke. "We didn't take none of that. We got six thousand and a little more. We can't give it all to you, but we'll fork up some."

Maritza smiled. "Fork up? Where did you get this handsome boy who talks so poorly? Fork up. Ah, at least you have a Redford and not a Frankenstein." She stared at Hector, who stared back.

"Ah—you," was all he could think of. It was hard to say if he was angry. He always looked angry. "I need two grand for tonight," he added. He held out his hand. When it was obvious he both meant it and wasn't going to drop his hand, Cheryl counted out two thousand of her mother's money.

Maritza put her hand atop Cheryl's. "Tell me everything you've been up to and not just what the pigs say in the papers. Start with after I left Greenwich. When was that? A year ago? I don't know."

Though Cheryl was as tired as Jackson, she went over the last year in detail. When she had finished, Maritza poured more coffee.

Jackson declined, preferring sleep. Hector had dozed off somewhere between the armory robbery and the Brinks heist.

"So," Maritza said, "you didn't bring Maritza that Brinks money and so now she can't go back to Colombia and start her business to help the rebels. Now she must stay here and wait for fugitives who won't come. Oh well, maybe Frankenstein will come through, maybe." She pointed at Jackson. "Hector wants your help tonight, you pretty thing. You help my Hector? I think you should."

Jackson held out his arms. "After some sleep, I'll do whatever the hell he wants me to."

Maritza pushed Cheryl's arm playfully. "Ah, you must keep this one. Such a dirty mouth. You watch him or I'll take him from you like you took poor Aaron from your sweet girlfriend."

"We're exhausted, baby," Cheryl said. She held up the coffee cup. "This isn't helping. Do you mind?"

"No, no, no. Why should I mind? Come with me, I'll show you two love cousins your room. The beds move together if you feel the tingle to mingle. Come."

Jackson felt no tingle and crashed when his head hit the cigarette-scented pillow. The IRA solider must have chain-smoked. When he woke, it was dark. Hector sat on the end of Cheryl's bed. Cheryl wasn't in it. Jackson didn't know if that was a good thing or not. All he knew is that it was the first time in his life he was jealous of a girl.

"Let's go, man," Hector said. "I know these guys, but it don't hurt to have somebody to watch out. This kinda business is tough, you know, but you're a tough guy. Cher says you're a tough guy. That right?"

Jackson wiped the sleep from his eyes. "What kinda business?"

"My kinda business. That's all you need to know."

"Let me get something to eat. I haven't had nothing since Laredo."

"Maritza made you a sandwich. It's in the car. There's a cooler with beer in the back seat."

Jackson washed his face, brushed his teeth, and had a cigarette. Maritza and Cheryl were out. Hector wouldn't say where and he didn't seem like the kind of guy to press the issue with. Once in the Beetle, Jackson ate his sandwich and drank two cold Mexican beers. He would be drinking a lot of them until his system got used to the water. Cheryl said it would take a week or so.

"Where are we going?" Jackson said.

Hector hung up his CB mic after Blue Bulling for five minutes, stopping only to breathe and drink half a beer.

"You know any of this place around here?" Hector asked.

"No. That's why I asked. Is Cheryl meeting us?"

Hector drank the rest of his beer. "You want me to tell you where we're going or where Cheryl's going, and I don't know where she's going. Maritza won't hurt her. We're here anyway. *Isla Dorado*."

A black cliff sloped down to a tremulous sea. Jackson couldn't see the ocean in the dark, but he heard it. Hector got out and looked over the edge of an outcrop of rock. "It's a cove. They're coming in a small boat, only way in without waves smacking you against the rocks. We're gonna meet them on the beach."

Jackson leaned over into the dark abyss. "How we supposed to get down there?"

"Hike down the path, Boy Scout. Hold my hand if you're scared, okay? Listen, like I said, I know the guy. Domingo. He's okay, but anybody go for their shirt or pocket or pants, you say *Jefe*. Got it?"

"What's a hefay?"

"Don't worry about it. You just say it. I'll do the rest. You're here to haul the stuff up the cliff with me."

"What stuff?"

"Weed. Three bales. We use your two thousand, my boy sells it in Tijuana, ten times that, maybe more. You keep the two, give the rest you brung to Maritza for room and board. *Comprende*?"

They slid more than hiked down the cliff, the sand slippery on the jagged rock. Jackson kept close to Hector, feeling his presence more than seeing him. They arrived at the bottom just as the boat motored in at near idle. The running lights were off, only the glow from the tip of a cigarette visible.

Jackson's eyes adjusted in the pale moonlight and he could make out two men, boys really, as they stepped out of the small motorboat and onto the beach. They had long, bleached-blond hair and wore T-shirts and baggies. The tall one was barefoot, the shorter one wore sandals. Hector put his hand in his pocket.

"Where's Domingo?" he said.

"Sick, dude," the taller one said. Both had muscular arms and barrel chests. Swimmers or surfers, Jackson guessed.

"Sick? Domingo? So he sends a couple of surfers?"

"Yeah, man. He's in Guatemala, you know. They're thinking malaria. Alma's got it, too. He might be out for a month. Domingo's our man when we're low on the good shit, you know, the Colombian, so he asked us to make the delivery. Five hundred for a day's work. How can you beat it? You got the money? We'll help you unload."

Hector kept his hand in his pocket.

"How's Maria Luisa? She sick too? I'm her godfather, so don't tell me my Maria Luisa's got malaria. That girl never gets sick."

The shorter surfer scratched his head and hacked a pot cough. "She a little sick, last we saw of her, but not like Domingo, man. Okay, we ready?"

They hauled out three bales wrapped in clear plastic and dropped them in front of Hector. Hector pulled out a jackknife and slit one of the bales on top. He stuck his hand in the slit.

"It's good, man," the tall one said, reaching down the front of his baggies. "Good Colombian."

Jackson couldn't remember the word Hector had told him to yell out. Something to do with a cow, he thought.

"Cow, man. Hector—cow!" he said.

Hector looked confused, at least from what Jackson could make of him in the dark. Then he took a pistol out of his pocket and shot the tall one in the head. "Domingo don't have no daughter, dude," he said. He fired twice at the other surfer, who had jumped back in the boat. The guy fired his own pistol three times at no one in particular. Jackson waded in to the shallow water near the back of the boat and crept to the front using the hull to hide. When the pistol came over the gunwale, he pulled the surfer out of the boat, pinning his neck on the sandy beach with his wet sneaker. The guy pounded Jackson's leg but stopped when Jackson kicked his stomach.

"Okay—okay," the surfer said. "It was Ray's idea. You keep the stuff and the money. Okay?"

"No problem," Hector said. He leaned over and shot that guy in the head, too. A mist of blood splattered Hector and Jackson. Jackson wiped it out of his eyes.

"Man," Jackson said. "He was giving it up. You should have let him go."

"If he's here, then Domingo's dead. I wasn't going to let him get away with that. You fuck with bad boys like me, you take the risk of not driving back to San Diego. Help me with the weed."

It seemed like everywhere Jackson went, he left a trail of dead bodies. It wasn't as bad in 'Nam. Screw it. He'd grab Cheryl and they'd find their own place. Blue Bull could do his own killing.

They had to take the backseat out of the Beetle to fit the bales. Hector strapped the third one on to the roof rack and covered it with an old sheet. He tied the backseat on top of it. Welcome to the third world. Hector downed half a beer before they found a real road to drive on.

"What's that cow shit thing you talking about?" he asked Jackson, who had finished off a beer himself.

"I couldn't remember the word. Heifer or something, so I said cow, figuring your word meant that in Spanish or something. I don't know, the guy had his hands in his pants, you know?"

"*Jefe*, man. It means boss. *Jesus, Maria y Jose.* You gotta be kidding me, man."

When they were at the house, the *jefe* ordered Jackson to help him unload the weed into the garage. Jackson should have let the surfer plug the bastard. He washed the blood off his face in the utility sink. Maritza's car was there, but they must not have heard them drive up in the tired Beetle. He went through the door that led to the kitchen, leaving Hector to his weed inventory.

Jackson took a beer out of the refrigerator and gulped it at the kitchen table. His hands still shook. Screw Hector and screw Maritza. They were getting out of there. He could get a job fishing or something in the tourist hotels along the beach. He called out for Cheryl and then heard voices from the other room. The kitchen led to a hallway and the bedrooms. Cheryl came out of a bathroom drying her hair, a bath towel wrapped around her body. He smiled.

"Hey, babe," he said.

She froze as the bathroom door opened behind her. A cloud of steam framed Maritza, who nearly bumped into Cheryl. Maritza had nothing wrapped around her body.

Chapter 39

THEIR FIRST SPAT

The only light came from the slit in the uneven door, casting a wedge of yellow on the adjacent wall. Jackson lay in one bed, Cheryl the other. From the repeated glow of her cigarette, she was smoking much faster than he was, an indication of anger, as he knew from watching his mother smoke after his latest arrest or lost job. He puffed faster. Cheryl couldn't possibly be as pissed as he was.

Mariachi music came in with the crooked light—Hector, drunk and singing off-key to a parade of guitars. Maybe he and Maritza were expecting fireworks from the gringos' bedroom, but Jackson and Cheryl said nothing, smoking in the dark, the minutes dragging on along with the background music and the aroma of spicy food from the kitchen. He wasn't hungry, the gory murders of the surfers still vivid in his head. Cheryl jumped in first.

"Are you ever going to say anything?"

No, he thought, but then he did, anyway. "What do you want me to say?"

"I don't care. Anything. Tell me how you feel about it."

Jackson leaned over and crushed the cigarette in the ashtray on the table. At least he thought it was an ashtray. Who the hell cared?

"How do you think I feel about it? I'm out there in the dark with Che Guevera, shooting kids over a botched drug deal, and then I come back covered head to foot in teenage blood to find you catching up with an old friend in the shower."

From the sound of the bed slamming against the plaster wall, she was now sitting up.

"Who are you to judge me? How long have we been together? Five, six days? What? Is that like a marriage or something in Charlotte? You can't tell me what to do and you can't tell me who I can or can't be with because of six damn days, Jackson. You know—maybe that's your problem. You think you have to control the girl you fall in love with, tell her what to do, when to do it. Is that the way you were with Karen? Is that why she left you? Why do you think you own me? Because we slept together?"

"That's like ten questions. Which one do you want me to answer?"

"How about telling me why you even care?"

His turn to sit up. "Maybe it's because you asked me a hundred times if I loved you or not. If you don't care about me, then what's up with that?"

"I do care about you. I love you, but what I do is my business."

"Did you ask Maritza if she loves you, if she'll *always* love you?"

"Oh, go fuck yourself. Maritza and I have been friends for years. She was there at the townhouse explosion. And you don't even know if we did anything while you were out, and if we did, it's our business."

"You're repeating yourself," Jackson said. "I don't feel like talking about it anymore." He felt for the cigarette pack, found it, took one out, and lit it.

"We have to talk about it," she said. "I don't want to sleep until it's all out. We've got enough problems. We don't need to create any more."

"You should have thought about that earlier."

Hector turned up the volume on the radio. Screw him and screw Maritza. They don't want to hear it, then *they* can go out. "And why is it everyone knows the details of this townhouse but me? Hector knows about it. Postlewait knows about it. Everybody except ol' Jackson."

She swung her legs over the bed, reached over, and held his hands. He pulled them away. She took them again, her thumbs massaging his knuckles. He wished he could see her face.

"I'll tell you about it if you tell me about that girl in Vietnam. Then you'll understand the way I feel about Maritza and you'll know I'm not who you think I am. You think I'm this innocent girl caught up in the movement because I want to hurt my mother. Maybe that was part of it, but not all of it. I care about the revolution and I want to do something to change the way this country works, the way they herd black men in prisons like animals, the way they start wars on whims, and beat and kill my sisters and brothers. Look at what they did at Kent State. They'll keep doing it until we stop them. You say you want the same thing, Jackson, but what you really want is vengeance, for your father's death, for Vietnam. You don't believe—I do."

She let go of his hands and sighed. "We used the money from the fake kidnapping to rent a townhouse in Greenwich Village." Her cigarette glowed as she paused, silhouetting her hand. "Haze wanted an innocent-looking place to make bombs without us seeming out of place with our clothes and hair. We looked like artists and fit in. They promised me they'd only use the bombs in the early morning, when there was no one around to get hurt. We targeted administration buildings at universities, recruiting offices, and police stations, anywhere they'd get the idea we were serious. But I knew Haze and the others wanted somebody to die. I knew it and I helped them, anyway, wanting to be part of the group—accepted.

"One Saturday, two of our members, Milt and Sammy, were building bombs in a back bedroom of the townhouse. Once they finished their part, they gave them to me, Janie, and Maritza to add the timers and wrap them for delivery. It was fun, just us girls, drinking a few beers as we assembled our deadly presents. We worked in the living room and, because of the heat, we wore only T-shirts and panties. The explosion came from the bedroom. A ball of fire raced into the living room, lighting up our hair and our underwear. Maritza's legs were burned, but she wasn't knocked out like Janie and I were. She dragged us outside and stripped us. When I came to, she was slapping at the flames on her legs. She has terrible scars on her calves. That's why she wears pants all the time."

Jackson had only seen the front of Maritza in the bathroom before he had stormed away.

Cheryl continued. "The three of us ran across the street, where a nice lady loaned us some of her clothes. When she went outside to see if others needed help, we ran a few blocks away to get a cab. We found out later Milt and Sammy had died in the explosion. That scared me enough to want out, but I participated, Jackson. I had the chance to go to the cops and stop Haze and the rest of them, but I didn't."

It was true, he thought. He wanted to believe she was this naïve kid caught up in an idealistic quest, manipulated by others, but it was more a wish than a reality. Maybe she was right about him.

Maybe he was fighting establishment and authority because of his father's death and the war. Maybe. "My turn?"

"Yeah," she said. "Yours can't be much worse than mine."

"Wanna bet?" He took a few puffs. The girl's eyes seemed to float in front of him, wide, full of fear. "We were ambushed on a bridge near a village. A bunch of villagers scooted from the huts, running down a path to get out of the crossfire. Beck—my sergeant—told us to round up the runaways into a gully. He ordered me and a corporal to shoot 'em. I couldn't do it, so the two of them did. Wiped 'em out, blown to hell. Beck gave me his .45 and ordered me to clean up. I went into the ditch and checked to see if they were dead. One lady, a girl, really, was still alive. She was pregnant. She begged me not to shoot her."

Jackson smoked during a long pause. Cheryl broke the silence. "Did you?"

He shook his head, and then realized Cheryl couldn't see him. "No. I held my finger to my lips and fired into the air. She still screamed when the gun went off, but I got her to calm down, finally. I motioned for her to lie still, but I don't think she understood me. When I climbed over the bodies to get out of the ditch, Beck was waiting for me. He'd come back for his .45." Jackson took another drag on his cigarette.

"What'd he do?"

"Nothing, at first. I gave him the .45 and he holstered it while we headed back to hook up. He threw me my 16—my rifle—and I followed him to the bridge. Then he stopped on the road and looked back at the gully. He must have seen some movement. He took my rifle back and sprayed a clip at the bodies."

"Did she"

"I don't know. I kept walking."

Cheryl squeezed his hands. "I'm sorry."

"Thanks."

"We can stay with Maritza for a few months," she said, "then get a small place, maybe near the beach, something cheap. Once they stop putting our pictures in the papers we can find some work, okay?"

"Sure. Maybe I can fish. Can't speak the tongue, but I can bait a hook."

"I speak it some," she said. "Enough anyway. In a couple of years I'll go back to the States and start a new life."

"With me?"

"Maybe. I don't know. I'm sorry. I still love you. Do you believe me?"

"Yeah, I guess."

Cheryl stood and pushed the beds together.

* * *

They stayed that couple of months with Maritza and Hector until the media stories of their flight from the law trickled to almost nothing. Jackson hadn't gone on any more of Hector's drug runs, and as far as he knew, Cheryl hadn't had any more steamy showers with Maritza. If she had, he wasn't sure he wanted to know.

Six months went by until they felt secure enough to reenter the world. Cheryl got a part-time job teaching English at a small school. With a pair of black-framed eyeglasses, dyed blonde hair, and a librarian's attire, she looked nothing like the anarchist in the papers. Jackson got his job on a fishing boat and kept his hair brown and short, hiding behind his sunglasses. By their one-year anniversary living in Manzanillo, they had established themselves as a nice gringo couple who couldn't make it in the States.

Almost every day around dusk, Jackson met Cheryl at Enrico's, a small open-air bar on the beach, for two or three drinks and whatever the catch of the day was, before heading home to their modest *casita*. He wanted it to stay that way for as long as it could until Cheryl felt safe enough to leave Mexico. Maybe he could talk her into staying a few more years. She seemed happy.

He filched the orange slice from her drink and ate it whole.

"You'll upset your tummy," she said.

Jackson held up two fingers to Enrico, who smiled and got to work on their second round. After all this time you'd think he would know to have them ready.

"Um—let's go home after the drink," Jackson said. "We can eat later. Is it our sex night?"

Cheryl sipped rudely at the last of her drink, her faux eyeglasses nearly slipping off from the effort. "I don't know. Is it a day that ends in Y?"

"Yup," he said.

"Well, then I guess so." She leaned over to kiss him.

A man in a black suit and tie sat down next to Cheryl. "Ah," he said. "Now, that's adorable."

It was Special Agent in Charge Postlewait. His partner, Special Agent Baker, sat on the stool beside Jackson.

"Keep your hands on top of the bar where we can see them, Mr. Hurst," Postlewait said. "You too, Miss Hebert."

They did as he said. Jackson was too stunned to say anything clever. Cheryl began to cry. Rebellious anarchist, she wasn't, at that moment.

Baker chimed in. "All right, Jackson, hands behind your back."

Jackson felt the muzzle of the agent's gun pressing against him. He complied and Baker cuffed him. Postlewait didn't need to use his gun to convince Cheryl. He just gently pulled her arms around her back and carefully clamped the handcuffs around her wrists.

Jackson chuckled. "You're good, Mr. Special Agent in Charge. Who dropped a dime? Hector?"

Postlewait smiled. "No, it wasn't Mr. Acevedo. He's in custody also. I wouldn't think someone with his outstanding warrants would seek a reward that could lead to his arrest. He was too smart for that. No, my friend, Miss Jimenez turned you two in for the $100,000. She's a bright lady. She gets the money, immunity from prosecution, and a free ticket back to Colombia after Miss Hebert's trial. If Miss Hebert doesn't wish to plead, that is."

Not likely, Jackson thought. Maybe he should have encouraged Cheryl to keep up her tryst with the Colombian beauty. It wouldn't have hurt.

Chapter 40

POSTLEWAIT BY THE BOOK

The FBI had everything planned out for the route from Manzanillo to Albany. Postlewait recruited three police cars from the Manzanillo Police Department to drive Jackson, Cheryl, and Hector separately to the airport. Maritza drove with the FBI agents in a rental car. Jackson wanted to talk to Cheryl, to reassure her. Fate had indeed been cruel to both of them, their ideal world ripped out from under them. Time to pay for past indiscretions. Nothing was free.

More agents came from Texas, each one assigned to escort a prisoner on a commercial flight to the States. Extradition of the fugitives had been worked out days in advance with Mexico so there was no delay ferreting them out of the country.

Two days later, they were interrogated in Albany. The Feds already knew everything except for the details of the gunfight at Lester Wester's ranch. They had apparently found the tunnel at Aunt Camille's house that same day Cheryl and he had escaped through it, but they hadn't told the media, hoping to give the fugitives a sense of security that they had a head start.

Postlewait brought up the Fitzpatricks, saying they had confessed to helping Jackson and Cheryl, but Jackson refuted the story, knowing Cheryl would do the same. No use screwing up more lives than necessary. By the end of the week, Cheryl had been hit with a twelve-count indictment including a first-degree murder charge for the deaths of the Brinks guards and the North Brook police officer. Jackson was tagged with second-degree murder for the gory death of Lester Wester by Jackson's wretched Fairlane. A lesser charge of accessory after the fact was also thrown in.

At their arraignment, all three pled not guilty and they were ordered held without bail until their trials in federal court, with Cheryl's to be first in about six months. Jackson's case would wait until after Cheryl's, since the outcome of her trial could affect his. He didn't give a damn. He'd been in prison before. It was Cheryl he was worried about.

Many things changed over the next six months. Cheryl retained the renowned lawyer Electus Canfield, a radical himself, arrested many times protesting everything from nuclear-plant construction to the war. He had already had her charges reduced to second-degree murder and unlawful flight. Cheryl paid for her and Jackson's defense with some of the three million left her by Aunt Camille. Cheryl was supposed to split it with Ethan, but Ethan was in no position to receive his share.

Cheryl lived in a private cell that was anything but, the media reporting the daily comings and goings of her legal counsel, from Canfield to lowly clerks. Jackson was grateful for his counsel also, especially since neither he nor his mother had any money at the moment. His lawyer met with him once, and that was to tell him that after a thorough investigation by the FBI and the New Hampshire State Police, they had decided he had told the truth about Lester Wester's death, and so the U.S. Attorney dropped the second-degree-murder charge. He'd still be tried for accessory after the fact, a charge that would get him five years in the state prison because of his record. Adios to the P.I. business. Maybe he'd get another fishing job in Mexico. Even ex-cons could make a living fishing.

Cheryl's trial was going to be a circus. Speculation by the media had it lasting from two to four weeks. They also speculated on the defense strategy. The *New York Times* said Canfield would use the brainwashing or Stockholm Syndrome defense, saying Haze had complete control of her mind. The *Daily News* thought there was no need for the elaborate brainwashing defense, since none of the witnesses who were in the van during the North Brook Brinks truck robbery were alive. No one. Not Haze or Aaron or Yardbird or Janie could dispute Cheryl's side of the story. There's your defense, they claimed.

There was one flaw in the story, though. If Cheryl was innocent, why did she flee to Mexico? Only one person knew that besides her and he was in a holding cell, spending most of his time reading newspapers and begging smokes. When Electus Canfield paid him a visit, Jackson did just that.

"Hey, man," Jackson said. "You got a cigarette?"

Canfield gave him a cigarillo that tasted like crap, but what the hell?

"Keep the whole pack, Jackson." He threw it to him across the table. Canfield was a contradiction of opposites with his long, gray, ponytailed hair, mutton chop sideburns, and a three-piece suit that probably cost as much as Jackson made in a year in his last job. "How are the pigs treating you, son?"

Jackson inhaled deeply on the skinny piece of crap. "Not like no rich girl, that's for sure. Anybody even know I'm here?"

"Of course. Listen, I only have a minute, so I'll get to the point. The US Attorney will attack Cheryl's story of why she headed for Mexico instead of turning herself in. Logical argument on his part, since if her claim of innocence is true, then she had nothing to fear by contacting the authorities. Now, Jackson, as you know, Cheryl's paying for your legal fees and—well, anything else you need. Here's what I'd like to propose. I was wondering if you remember telling Cheryl it was in her best interest to run, that the government wouldn't believe her story, that history shows the establishment would punish her regardless of her guilt or innocence."

Jackson lit another. They didn't last long. "I remember some of them words being said and all, man, but I don't remember saying 'em."

"Oh, for Christ's sake. If Cheryl's convicted she'll get a minimum of twenty-five years. She'll be fifty, man, fifty, and that's only if it's a minimum. The most you can expect is five years, and I can tell you right now I will guarantee you I can have that reduced to one—maybe two."

"If," Jackson said.

"Yes—if."

Jackson was starting to like the little cancer sticks. "I tell you what, Mr. Electus Canfield. I will indeed testify that I was the miscreant who convinced the young lady to flee the pigs, but it ain't because you're gonna get me a lighter sentence, and it ain't because my dead aunt is paying for some lawyer to defend her shit-for-brains nephew, and it ain't because I don't wanna see Cheryl go through menopause in a federal prison. It's because I love her and that's the *only* damn reason. You tell her that and then you get one of them flunkies of yours to get me a carton of these fine cigarillos."

Canfield agreed and told Jackson he'd need him to testify at Cheryl's trial.

"Whatever," Jackson said.

Chapter 41

THE TRIAL

Jackson's guards broke a few rules and supplied him with newspapers so he could keep up with Cheryl's trial. The local rag printed prosecuting attorney Daniel Hunt, as well as defense lawyer, Electus Canfield's, opening statements. An opinionated reporter wrote that Hunt's statement seemed pedantic and stiff and the prosecutor's long list of facts surely put the jury to sleep. Hunt emphasized Cheryl was as guilty as the ones who had actually killed guards Thomas Elder, Bobby Weller, Samuel Young, and North Brook patrolman Dave Brown. His strategy, he told the jury, was to prove Miss Cheryl Hebert was a willing participant in the brutal slayings and had every opportunity to turn herself over to the federal authorities. Instead, she fled to Mexico, the actions not of the innocent, but of the guilty.

The longhaired and hyperactive Electus Canfield would not use the brainwashing defense as far as Jackson could tell from his opening statement. Canfield portrayed Cheryl as a naïve child, spoiled by a wealthy mother who had in fact kidnapped her from a loving family two decades before. He went on to say Cheryl found herself accepted by the radical revolutionaries and thrived with their attention. But the point he wanted to stress most to the jury was that his client tried to stop the robbery with her actions and took no part in the murders of these honorable heroes during that horrible crime in North Brook.

As he closed, he emphasized, it was not the defense's job to prove its client did not commit the crimes she was charged with. It was the prosecution's job to prove she did commit them, and if the jury had any doubt of her guilt then they would have to side with the defense.

A large photo of Cheryl was on the front page. Her short, dark hair had been layered to fall just to the top of her ears. Jackson supposed Canfield wanted to make sure the jury saw the severed earlobe, proof she was a victim and not a willing participant. She still wore the glasses she didn't need and a suit that made her look like the lawyers who surrounded her at the table. She was studying papers on the desk, a bright, pretty, conscientious girl who undoubtedly had been duped by the radical left. An everyman's daughter. Hell, if he were on the jury, he'd vote not guilty just because of her looks. He'd see her soon when he testified. Would he be able to sleep until then?

Cheryl felt at peace. There was good karma coming from Electus and she felt as if his upbeat attitude had somehow rubbed off on her or maybe even entered her through osmosis. Either way, the trial would have a successful conclusion once Jackson testified. She knew he'd come through. He loved her. He'd told her that every night when they were together and she knew he meant it. Very good karma.

US Attorney Daniel P. Hunt called Sergeant Loyal Kendricks of the North Brook Police Department to the witness stand, the only true eyewitness, besides Cheryl, to the carnage in front of the bank that day. The black officer's left arm was in a cast that jutted out obscenely to his left. His third surgery since the robbery, according to the newspapers.

He didn't need the broken arm. He used his good one to swear an oath on the Bible, an oath he then proceeded to break.

"Sergeant Kendricks, you told investigators that when you drove your cruiser by the white van parked behind the Brinks truck, you saw a woman waving her hand out of the window."

"Yes, sir, but what I meant to say was that I believe she was just holding it out of the van, not waving. I believe she may have had a cigarette in her hand. Might have been flicking ashes, you know?"

"So she wasn't trying to get your attention?"

"No, sir. I don't believe so."

Canfield stood. "I object, Your Honor. Is Sergeant Kendricks now changing his testimony?"

The judge shook his head. "Mr. Canfield, you will be able to cross-examine this witness when Mr. Hunt is through with him. You do remember that, don't you? Objection overruled."

"Thank you, Your Honor," Hunt said. "So, Sergeant, you believe Miss Hebert was cooperating with the other perpetrators and—"

"Objection," Canfield said.

The judge nodded. "Sustained. Mr. Hunt, we are not interested in Sergeant Kendricks's opinion."

"Yes, Your Honor. I retract the question."

"The statement, you mean," Canfield said.

Hunt ignored the defense attorney. "Is there anything else you can tell us about Miss Hebert's actions during the shootout?"

"That's about it, except after I shot out the van's windshield, she nearly ran over me trying to scoot out of there."

The US Attorney turned the witness over to Canfield, who paced in front of Sergeant Kendricks for a few moments as if thinking of a question. Kendricks followed the attorney with his head as if he were at a tennis match.

Finally, Canfield spoke. "Sergeant Kendricks."

"Yes, sir."

"In a written statement you said, and I quote, 'The girl looked like she was trying to wave us down.' Are those your words?"

"Yes, sir."

"So was she or wasn't she?"

"Well, sir, what I said was it *looked* like she was trying to wave us down. Later, when I had time to think about it, it became clearer in my mind and I realized she wasn't doing that at all. She was, like I said a few minutes ago, just flicking a cigarette."

Canfield held his hands up and shook his head at the jury. After a deliberate pause he walked back to Sergeant Kendricks, who looked as if his plaster cast might be getting heavier.

"You know what I think, Sergeant?"

"No, sir."

"I think you realized she was flicking a cigarette when you started thinking about your dead partner and the wife and child he left behind. That's what I think."

"Objection, Your Honor," Hunt said. "Mr. Canfield is the one giving testimony now."

"Sustained. Do you have any more questions for the witness, Mr. Canfield?"

"No, Your Honor."

Sergeant Kendricks awkwardly left the witness stand, banging the ungainly cast twice on the railing. His gaze met Cheryl's, though he quickly lowered it to the floor.

Maritza Jimenez wore a peach miniskirt, the first in a long time Cheryl had seen her in anything other than men's slacks, unless she included the time when they were together in the shower. That memory made Cheryl smile at Maritza, who smiled back, knowingly. The burn scars on the back of Maritza's legs were visible. Hunt probably told her to wear the short skirt to get a little sympathy from the jury. She'd have to ask Electus later to see what he thought.

The US Attorney asked Maritza how she knew Cheryl and then had her go over in detail the townhouse explosion in Greenwich Village, where she, Cheryl, and Janie escaped the bomb-making factory as it burned to the ground.

"Did Miss Hebert express her concerns to you about assembling bombs to be used by the Weather Underground and the Black Liberation Army?"

"No. She never said nothing to me. We smoked a little dope, drank a few, and had a good time, you know, putting in timers and telling jokes."

"Telling jokes?"

"Yeah, a few."

Hunt turned to narrow his eyes at Cheryl. Then he faced the jury.

"They told a few jokes," he said.

"Objection," Canfield said.

"Sustained. Mr. Hunt. Please direct your questions to your witness."

"Yes, Your Honor. All right, Miss Jimenez. And so, you didn't hear from Miss Hebert after that until a year ago in Manzanillo, Mexico. Is that correct?"

"Yeah."

"And how did she contact you?"

"She called me from the States, said she needed a place to hide out."

"So it was her and not Jackson Hurst who called you?"

"Yeah."

"That doesn't sound like somebody having trouble deciding whether or not to turn herself in, does it, Miss Jimenez?"

"No, it doesn't sound like it."

"Objection." Canfield stood. "Leading the witness."

"Sustained. Put it in a question, Counselor."

"That won't be necessary, Your Honor. I'm finished with Miss Jimenez."

The judge pointed to Canfield. "Your witness, Mr. Canfield."

Canfield thanked the judge and asked only one question. "Did my client tell you after the explosion that she wanted to get the hell out of the Weathermen?"

Maritza shrugged and smiled at Cheryl. "Yeah. I guess so."

"Thank you, Miss Jimenez. That's all."

The rest of the prosecution witnesses neither helped nor hurt the Feds' case against Cheryl. The waitress who had fingered them in Vermont could only recall that the pretty girl in the car really enjoyed her pancakes and butter. Canfield destroyed Joshua Robert Prebor's testimony by portraying the dense farmer's son as a sadist and a pervert. The prosecution rested. Although Electus rubbed his chin nervously, Cheryl still felt the good vibes. Tomorrow, her lover would save her.

The next day, two federal agents escorted Jackson into an enormous four-story art-deco courthouse that Jackson decided had to be enormous in order to display its chiseled title: *The United States District Court for the Northern District of New York*. The agents placed him in a back row and sat on either side of him. His lawyer managed to talk the judge and prosecuting attorney into allowing Jackson to watch the day's proceedings after he testified. It would inconvenience his escorts, but he didn't give a shit, he just wanted to see Cheryl for as long as he could. He'd have a good view of the trial, though. One advantage of being over six feet tall.

Cheryl sat next to Canfield, who whispered in her ear. She turned in her seat and smiled at Jackson. Canfield gave Jackson a half-hearted salute, the counselor's ponytail flapping against his shoulder.

"Jackson Hurst," the bailiff called.

It was a long walk to the witness stand. When he sat and saw the large crowd staring at him, his heart raced. So much for a career in public speaking. Canfield started out with a few softball questions about his motivation for helping Cheryl and the like. Jackson said initially it was for his aunt's money, but after a while he grew fond of Cheryl.

"Do you love her?"

Jackson said nothing, preferring the question to go away.

"It's an easy question, Jackson. Yes or no?"

"Then, yes, I guess."

"Do you love her enough to lie for her?"

He almost said, "You're damn right I'd lie for her," but, instead, he gave the dude the answer he expected. "No, I wouldn't lie for her."

Canfield walked back to look at some notes on the table next to Cheryl and then turned to face Jackson. "Did you insist Cheryl flee to Mexico with you instead of turning herself over to the authorities?"

Jackson hesitated until he met Cheryl's gaze. It was pleading and apologetic at the same time. "Yeah. I figured—I figured the cops would find a way to shoot her, you know, say she had a gun or some bullshit like that."

The judge leaned forward, looking more than a little pissed. "Mr. Hurst."

"Sorry, man—Your Honor," Jackson said.

Canfield came to the rescue. "Thank you, Jackson. I appreciate your candor." The attorney looked up at the judge who seemed appeased. "That's all I have, Your Honor."

As Canfield walked back to his table, the prosecutor, Hunt, shook his head like one of those toy dogs in a car rear window. He stood from his table, walked slowly over to Jackson, and paced in front of him.

"Mr. Hurst, for the life of me I can't figure you out. You've been arrested many times in Charlotte for . . . let's see . . ." He read from a sheet of paper. "Drug possession, drug peddling, robbery, assault. You've been incarcerated for a year and now, sir, you are up to your elbows in trouble and all because of an infatuation with a pretty girl. All you can hope to accomplish by lying about Miss Hebert's crimes is to get yourself a significant amount of jail time added to your inevitable conviction. Is it worth it? Do you really want to fall on your sword to protect the guilty?"

Jackson wanted to say, "Yeah, and I'd do it a hundred times over. You don't know what it's like to hear her ask you if you love her. You don't know what it's like to fall asleep in her arms." But, instead, he said, "I swore to tell the truth, man. I may be a criminal, but my momma never let me lie and I ain't gonna get my momma upset by doing it now."

It got a few laughs from the tired spectators. As Jackson sat back down next to the agents, Canfield caused a commotion among the crowd when he called Cheryl to the witness stand. Jackson couldn't see US Attorney Hunt's face, but he'd bet he was smiling.

Canfield questioned her for what seemed like forever, the questions more of a prompt than anything else. She went over her life from the day she was kidnapped as a baby to the day she was caught. Canfield obviously wanted to leave doubt in the jurors' heads, so he kept the pertinent questions for last.

"Were you brainwashed by Mr. Willis?"

"No—I was never brainwashed. I believed I was championing a noble cause, that what I was doing would make a difference."

"Did you try to wave down Officer Kendricks in front of the North Brook Bank?"

"Yes. And when I saw him make a U-turn, I regretted it."

"Why?"

"Because I realized Haze would kill him along with the guards and it would be my fault."

"Did you want to turn yourself in after Jackson Hurst rescued you from Mr. Willis, Miss Anderson, and Mr. Wester?"

"Yes."

"But you didn't. You fled to Mexico. Is that right?"

"Yes."

"May I ask why?"

She tugged at her damaged ear, looked at Jackson, and then at the jury. "I just did, that's all."

"Was it because Jackson Hurst talked you into it?"

"I'd rather not say."

"I think you just did. No more questions, Your Honor." Canfield motioned to Hunt that he was through with his star witness.

The prosecution rehashed everything he had already gone over with the other witnesses, portraying Cheryl as a willing soldier who participated in illegal operations, all of which led to the deaths of the guards and the policeman.

"You were in Mexico for over a year?" Hunt asked.

"Yes."

"You could have left, Miss Hebert. If you were innocent, why stay?"

"I—I wasn't sure. I wanted to, but—well, Jackson didn't want me to get hurt. We were sure the FBI would shoot me even if I surrendered.

Maybe we were wrong, but that's what we thought. Listen, I'm sorry for what I did. I never wanted to hurt anyone."

Hunt shook his head. "Oh, I'm sure you are, Miss Hebert, but I'm not the one you should be apologizing to. You should be apologizing to the loved ones of the men you killed."

"Objection," Canfield said.

Hunt walked back to his table. "I'm finished with the witness."

Jackson thought the trial was over as Cheryl exited the witness stand. It seemed like everybody else did, too, until Mr. Electus Canfield pulled a rabbit out of his hat.

"Your Honor, I'd like to call Sergeant Kendricks back to the stand as a witness for the defense."

Hunt stood. "He can't do that."

"Sure he can," the judge said. "I can cite several precedents, Mr. Hunt, if you wish. Would you like me to call a four-hour recess so I can go through my case books?"

"No, Your Honor, but I wish to declare Sergeant Kendricks as a hostile witness."

"So declared, Prosecutor. Okay, Mr. Canfield. We're waiting on you, sir."

"Thank you, Your Honor," Canfield said from his seat. He waited until Kendricks was sworn in again before approaching the witness stand. "Now, Sergeant, you told one of my associates a little while ago that you wished to change your testimony. Is that correct?"

"Not necessarily change it, sir. Just—clarify it a little."

"You do know you were under oath when you gave that testimony."

"Yes, sir, I know."

"All right then. Go ahead."

"Well, sir. I got to thinking about what I saw that day, the day of the robbery. In my testimony I said I *believed* Miss Hebert was flicking a cigarette, but when I thought about it better, I was sure she was trying to wave me down."

"She was trying to wave you down."

"Yes, sir."

"Thank you, Sergeant." Canfield turned to Hunt and smiled. "Counselor?"

Hunt moved in close to the big police sergeant. "You can be charged with perjury for lying on the witness stand."

"Yes, sir, but like I said, during my initial testimony, I said I *believed* I saw her flick a cigarette. I didn't say for sure she did."

"So, why'd you change your mind, Sergeant? Tell the court. Tell the jurors. I'm sure we all want to hear what you have fabricated."

"Dave Brown was my partner, sir, but he was also my best friend. Somebody needed to be punished for killing him, for making Cyndi a widow, for taking a daddy away from Kathleen. I wanted justice and I think the blood in my eyes clouded what I know is the truth. Nothing good's gonna happen putting a young, stupid girl in prison for the rest of her life because one pissed-off sergeant believed he saw something he didn't. I didn't change my testimony, sir. I just made it clear."

And that was it. The case just went from 50-50 to a sure thing because of a cop with a conscience. Canfield gave a strong closing argument, as did Hunt, but the verdict was decided when that big, wounded cop stepped down from the witness stand.

"Not guilty."

As the crowd of lawyers and spectators gathered around Cheryl in jubilation, the two agents led Jackson away.

Chapter 42

OUT OF JAIL

It had been almost three years since Jackson had been to his little office on South Hero. Yellow and orange maple leaves filled the street gutters, signaling the change of season. He had neighbors now, a deli on one side and a grinder shop on the other. He'd never have to go far for lunch. Outside on the plate-glass window were the words, Hurst Private Investigation Agency, etched in modern type, a foot high. Nice. Very nice.

He used the office key the landlord had dropped off at his apartment. The entrance door opened with a flick of a shopkeeper's bell that hung above it. Another nice surprise.

The week had been full of surprises, thanks to Cheryl. It seemed she had kept up the rent on both his apartment and his office and had made quite a few improvements on the latter. He wasn't sure if her motivation was to make him happy or to keep him in Vermont.

The chill went away as he shut the door. The room had been partitioned into two sections. The front was a waiting area with a reception desk, a phone, a coffee table, and a few chairs. The back of the room was an enclosed office with a door that had a smoky glass window with the words, *Jackson Hurst PI* etched on it. Better and better.

He opened his office door and walked inside, half expecting to see Humphrey Bogart with his feet up on the desk. No Humphrey, but along with the new desk, Cheryl had furnished the room with a high-backed leather chair, a coat rack, and a few, small oil paintings depicting idyllic Vermont scenes, including one of the Brookfield floating bridge.

Jackson sat in the comfy chair and lit a cigarette, a Camel, not a rolled one like the kind Bogart fancied. He did put his feet up on the desk, though. Jackson Hurst, the Sam Spade of Vermont.

He looked around and gave his approval with a ring of smoke that expanded to twice its size before dissipating on the plaster ceiling. As his ma would say, he did good by the girl.

Cheryl had visited him only once in prison, three months after her trial. The US Attorney had refused to drop the unlawful flight charges against her, so on the advice of her lawyer, the esteemed Electus Canfield, she pled guilty and was sentenced to time served. Jackson hadn't been so lucky, still charged with accessory after the fact. Jackson's lawyer, along with Canfield, also advised him to plead guilty, which he did. But even with a plea bargain, he still got hit with two years because of his record. Hector got ten years for a slew of crimes, though Jackson figured the big guy would never get out. Maritza had better hope he didn't. Hector didn't seem like the kind of guy who forgave and forgot.

Prison wasn't so bad, a breeze really. Federal pen was nothing like the state ones. Jackson spent most of his time reading and watching television, when he wasn't playing baseball or basketball. The Feds kept the really bad dudes off by themselves, away from the prison population, which seemed to have a lot of paunchy middle-agers who looked like Ehrlichman.

Jackson's big regret was knowing he couldn't possess a gun, being a felon and all, once he got out. Being a private investigator without a gun could be a challenge. Maybe he'd walk around with a Louisville slugger like that *Walking Tall* badass. Or maybe not. It was Vermont, after all, not exactly a hotbed of violent crime.

They had let him see Cheryl in a visitor's room, the guard standing close enough to hear everything. Cheryl had leaned across the table and kissed him passionately.

"This isn't a conjugal visit," the guard reminded them.

"Sorry," she said, and smiled brightly.

The guard smiled back.

"How you doing?" she said.

"Ah, can't complain. Good food, lots of exercise, and nobody in here I can't beat up. It's like summer camp. No reason to ask about you. I see you in the papers and on TV all the time."

"Yeah, but that won't last. I'm officially on the lecture circuit, mostly universities and some political events. Everyone wants to see the little rich radical. I want to talk about the state of the nation and all they want to hear about is the robbery and the bombings and the kidnappings and about—about you and me."

"Really? Is there a you and me anymore, babe?"

She held his hands softly. "Listen, Jackson—"

"Oh, Christ. Every time you start with 'Listen, Jackson,' I get screwed."

"Seriously. I'm going back to school after all this winds down. UC Berkeley offered me a position as a teaching assistant while I go for my master's in political science. This is my chance to do something with my life and use my influence to make the changes we wanted. I'm not sure how long I'll stay there. I might run for office, local at first, but who knows?"

Jackson lit a cigarette. He offered one to Cheryl, but she refused.

"I guess this is leading up to something," he said. "You're going to explain there's only so much room in your life for that and me too. Am I close?"

"You're a good investigator, Jackson. You proved it when you helped me, and when you tracked down my parents. I still love you. I know you don't believe me, but I do. I'll visit my family several times a year and you're not that far away. I guess the question is, will you want to see me?"

He kissed her hands. "Only if you aren't married."

"No love interest at the moment," she said.

He almost asked her if she meant male or female. Why spoil the lousy mood?

"I have to go," she said. "You write me, I'll write you. I know you love me or—" She leaned in to whisper, "—or you wouldn't have lied for me."

She kissed him again. The guard harrumphed. As she got up to leave, Jackson rubbed the stubble on his chin. She turned back to wave.

She didn't write. If she went to visit the Fitzpatricks in Vermont, she didn't stop in New York to check on him first. He didn't mind all that much. His ma said all wounds healed, all things would pass. Ma was always right.

Now, Jackson played with the six buttons on his fancy speakerphone, which was just like the one in the reception area. Why so many buttons? You could only take one call at a time.

He stared down at his blue jeans. It was 1978. He needed to stop dressing like it was 1968. He still wore his hair long, more Allman Brothers than disco. It was okay in prison, but how would it hang in Burlington? He'd get some new clothes and a baseball bat. Right after a few joints. He didn't see his parole officer for two days, so what the hell?

He looked in the top drawer of his desk, hoping Cheryl might have thought of the possibility he'd want to get stoned after two years in the slammer. He'd always wanted to say *slammer*.

"That's right," Jackson said aloud. "Two years in the slammer, doll, and the better for it."

No weed in the drawer but there was a wrapped package and envelope. He opened the package first. It was the latest version of the *Private Investigation Training Manual*.

Cheryl had written inside. *I remembered you left yours in the Fairlane. Use this wisely, my beautiful white knight. Love, Cheryl.*

It was hard not to grin at that, and his heart began racing—just a little. He opened the envelope.

> *I hope you like the improvements to your office. You don't owe me anything. My mother—my first mother—owes you for all you've done. I plan to visit my family soon. I was wondering if you wanted to drive up to the Maple Inn for some pancakes with butter!! Oh, and maybe we stop at some motel and play a little poker. You know the kind I like.*
>
> *Love,*
> *Cheryl*

His grin turned into a wide smile.

The bell over the door jingled. Through a crack in his office door, he saw an attractive woman adjusting the hem of her little girl's dress. The girl had his blue eyes and her mother's dimple.

Acknowledgments

Thanks to my good friends and editors, Mary Brotherton, Athena Sasso, and Hank Rhodes. Also thanks to my readers, Edward White and Patricia Thomas and my agent, Jeanie Loiacono of the Loiacono Literary Agency. And a special thanks to Sterling Watson.

About the Author

J.J. White has had articles and stories published in several anthologies and magazines including, *Wordsmith*, the *Homestead Review*, the *Seven Hills Review*, *Bacopa Review*, and the *Grey Sparrow Journal*. His story, "The Adventure of the Nine Hole League," was published in the *Sherlock Holmes Mystery Magazine*, and his story, "Lucky Bastard Club," was published in the *Saturday Evening Post*'s 2016 Great American Fiction Contest anthology. His debut novel, *Prodigious Savant*, was published in 2014, followed by *Deviant Acts* (2015), and *Nisei* (2016). He was nominated for the Pushcart Prize for his short story "Tour Bus." He lives in Merritt Island, Florida, with his wife and editor, Pamela.

J.J. WHITE

FROM OPEN ROAD MEDIA

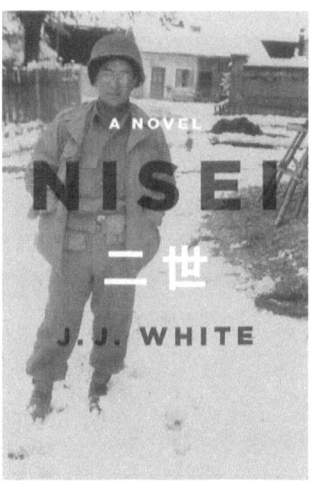

OPEN ROAD

INTEGRATED MEDIA

Find a full list of our authors and
titles at www.openroadmedia.com

FOLLOW US
@OpenRoadMedia